GOING WHERE IT'S DARK

NOVELS BY PHYLLIS REYNOLDS NAYLOR

Going Where It's Dark
Faith, Hope, and Ivy June
Emily's Fortune
Emily and Jackson Hiding Out

THE BOY/GIRL BATTLE BOOKS

The Boys Start the War
The Girls Get Even
Boys Against Girls
The Girls' Revenge
A Traitor Among the Boys
A Spy Among the Girls
The Boys Return
The Girls Take Over
Boys in Control
Girls Rule!
Boys Rock!
Who Won the War?

GOING WHERE IT'S DARK

Phyllis Reynolds Naylor

DELACORTE PRESS

With special thanks to Richard Christin for his caving expertise

Text copyright © 2016 by Phyllis Reynolds Naylor
Jacket art copyright © 2016 by Cliff Nielsen

Visit us on the Web! randomhousekids.com

Educators and librarians, for a variety of teaching tools, visit us at
RHTeachersLibrarians.com

Library of Congress Cataloging-in-Publication Data
Naylor, Phyllis Reynolds.
Going where it's dark / Phyllis Reynolds Naylor.
pages cm
Summary: "A coming-of-age novel about a boy whose daily life is difficult
because he stutters but who discovers enormous courage when he goes on
heart-pounding cave adventures"—Provided by publisher.
ISBN 978-0-553-51242-7 (trade hardcover) — ISBN 978-0-553-51243-4
(library binding) — ISBN 978-0-553-51244-1 (ebook) [1. Stuttering—Fiction.
2. Caving—Fiction.] I. Title. II. Title: Going where it is dark.
PZ7.N24Go 2016
[Fic]—dc23
2014033204

The text of this book is set in 11-point New Aster.
Jacket design by Kate Gartner
Interior design by Trish Parcell

Printed in the United States of America
10 9 8 7 6 5 4 3 2 1
First Edition

Random House Children's Books
supports the First Amendment and celebrates the right to read.

TO REX

CONTENTS

1. The Hole 1

2. It's Real 8

3. Jacob Wall 19

4. Pukeman 29

5. Secrets 37

6. Stand Off 46

7. Theft 54

8. The Unexpected 64

9. Pukeman Makes Spaghetti 76

10. Sister Pearson 86

11. Running Backward 97

12. David to Buck, Buck to David 110

13. A Taste of Bud 112

14. In the Woods 126

15. Dinner Conversation 141

16. Buck to David, David to Buck 147

17. Surveillance 149

18. Buck to David, David to Buck 156

19. In the Hole 158

20. All That Way 168

21. Buck to David, David to Buck   176

22. Torture   178

23. Pukeman Goes Exploring   188

24. The Suspect   190

25. Questions   202

26. Discovery   208

27. Confrontation   217

28. Wildcat   227

29. Duck and Cover   233

30. Buck to David, David to Buck   238

31. Jacob's Story   240

32. Facedown   248

33. Dark   257

34. Too Late   265

35. Passages   273

36. The Last of Everything   281

37. Rope Trick   291

38. Imprints on Stone   299

39. Buck to David, David to Buck   317

1

THE HOLE

Buck couldn't raise his head any higher. Lying there on his stomach, helmet scraping the boulder above, his chin on the clammy surface beneath him, he wriggled his way around the turn. Then he eased the flashlight into position and directed the beam along the passage.

Rocks jutted out on every side, and the path, if there was one, was irregular, sloping downward. Beyond, the light dwindled off into blackness. Whether it would reveal a wall, a curve, or a drop-off, he didn't know. His nostrils were filled with the scent of mud and mold and insect droppings.

But still he felt it, the draft of cold air that had first caught his attention. Maybe it led down a short ways, then up and out, and that was that, yet Buck didn't think so. Something about the chill of the rock around him the farther he'd gone in, the dank smell of undisturbed roots and moss, encouraged him to feel—to hope—that there was more, a lot more.

It proved nothing, but he felt the urge to yell:

"Hey!"

Then he filled his lungs and yelled again: "Hey!"

There was no echo, but the draft that brushed his face each time he lifted his head told Buck that this was no dead end. There was something else, far off. . . .

Wow! he said to himself, even as he began inching his way backward. Then *Wow!* again, and couldn't help smiling. He'd known that once he'd made the turn, he wouldn't go any farther. Buck had already disobeyed the first rule of caving: never—*not ever*—do it alone. But he wasn't about to disobey the second—the one he and David had decided on for themselves: never lose sight of a cave entrance.

Not yet. Not until they were far more experienced than they were. And then, just as things were getting interesting for them, David had moved to Pittsburgh.

Buck Anderson was nervy, but he wasn't nuts. His fascination with caves had begun when his family took a trip to Luray Caverns when he was seven. He and David Weinstein had been reading up on local caves—and trying to find those that were close—since spring of fifth grade, when the teacher had made them partners for an Earth Science project.

"Rock, sky, or water," she had said to the class.

And David immediately piped up, "How about rock, paper, scissors?" and everyone laughed, even the teacher.

"Rock includes caves, sky includes space travel, water includes the ocean bottom," she had said. "You can expand whatever category you choose."

Buck had turned around to face the large boy seated behind him. Both he and his friend said together, "Caves?"

Their interest only grew stronger after the project had ended, and now—two years later—they'd both be starting eighth grade come fall. Two hundred miles apart.

They knew some of the things that could happen to you—to even the most professional cavers. You could get lost in a maze, sure you knew your way out, and realize you were passing the same marker you'd left two hours before. You could slip on a rock covered with wet clay and break a leg. You could run out of batteries, get hit by falling rock, find your boot stuck in a crevice and not be able to reach down and free your foot.

To his advantage, Buck was small for thirteen, and strong—lean, but not skinny. It had always been Buck who crawled into an opening first and gave the okay. David, thirty pounds heavier, once said he'd seen all of Buck's backside he cared to see, but he never suggested trading places.

So far, of course, most of their "caves" had been more like overhangs under a cliff, with maybe a smaller cavity or two that didn't go far, and cigarette butts or graffiti meant you were only the next in a long line of explorers who had been there. It was always the hole, the deep crevasse, or the gaping mouth of a hidden cave that they hoped to discover.

"You'll just have to find another guy to go caving with, I guess," David had said morosely the day the moving van arrived. But that probably wasn't about to happen. And now—on one of the most exciting days of his life—Buck had found a hole. And he had no one to tell.

He continued his backward crawl, rocks bruising his knees, his forearms, until he reached the place he could turn around. A patch of sky shone through a tangle of weeds above, the opening no bigger than a car door window.

Buck crouched there, breathing heavily, his back against the cool wall of rock. He still couldn't believe he'd found this—wouldn't have, if he hadn't felt that draft of cold air coming up through a web of brush and roots between the rocks. Virginia was riddled with limestone caverns, but they were usually discovered by farmers, quarrymen, hunters, or caving clubs, not guys like him, out tramping around solo on a Saturday afternoon.

Now he had to remember exactly where this was. The worst thing he could do was to ride off half crazy and then not be able to find it again.

He straightened to a standing position and looked for the roots he'd used as footholds coming down. Then, reaching up and clawing out handfuls of dirt to get a better grip, his feet scrabbling against the rock, he made the climb and reached the opening. He could feel the warmth of the May afternoon already. Could smell the clover. One hand grasped the low branch of a bush and then his head was up, his elbows were out, and finally he was sitting on the rocky ground that rimmed the opening of the hole, squinting out over a forsaken cow pasture.

• • •

The old Wilmer place was mostly that: old. The frame house had long given way to termites, the barn had collapsed on a rusty Buick, and the two hundred seventy acres were far from the interstate.

Okay. Working backward, Buck tried to reconfigure. He'd left his bike in the gulley beside the road and started across the property, following the tree line to keep in the shade. He'd tramped past outcroppings of rock that separated the field from the slow rise of forested mountain—just a sliver of mountain—a spur of the Blue Ridge.

At some point, however, the ground had dipped into a shallow bowl, suddenly propelling his legs forward. But then he had walked on, just past the sun-roasted carcass of a dog or a fox. And climbing over the second—or was it the third?—rocky pile, he had felt the draft of cold air.

There was no fence here, no sign that anyone had paid much attention to this corner of the property, which was overgrown with weeds and brush. Beside the woods, smaller trees encroached upon the pasture, like children straying from their parents. If the Wilmers had known the hole was here, though, wouldn't they have plugged it up or boarded it off, afraid a sheep or even a cow might amble up the rocks and fall in? Break a leg? Next time he went down, he'd . . .

Next time. Buck already knew he was going again, even though his brain screamed *Stop!* One stubborn dude, Uncle Mel always said of him, and he was right.

Okay. He took a couple of deep breaths. He wouldn't go down again until he had everything he needed—everything he could afford, anyway. He'd make a list. How many times had he and David scoured the countryside for caves? They usually didn't find one deep enough to need a flashlight. And today . . .

Buck examined the hole again. The break in the weeds

5

was barely visible, but he covered it with sticks and brush so that no one else would find it. And then, his heart still thumping wildly, he headed back to his bike.

• • •

His arms were streaked with dirt, his jeans caked with mud, but he always had an excuse ready just in case: he'd fallen in Cloister Creek, he was hiking through Miner's Gulley when it started raining, he slipped going up Buzzard's Roost. . . . He'd done all these things at one time or another, so it wasn't exactly a lie.

"You're not going in any caves, are you?" his mom had said once, wrinkling her nose at the mud-stained sweatshirt he'd left on top of the washer.

"No," he'd answered, simply because he hadn't found any to go in. Most of the caves seemed to be in the northern part of the state, and the ones in southwest Virginia had either been discovered by someone else or were doing a good job of staying hidden.

But now Buck was smiling again, feeling the late spring breeze on his face as he pedaled. What a caver dreamed about was being the first to ever explore a place.

"I mean, *think* about it!" David had said when they'd first begun searching for caves on their own. When David was excited about something, his wide face had a constant look of surprise. "There are thousands of caves in Virginia, and probably zillions that people don't even know about. You could go down in one and find prehistoric bones or something."

For Buck, it was the "going down in" that was the main

6

attraction, never mind the bones. Sometimes, he'd read, holes had been detected because animals gathered around them on a hot summer day, wanting to cool themselves. He was glad there were no cows in the pasture now to give it away. A few feet to the right or left and Buck wouldn't have felt the draft. And if he hadn't chosen the shade along the tree line, he would have missed it.

"YES!" he yelled, unable to contain it any longer. Then, throwing back his head, "YES! *Wheeeeeee!*"

If Mom knew where he'd been, she'd say the same thing she'd said when Buck was little and had run outside after a cold spring rain to glop around barefoot in the newly plowed field: *Get in here, Buck, or you'll catch pneumonia. You want to die?*

Of course he didn't want to die. He'd just wanted to feel what it was like to have four inches of newly plowed earth squishing up between his toes.

If Dad knew, he'd grumble: *Stubborn as the day is long.* And he was right about that.

Gramps, however, would hit the nail on the head: *He's a risk taker, that boy,* he'd say. But like the other comments, it was a complaint, not a compliment.

No, Buck's family would never in this world allow him to do what he planned to do next.

2

IT'S REAL

When Buck got home about four, only Dad was there, his old Chevy parked at an angle in the clearing. The shower was running upstairs, and then Buck heard it cut off.

Mom had the day shift at Holly's Homestyle, so she'd be back around five, and Joel and Gramps closed the sawmill at six on Saturdays. If Katie, Buck's twin, was there, she'd be either at the large farm table with her sketchpad and magazines or watching TV. The kitchen was empty and the television was off. This meant that Buck had the downstairs to himself, long enough to eat some peanut butter crackers and get his muddy clothes in the washer before his dad came down.

He opened a Coke and had just started toward the table when the phone rang.

Buck stood holding the soda in one hand, crackers in the other. If he was alone, he had to answer. If he wasn't, he let someone else pick up. The phone rang again. Then again.

Upstairs, the bathroom door opened.

"Buck?" yelled his dad. "You home?"

Another ring.

"Yeah . . . ," Buck answered.

"Well, get the phone, darn it!"

Buck set his can on the counter and walked across the green-and-white-flecked linoleum to the wall phone. Mom's cuckoo clock hung just above it, except that the bird didn't come out on the hour as it was supposed to. Uncle Mel kept promising to fix it, but he hadn't yet.

Buck watched his left hand reach forward and interrupt the phone in mid-ring. "'Lo," he said.

"Joel?" came a young man's voice.

"N . . . no. This is B . . . B . . . Buck," Buck answered.

"Oh. Hi, Buck. It's Larry," said the voice. "What time do you think he'll get home?"

Buck felt the familiar ache in his jaws as his muscles tightened, and there was perspiration between his fingers and the handset. "I s . . . s . . . suppose around . . . ssssix-th . . . th . . ."

"Great," Larry said. "Have him call me, would you? See if he wants to watch some wrestling tonight."

"Okay," Buck said, and hung up.

"That for me?" his dad called from the top of the stairs.

"No. J . . . Joel."

"All right." And then his dad said, "You've got the rest of that carrot row to weed, you know. Don't go putting it off."

"Uh . . . I won't," said Buck, knowing his dad meant, like,

right now, before dinner. When he'd set off that morning, he'd forgotten that he hadn't finished his work, and now he was going to have to hustle before Mom got home. First the hoeing. Then his clothes in the washer.

"We've all got our jobs, and this one's yours," Dad had told him once. "Nothing prettier than a long straight row of beans or lettuce, not a weed in sight. You should get your work done in the mornings when it's cooler, Buck. Then you'd have the afternoons this summer for yourself."

Buck agreed with him about working when it was cool, but he could think of a lot of things prettier than a row of carrots. Their fine lacy tops were hard to distinguish from weeds, and occasionally Buck pulled up a whole plant by mistake. Sometimes he wished he worked at the sawmill instead, like Dad and Gramps and Joel. Still, working alone, he never had to take orders, or worse, answer the phone.

"I'm going to pick up a few things at the store," Dad called down. "You want anything?"

Flashlight batteries! Buck thought, but then Dad would ask what for.

"No."

"Okay."

Buck went outside, picked up a hoe, and tramped to the back of the garden.

Today, not even weeding carrots could dampen his excitement. Not even a phone humiliation. He dropped clumps of weeds into a bucket without even thinking about the scrapes and blisters on his hands from all that rock crawling. Man, what he had to tell David! And only David.

• • •

Except for Thanksgiving and Christmas, the Andersons ate their meals in the kitchen. No one had an official seat at the large, rectangular table, except for Gramps at one end, Dad at the other. Mom and Joel, Buck and Katie sat in varied arrangements on either side, and Mel pulled up a stray chair wherever he could find a spot when he was home. Katie's main job was to start dinner, following whatever instructions her mom had left for her that morning—put a casserole in the oven, boil some potatoes, make a salad. . . .

Tonight it was spareribs, and nineteen-year-old Joel was in a good mood because it was Saturday and he'd be meeting up with his buddies later. No matter how much he ate, he still remained the tall, slim young man with a slight bump on his nose where a baseball had hit it when he was nine. He had a smile that turned one side of his mouth up a fraction, the other side down, and he was smiling now.

"Had a pencil tucked under two fingers when I measured a board for Mrs. Ebert today," he said, grinning down at the red-skinned potatoes he'd just heaped on his plate. "She says, 'Joel! What happened to your hand?'—she can't see worth a hoot—and I say, just as quick, 'Lost a couple fingers to the saw last week,' and she pret' near' died."

Everyone laughed.

"So that's what all that screechin' was about," said Gramps. His shaky hands made the wooden fork he was holding vibrate against the rim of the salad bowl. He fished out a couple of snap peas and passed it on.

"Oh, she's a good sport. And she's teased me plenty when I was little," Joel said.

11

"She told me I was pretty once," said Katie, her saucy eyes daring her brothers to contradict her.

"Well, you are, but pretty on the inside is what's important," said Mom. A short, sturdy woman, Doris Anderson was still wearing her green and gray Holly's Homestyle uniform, and after she buttered a roll, she turned her attention to Buck. "What did you do today, Buck? Saw your sneakers there on the back porch. Looked like you'd been through a swamp."

His sneakers! He'd forgotten about those. "J-just riding around," Buck answered.

"Alone?"

"Yeah. Wish D . . . D . . . David was here."

Without looking up from his plate, Dad said, "Good chance to make friends with some other boys."

"Way out here?" Buck said.

Dad's voice was as deep as he was big. He and Mom made quite a pair, because she was five foot two and he was six foot one. "You got a new bike, and you ride all over the county. Not like I work you to death."

That was true, and they'd lived here all Buck's life. Not like he was new in town either. But David was easy. With David he could talk or not talk. If he stuttered on a word, David didn't get antsy. Didn't jump in and say it for him.

Gramps, though, had turned the conversation to the sawmill. "Think sometimes I should've gone into the plywood business. Can't hardly keep it in stock. Used to be we could make a living out of the wood we cut. Now we've got to sell plywood too, and I don't know what-all."

Buck gratefully reached for his iced tea. His grandfather

had the typical Anderson face—narrow, with an especially long distance between the nose and upper lip. "A horse face," he'd once said of himself. But a gentle horse, Buck thought. There were lines on both sides of his mouth, so deep they'd hold a penny, Buck figured.

Mom and Katie, with their round faces and puffed cheeks, were the exception, but everyone shared at least a few characteristics with the others—smile or hair pattern or the way they laughed.

So how was it that out of the six members of this family—seven if you counted Uncle Mel, twenty-three if you counted Grandma, who was gone, and all of Buck's assorted aunts and uncles and cousins—he was the only one who stuttered? For the rest of the family, talking was as natural as breathing.

"How hard is it to just open your danged mouth and get the word out?" Dad had asked Buck once in exasperation.

Harder than anyone knows, Buck had thought.

• • •

He had texted David right after dinner and was waiting for him to answer. Now he sat on the edge of his bed, trying to stop the jitters in his chest. He felt like he had the day he and David jumped over a four-foot gap in the rocks with a twenty-foot drop below. The same way his heart was thumping when he balanced his way across Hazard Creek on a poplar that had fallen over in a storm.

How could everything in his room look so ordinary when he felt so different inside? The small red radio on the top of his bookcase was the same; the catcher's mitt and the photo of him and Gramps holding a string of fish. The racing car model, the football helmet Uncle Mel had worn back in the eighties, and the *National Geographic* poster of mountain climbers next to the window. His excitement dimmed a little as his eyes scanned the Baltimore Ravens calendar above the dresser, because it was almost summer, and his goal had been to stop stuttering by his last semester of middle school. That was only one year off, and he wasn't even close.

But that was beside the point at the moment. He had to plan. Carefully. The right time. The right stuff. His eyes traveled back to the football helmet Mel had given him as a souvenir of his quarterback days in high school. He wished he had a caving helmet with a headlamp, but he didn't. For now his bicycle helmet and flashlight would have to do.

Okay. What else? Professional cavers were equipped with rope, duct tape, electrical tape, knives, headlamps, flashlights, wet suits, gloves, canteen, knee pads, elbow pads, matches, goggles. . . . He sure could have used a headlamp when he was down there today, and wondered how much they cost. Dad was going to pay him a dollar a row to keep the garden weeded, and each row reached from the edge of the backyard to the creek. It might take all summer before he could afford one.

Buck opened his notebook and started a list.

• • •

What was taking David so long? When he hadn't immediately responded to Buck's text, Buck had simply thumbed in the words **NEWS! r u there?** and waited. After the Weinsteins had moved away, Uncle Mel gave Buck his old cell phone, and the boys usually texted at least once a week. Sometimes once a day.

Buck didn't like to admit it, but he worried sometimes that David had made a new friend—someone who was taking up time David could have been using to text him. It wasn't that he wanted David to remain friendless. And he knew that David's mom was filling his life as full as possible to make up for yanking the boys apart when she got a job transfer. It was just that Buck had had more fun with David than any friend he'd ever had.

He rarely spoke to him on the phone, though. Never spoke to anyone by phone if he could help it. The minute he tried to speak, his vocal cords went into spasms of paralysis, and every word was a struggle. When Buck had to carry on a phone conversation, he could sense his jaws tightening, his teeth clenching, his lips quivering. Sometimes at school, especially if he had to speak in front of the class, he could feel his face and neck burn. He would blink repeatedly, and his mouth and lips felt as though they were cast in concrete.

"Stupid freak," Ethan had called him once.

But now, sitting on the floor of his room, his back against the bed, Buck could punch in the letters faster than he could talk, and tonight Buck willed his cell phone to buzz. Tonight, he'd even try talking if he had to.

David always had the most to say, even with thumbs. How he hated his new school but liked their apartment; that they were buying a dog; that he'd just seen *The Man Without a Face;* that his mom's boss was a dork.

Even when they'd been together, it was David who talked

the most, and when Buck stuttered a reply, David waited him out. Sometimes, if he asked a question and it was taking Buck more time than usual to answer, David would say, "One . . . one thousand, two . . . one thousand . . . ," and they'd both laugh. That was as far as it went. In the two years they'd been friends, David had never once asked Buck about his stuttering. David jiggled one knee when he talked; Buck stuttered. That was just the way they were.

His cell phone buzzed and Buck texted in seconds: **yo!**
hey dude u must have been sitting on it whuzzup?
u won't believe
what? WHAT????
i found something. a hole. and i went in
alone? how far?

And then . . . slowly . . . sentence by sentence, Buck told him about the Hole. About sticking his head in as far as it would go and shining the flashlight, climbing down about eight feet, then crawling, sliding, following the draft, and wriggling to where the passage made the first turn.

And every so often David interrupted with a **u got to b kidding!**

When Buck finished at last and gave his thumbs a rest, there was no reply for some time. Then David's words on the screen,

is this 4 real?

And Buck answered, **it's real.**

• • •

The question they kept coming back to was whether Buck should be going in there alone. Discussion was pointless be-

16

cause they both knew that, number one, he shouldn't, and number two, he would.

He *had* to. Someone else might discover the Hole if he didn't explore it first. What if that dip in the earth he'd come to meant that water erosion was the beginning of a sinkhole? What if the ground just collapsed someday, and when the Wilmer place was sold and the property surveyed, the new owners could walk right into a cave, no exploring necessary?

Or what about "the Pit," an underground chamber out near an old quarry? The police had found some college kids partying in it a month or two ago. Before anyone could explore it, the county declared it unsafe and boarded it up, with a space for bats to go in and out, Buck had heard, until they could put a metal grill over it. They might do the same to the Hole if they found it.

Was it too much to want to discover *something*? Buck wondered, keeping this particular thought to himself. They didn't have to name a cave after him. It didn't have to make him famous. All he wanted was to be the one who found it. How many places were left on earth where no one else had ever been? Oh, yeah, mountains and the ocean floor, but somewhere he had a chance to get to, he meant. And he'd never had a chance to go far.

Their discussion had even made David nervous, though.

r u sure u can find it again? he asked.

Of course, Buck told him. It was either the second or third outcropping of rock into the meadow, and he had counted off fifty-two paces from the sun-bleached skeleton of a dog or a fox, he wasn't sure, to the Hole.

a pile of bones? David had texted back. **dude, any animal could come along and carry those off before u got there again**

Embarrassed, Buck punched in, **don't worry i'll find it**

i'm making notes, David texted.

Before they signed off, however, he wanted a promise: that when Buck went in the Hole again, he would leave a note in his room that if he didn't come back, his folks should call David. That only David could tell them where to look.

And Buck had promised.

3

JACOB WALL

Uncle Mel got back two hours after the family returned from church on Sunday. The big noon meal was over, and Buck sat at the kitchen table eating his second piece of butterscotch pie. Although his uncle usually knew before he started a long-distance trip just how many days it would take, there was always the possibility of mechanical problems with the big semi, or a delay in unloading at a docking station.

"Well, look who's just in time to do the dishes," said Mom when Mel came through the back door. "Should have called and told us to keep a plate warm for you."

Her brother grinned as he set his thermos on the counter. "Don't trouble yourself," he told her. "I stopped at Holly's for some fried chicken."

"You *what*?" Mom whirled about. "Ten minutes from home and you stop at a restaurant to eat?"

Curly-haired Mel broke into laughter.

"Don't get your britches in a twist. Naw, I met up with a buddy of mine in Hanover and we had lunch. Even got my truck back on time. I'll heat up your leftovers for supper. Be just as good then."

"Oh, *you*!" said Mom, and she gave him a swat with the dish towel.

Buck smiled at his uncle as Mel hung his cap behind the door, where a faded assortment of jackets, raincoats, hoodies, and an apron or two dangled limply on painted white pegs, waiting to be claimed. Except for Mel's dark curly hair and Mom's straight, they looked a lot like each other. Both had eyes that squeezed into slits when they laughed, and both were slightly plump in the midsection. Because Mel was divorced and supporting an ex-wife and daughter in Cincinnati, he'd been glad to make his home with his sister and her family. And being a long-distance trucker meant he couldn't have kept up a house and yard even if he'd had one.

"How's everyone here?" he asked. "Been away for five days. Anything exciting happen?"

Yes! Buck was thinking, but he couldn't tell it.

"Not much," Mom answered. "Garden's going good. Don and Gramps are watching the Nationals. Go on in."

"Naw. The Ford's acting up. I'm gonna try cleaning the spark plugs. Then I need to look in on Jacob. Like to stay off my fanny for a while, anyway. Grab me a rag, will you, Buck?"

Buck scraped his fork sideways across the plate to get the

last of the butterscotch, then put his plate in the sink, got some old rags from the pantry, and followed his uncle outside. He liked to hang around when Mel worked on his car.

"N . . . need any help?" he asked.

"Not unless you got a batch of new spark plugs for this sucker," Mel said, and opened the hood of the old green sedan. "So how you doin'?"

"Doing okay," Buck said, resting his hands on the side of the car and looking down into the belly of the Ford. More than okay, but he couldn't say it. He watched as his uncle removed a spark plug, wrapped a rag around it, then stood, twisting it back and forth.

"Doing anything special this summer?"

Buck avoided Mel's eyes. He couldn't guess, could he? He shrugged.

Mel inspected the plug in his hand, then glanced over at Buck again. "Got a favor to ask. I know your dad needs help in the garden, with vegetables coming up overnight, almost. I was thinking about something the other day, though, if you've got some extra time. It's another job for you, but the kind you do partly because you want to, not just because you're getting paid."

"Like what?"

"Well, one of our drivers quit last week and another's going to retire. I'll be getting some of their cross-country runs, and that means I'll be on the road a lot more. I've been looking in on Jacob Wall a couple times a week. But if I'm going to be gone four and five days at a time, maybe you could look in on him for me when I'm away."

Buck tried to remember if he'd ever seen the man who'd

moved into the small yellow house halfway between the Andersons and the general store. "What do you m . . . mean, 'look in on'?"

"Take in his mail, see if he needs any groceries, get something off a shelf for him—just see if he's okay. He's not an easy man to get along with; doesn't even want me there half the time. But he needs me—needs someone—and he knows it."

"What's wrong with him?"

"Not sure. Moved in last year. Rheumatoid arthritis or something. Walks like every joint in his body gives him pain. Gets disability checks, Ted Beall told me. The only way he'll accept help is to give me a five-dollar bill on Fridays. Hands it to me without a word, and I take it without a word. Doesn't want thanks from anyone, and sure as heck doesn't want pity."

"You d . . . don't ever talk to him?"

"Oh sure, but not much. If you take over for me when I'm out of town, you can keep the five on Fridays. Any big repairs he needs, I'll do when I get back."

Buck shifted his weight to the other foot. "I d . . . don't know. . . ."

"Well, I don't either, and I'm not about to make up your mind for you. I'll get Joel to do it if you can't."

Buck thought about that garden. If he weeded five rows a week, got a five on Fridays . . . Buy that headlamp sooner than he thought. More than that, though, he didn't like saying no to Uncle Mel.

"I'll g . . . g . . . give it a try," he said.

"Good." Mel closed the hood of the car, handed the rag

to Buck, then reached in the backseat and grabbed an old pair of overalls rolled up in a bundle. He gave those to Buck as well. "Those can go in the trash. So torn up I'm embarrassed to wear 'em even when I'm changing a tire."

No way, Buck thought. No matter if they were four sizes too big; he could cut them down and wear them over his clothes the next time he crawled in the Hole.

• • •

They walked a half mile down the road to Jacob's house. Buck was still in his Sunday pants, but had traded his white shirt for a brown tee from Bealls'. Printed on the front were the words *Bealls' Country Store* in yellow, with the outline of a rooster beneath.

Mel bent his elbows and pulled his shoulders back in a giant stretch.

"Whoo!" he said. "Sure does feel good to walk around. Someday I'll be trying to get out of that semi and find my butt's sprouted roots to the seat."

Buck laughed. He and his uncle both had the same sort of loping walk. Like Buck, Mel was on the short side, but he was definitely muscular. He might have spent a good part of his week sitting in the cab of a truck, but the hauling of freight on and off when he got to where he was going kept the muscles in his arms and legs as thick as a boxer's.

"You like your j . . . job, though," Buck reminded him.

Mel nodded. "Like sitting up high while I drive, seeing the country, the way it changes, south to north and east to west. Like talking with other truckers on our radios. Makes me feel for Jacob all the more, trapped inside that little place."

The sun shone through the trees and made leaf shadows on the pavement. Buck and his uncle kept to the side of the road and shifted over even farther when a car went by.

"How'd you meet him?" Buck asked.

"Remember that big windstorm we had last September? I was coming back from the gas station and I see the screen door on this house flopping back and forth. And here's this crippled man holding a hammer in one hand, the other on the screen, trying to set it straight. So I stopped."

Uncle Mel reached up to push some branches out of their way. "Can't say he was glad to see me. In fact, I wasn't sure he saw me at all, 'cause when I asked if I could help, he didn't even look my way. But a hinge had lost its pin, so I found it, wrestled the screen in place, then let him hammer the pin back in. . . ."

"D . . . did he thank you?"

"Nope. I'd been studying the way his legs shook, and the spotty way he'd shaved that morning. I put out my hand and said, 'I'm Mel Turner. Live with the Andersons down the road there.' And all he did was give me a nod and hobble back into the house."

Buck waited until a pickup without a muffler roared by. Then he said, "I wouldn't have ever g . . . g . . . gone back."

"I sort of felt the same way. But when I walked out to the road again, I saw how the flap on his mailbox had been blown open too, and the box was full. Stuff had been there a week, maybe. So I pulled out all the mail, walked it back to the house, and set it between the screen and the door. One envelope read *Jacob Wall,* so at least I had his name."

The small square house was coming into view now. Like

many of the other houses along the road, it was dwarfed by the land on which it sat. Folks along here were said to be land-rich and house-poor, Buck had heard.

When he and his uncle turned up the gravel drive, an old Volvo crookedly parked at the head of it, Mel said, "So . . . I just started dropping by couple times a week, walking the mail up to the house. And one day I knocked and said, 'Jacob, it's Mel. You got a pliers and screwdriver handy, I could fix the flap on your mailbox.' And after that—maybe because I was asking *his* help, wanting to borrow his tools—he thawed a little."

"Like you were friends?"

"Naw. Never that. But when I'd ask if he needed anything, he'd let me pick up something from the store, mail a letter, fix a leak. The Bealls say he comes into town 'bout once a month, but driving's a chore for him. I never learned much more about him than I'm telling you now. But every Friday he hands me a five-dollar bill. Told me I couldn't come back if I didn't take it, and he doesn't want any thank-yous. Strange, though. The inside of the house doesn't fit with the outside, and he doesn't quite fit with either one."

Buck wondered if Jacob heard the gravel crunching underfoot as they approached the house—if he'd been watching from a window, maybe. It seemed a long time before the door opened, though. Then he found himself staring up into two fading blue eyes, half hidden by bushy white eyebrows that matched the thick thatch of hair reaching down under his collar. Jacob's face had so many wrinkles it looked like a shriveled apple.

"Afternoon, Jacob. Brought the lightbulbs you needed.

This is my nephew, Buck. He's going to give me a hand. Buck, this is Mr. Wall."

"Hi," said Buck, and waited.

In response the man stared at him two seconds longer, then shakily turned himself around and wordlessly set off for the kitchen.

Buck looked up at his uncle, but Mel only shrugged and followed Jacob through the house.

• • •

It was more like an antique store than a house. So much furniture that in places Buck had to turn sideways to get through. Two large leather couches, when the living room was only suited for one. Two leather armchairs, three end tables, and bookcases that not only lined the walls but covered one window as well. Only a few of the framed pictures had actually been hung, the others propped against a buffet.

Uncle Mel stepped up on a low stool, removing a glass globe on the ceiling and handing it to Buck. And Buck had never felt so unwelcome. He could see himself reflected in the tall framed mirror leaning against the wall, looking as stiff and awkward as he felt. He could sense the glare of Jacob's deep-set eyes boring into his back. When he glanced at the old man once, it made him so uncomfortable, he had to look away.

"Here's the thing," Mel said, when he stepped down again and they moved toward the bedroom to replace a bulb there. "Since I've got a few longer hauls coming up, I'd like you to let Buck come in my place when I'm not here. He'll pick up the mail, run errands. . . . Any repairs you got, I'll do when I get back."

Jacob's face didn't change, and he said nothing.

"He's a good worker," Mel continued, positioning the stool at the foot of the large bed, the headboard shaped like a scroll, and climbing up a couple of steps. "Won't touch anything he shouldn't. He's got a bike, so he could ride to the store for you." He looked at Buck. "Where's that wire basket you can hook on a bike if Jacob needs a few things from Bealls'?"

Buck fought that old, familiar tightening of his jaws that clamped them together, locking the words in. "I th . . . th . . . think it's in the c . . . c . . . c . . . cellar," he struggled to say, and wasn't all that surprised when Jacob turned himself around, stared at Buck a moment or two, then turned his back on them both and limped out of the room.

Buck let out his breath. He did not want to work for this man, and obviously, the man didn't want him to.

After the lightbulbs were replaced and Mel had tied up the trash and deposited it outside, and after Buck had emptied a mousetrap under the sink and scrubbed out the shower stall, he followed his uncle to the front door.

"Buck will be by in a few days, then," Mel said. "He's as handy with a mop as a lawn mower, so if you need any housekeeping done here inside, you just tell him. Take care, Jacob."

Jacob gave an almost imperceptible nod and closed the door behind them.

Buck didn't say anything until they were almost to the road. Then, "Wow. How old d . . . do you think he is? I fig-ure ninety."

"Naw," said Mel, "He's weathered, that's all. Weathered and worn."

"What kind of house did he have b . . . before? Had to be b . . . bigger than what he has now."

"Appears that way."

"Looked like he c . . . could chew me up and s . . . spit me out. Where'd he c . . . come from?"

"I don't know and I don't ask," said Mel. "Think you can handle this now?"

"He doesn't want me there."

"Wants you or not, he needs help."

When Buck made no reply, Mel glanced over. "Not afraid of him, are you?"

"No," Buck said. But he sure didn't like him.

4

PUKEMAN

He hated the bus ride to school without David. Some of the boys in eighth, and a few in seventh, used to joke about the two of them—David, with his shaggy hair and stocky frame; Buck, the smallest in the class.

"Here come the sheepdog and his Chihuahua," someone would say.

Now that Buck rode alone, the hassling became more specific. Whenever he could, Buck sat with a boy, any boy. Failing that, he took an empty seat near the front. But usually one of the girls had snagged it and saved it for Katie, and then Buck settled for whatever he could find.

This morning, with two weeks of school yet to go, the only seat the girls hadn't preempted was second from the back, directly in front of Pete Ketterman and his buddies. And no one made jokes about them. Pete Ketterman, Ethan Holt, Isaac Lewis, and Rob Moss were the *It* guys, and all but Rob were in eighth grade.

"Pete and his ducks," David used to say. "You ever notice how they follow him around? Pete says 'jump' and they say 'how high?'"

"Ducks can jump?" Buck had said, and David elbowed him in the ribs. Buck knew what he meant, though: Pete called the shots and the others fell in line.

Buck slid into the empty seat, his Nationals cap partially obscuring his eyes. Already one of the boys had his knees digging into the back of Buck's seat. The bulge receded, then came back again with a hard *whump*. Outwardly Buck didn't react, but he took a long, silent breath and let it out again. It was a seventeen-minute ride to school, and the pranks had only begun.

"H . . . h . . . hi, B . . . B . . . Buck. H . . . h . . . how y . . . y . . . you d . . . d . . . doin'?" Pete said to a chorus of snickers.

Not even half authentic, Buck was thinking.

One of the girls in the seat across from him pivoted and glared in Pete's direction, but that made it all the worse somehow. Buck could feel the heat rising in his neck. He turned his face toward the window.

Trees were so close to the road that all he could see was a blur of green, broken open now and then by a patch of sunlight, then closing again. JESUS SAVES AND HEALS, read a sign. Occasionally branches scraped against the roof of the bus, adding to the chatter of the riders.

"C . . . cat g . . . got . . . y . . . your t . . . tongue?" came Isaac's voice this time.

Then Pete's: "He can't help it." His voice rose higher and higher with each word until it sounded like a three-year-old's. "He's so short his words get stuck in his windpipe." All the guys laughed, even a couple of boys sitting a few rows ahead.

Rob asked if they remembered the teacher back in sixth grade who lost his voice for a week and had to signal with his hands. And finally, the conversation turned to teachers in general.

Buck relaxed a little. Sometimes, if he ignored them long enough, they'd quit. The bus had reached an open stretch, and beyond the field, Buck saw a few dogwoods still in bloom. The hills in the distance were every shade of green he could imagine, with a few dots of white or yellow.

Still, Buck liked the colors of fall best. He and David used to climb to the top of Buzzard's Roost in October and look down at the valley—watch the reds and yellows lighten or darken when a cloud cast a shadow. He could almost see David sitting beside him on a rock—the heavy clump of dark hair hanging down over one eye, matching the brown of his pupils—his large chin like a paperweight at the bottom of his face. And the grin—always the grin—because they had a good time when they were hanging out, tramping around the countryside.

The seat-poking behind Buck had stopped, but so had the conversation, and that was a bad sign. And then he felt it—the soft *scritch-scritch* of something crawling up the side of his neck.

He reached up to flick it off, but nothing was there. Moments later, *scritch-scritch* on the other side, just behind his ear. His hand shot back but, once again, nothing. He brushed off his shoulder to get rid of whatever insect it might be. But when the scratching came again, this time accompanied by a guffaw, Buck was quick enough to grasp the end of a ruler and push it away.

"Kn . . . knock it off," he said, half turning.

"What? Okay," said Isaac, and the ruler lifted the Nationals cap off Buck's head and sent it flying.

"You guys cut it out back there!" ordered the driver, and Buck could see his small eyes glaring at them in the rearview mirror.

"Sorry. Don't have any scissors," Isaac murmured, and again the boys laughed.

The cap had landed between some girls three rows up, and one of them passed it row by row back to Buck, sympathy in her eyes. Pity was the worst, and Buck could feel the heat in his face and neck again.

You've got to stand up for yourself, Buck, his dad had said when Buck was in fourth grade and complained of bullies. "Give as good as you get."

"And a punch in the mouth now and then might show 'em you mean business," Uncle Mel had added.

Except that neither Dad nor Mel had ever stuttered, as far as Buck knew. He was strong despite his size and he could punch pretty well, but the first time he'd tried it, he was kept in over lunch period for a week, emptying wastebaskets for all the teachers, and had missed out on soccer.

"Just because someone says something that upsets you doesn't mean you can split his lip," the principal had said.

It had helped to have a buddy. In that same fourth grade, David had been watching from the swings when two boys

32

penned Buck against a wall, their arms making a cage around him. With a small audience looking on, they accused him of stuttering so he wouldn't have to read aloud in class.

For Buck, *never* being called on was almost as embarrassing as stuttering his way through it.

"Oh, *p . . . please,* M . . . Mrs. Sellers, I c . . . can't read it b . . . because I s . . . stutter," one of the boys was saying, his nose five inches from Buck's face.

Some of the other kids had laughed.

And suddenly David Weinstein was there, grabbing hold of both boys by their shirts and throwing them to the ground. The little crowd had scattered, and the astonished boys picked themselves up, muttering accusations. But they backed off, and from then on, Buck knew he had a friend.

• • •

The bus pulled into the circular drive at East Bend Middle, and the large boys behind Buck crowded into the aisles, not giving him a second glance this time. Pete was in the lead, his thick short hair standing straight up in a style all its own, and when he grinned at the girls, he displayed the slight gap between his two front teeth.

If David had still been there, he and Buck would have sat together and talked all the way to school. David could discuss almost anything at all because he read everything from *Scientific American* to horror comics, like the one about the giant amoeba that oozed into a town, leaving a DNA marker on everyone it touched, turning them into amoebas too.

Last fall when the class was assigned to write essays on

imaginary science experiments, Buck had written about living in a pressure-controlled community at the bottom of the ocean, while David wrote about being frozen in a cryonics lab, having his head removed and attached to a muscle-builder's body. The class loved it.

And then, of course, David's mom got a job transfer and they had to move.

But Buck had a story going of his own that only David had ever seen—a comic strip, actually—and he was thinking about a new adventure for Pukeman as he put a couple of books in his locker. Taking out the one he'd need for first period, he walked down the noisy hallway to homeroom. Someone was having a birthday because a bunch of balloons were tied to a locker door handle.

"Hey, Buck-a-roo!" one of the guys from civics class said in passing. Buck raised one hand in greeting and went on, reminding himself that not everyone was a jerk. But that guy lived on the other side of the county, practically—not a couple miles away, as David had.

The morning announcements on the PA system began with the Pledge of Allegiance. Buck stood with everyone else and, like everyone else, recited it flawlessly, without the trace of a stammer. ". . . with liberty and justice for all." That was what he couldn't understand. No one else could either.

Then, when they sat down again, and the principal talked about test results for May, Buck turned to a sheaf of well-fingered papers at the back of his three-ring binder. *The Life of Pukeman*, the ink-smudged title read, and beneath that, two rows of comic strips spanned the page so far, with others in the preceding pages.

The first strip, "Pukeman Rides His Motorcycle," showed a ferocious guy with thick short hair that stood straight up, bent over the handlebars of his cycle. His wide mouth, showing the gap between the two front teeth was bellowing, "I want the whole world to worship me." In the second frame, the wind whipped at his jacket and he continued ". . . I want the whole, whole . . ."

And in the final frame, his motorcycle is falling into an open manhole in the street, and a small mouse in the bottom right corner with bug eyes, holding a manhole cover, says, "You got it, Pukeman," and grins.

The student council president was announcing the last meeting of the semester, and Buck smiled to himself, remembering when he'd drawn the first Pukeman strip.

"Make his eyebrows slant down in the middle," David had said. "And his mouth's gotta be sort of open, so when he falls into the hole you can see his teeth flying all over the place."

They had worked on the strip in study hall, handing it back and forth, each adding little touches until they were satisfied—the helmet and leather jacket, the gap-toothed grin . . .

There was a "Pukeman Goes Skiing" and "Pukeman Plays Football" on some of the other pages.

Over the PA system, the coach was reminding the basketball team to turn in their uniforms before the last day of school, and as Buck started a new strip called "Pukeman Likes Heavy Metal," the cheerleaders ended the morning announcements with a rousing cheer for East Bend Middle School.

"Have a great day," the principal said, "and make it count."

The microphone clicked off, then clicked on again and the school secretary's voice came through the speakers: "Excuse me, students," she said over the ringing of the first bell, "but would Buck Anderson come down to the front office, please?"

"What'd you do now, Buck?" a girl teased good-naturedly as she passed his seat.

Buck gathered up his stuff and started for the door.

5

SECRETS

What now?

Buck weaved in and out of the swarms of students in the hallway. Had someone seen him at the old Wilmer place on Saturday and reported it to the school? Who would know? And who would care?

Two eighth-grade girls made way for him as he mindlessly plowed between them. "Well, excuse *me!*" one of them said.

"Sorry," Buck murmured, and went on.

He opened the glass doors to the office and stepped inside. The red-haired secretary looked up. Her earrings were little ceramic cats in the pounce position, and they jiggled each time she moved her head.

"Hi, Buck," she said. "Would you believe that a speech therapist is finally going to see you?"

He stared at her, at the way her arched eyebrows, drawn with pencil, extended up onto her forehead. He'd been on the waiting list since September of last year—Mom had seen to that. "There's only t . . . two more weeks to g . . . go," he said.

"I know. She has three other schools besides this one, and she's doing the best she can." The secretary nodded toward the row of chairs along one wall. "Want to take a seat? She'll be with you shortly."

"I've g . . . got English. . . ."

"This is only a preliminary interview," the earring woman said. "She just wants to set something up for next year. Then you can go."

Buck shuffled over to the orange plastic chairs and dropped his backpack. Maybe he'd hoped they'd forget about him. Maybe he'd figured he could deal with the stuttering himself, though nothing had worked so far. But this meant he'd be called out of class all through eighth grade to work with a speech therapist, as though he couldn't even manage one of the basic abilities of being human.

He sat with elbows resting on his knees, remembering the therapist who had seen him periodically back in third grade. She was a slim young woman named Miss Saunders, with a thin face and a smile that exposed her upper gums.

Buck had seen her only a half-dozen times before the county cut off funds for speech therapy. They had spent much of their sessions trying to get Buck to relax. Miss Saunders said that stuttering was caused by the vocal cords clamping shut, and she had tried to teach him the airflow method of speaking—to sigh inaudibly just before saying a difficult word, and letting the word sort of slide out on the rush of air—"A free ride," she had called it.

Except sometimes it worked and sometimes it didn't, and Buck had other tricks of his own. Sometimes if the word was in the middle of a sentence, he'd just back up and use a different word. Sometimes he'd cough to hide the stutter.

"Buck?" Another woman was facing him now from the doorway of the conference room. She had a wide smile that matched a wide body and was wearing a crazy pin on her shirt with googly eyes and the words *Try me. I don't bite.*

"You can call me Connie," she said as she led him into the room and closed the door after them, motioning for him to take a seat. "I'm so sorry I couldn't get to you before this, but as you probably know, the county budget has been cut, and I can't see any of my referrals nearly enough. But you are definitely on my radar for September. We can meet over your lunch period if that will help."

Buck shrugged. "I guess."

"They tell me you've been stuttering for some time, and I plan to help you with that. But I'd like to get to know you better." She leaned back in her chair and smiled at him. "Tell me something exciting about yourself. What do you do best?"

I should be in English class, Buck was thinking. *I'll have an assignment to make up.* "I d . . . don't know," he said. He found he had turned one foot sideways and was resting the other foot on top of it. He put both feet flat on the floor.

She tried again. "What do you *enjoy* doing the most?"

As though he'd tell her. Buck shrugged again and glanced at the clock.

. . .

He was already thinking of going back into the Hole, even
though he had vowed he wouldn't go again without a good
headlamp. There could be all kinds of things he might miss
in the beam of an ordinary flashlight—rocks about to fall,
places he shouldn't step, creatures he shouldn't disturb,
formations he shouldn't touch. And, most important, he
needed both hands free to steady himself.

But how could he stay away for days? Weeks, even? Summer would be over. If he didn't go farther than he'd gone
before, if he just went back to check it out more carefully,
the part where he'd already been, what could be the harm?

On the bus that afternoon, Buck was one of the first on
board, and took a seat only halfway back. Katie was in a
huddle with her girlfriends, all of them excited about something, and when she and Buck got off at the mailbox and
started the long walk up the lane to the house, she said,
"Guess what?"

Buck glanced over.

Katie gave him a secretive smile and her eyes sparkled.

"Yeah? What?" he asked.

She giggled. "Somebody asked me out."

"Well, hey!" said Buck. "Who's the g . . . guy?"

Katie tossed her head and her long brown hair flew
around and covered one cheek. "You don't know him."

"M . . . maybe I do."

She brushed her hair back. "He's an eighth grader."

"*Who?*"

"Colby Leisinger."

Katie was right. Buck didn't know him.

"He's on the basketball team. Second string," Katie said. She was walking slightly ahead of Buck now, avoiding his eyes. Born seven minutes apart, Katie was about an inch taller than Buck, and heavier, but because he was born first, she sometimes referred to him as her "older brother," and that made them laugh.

Buck was grinning now too. "How'd you meet him?"

"After practice once. When the cheerleaders were rehearsing. He seems nice."

"So where you g . . . going?"

"I don't know. He just asked if I'd go out with him sometime, and I said yes."

"Mom know?"

Katie came to a dead stop and faced him, then moved on again. "No, and you'd better not tell her. Dad either."

"Course not."

Buck had no problem keeping Katie's secret. Somehow they'd always gotten along, probably because the Andersons never treated them as twins. Katie usually took his side in arguments at the dinner table, and Buck had earned more than one bloody nose defending her on the playground when they were younger.

One of the ways Buck and his twin were alike was also one of the things that made them different: Buck was a risk taker when it came to crawling into places he shouldn't be, jumping boulder to boulder, or crossing a river on a slippery log.

Katie took chances too, but not physically. She liked to write and draw, to try out for plays and enter contests. The risks she took were being rejected or laughed at in public. Buck had enough of that without half trying. She especially enjoyed designing things: houses, parks, malls—these were her specialty. Her walls were covered with sketches of *Katie's Condo*.

Their large white farmhouse sat on eighty acres of land. The old Anderson farm had been subdivided decades ago, and four homesteads now occupied the ground where the first Andersons had raised cattle. Much of the land was too hilly for farming, and Gramps leased out the south pasture for grazing.

The asphalt on the long lane was worn thin, and Buck was so familiar with the location of bumps in the paving that he could probably have walked it blindfolded.

Katie, in fact, was walking backward now, facing him on his left, and suddenly she sniffed the air and said, "Are the lilacs blooming? I can tell without even looking."

Buck glanced over at the bushes Mom had planted two years ago. There were alternate white and lavender clumps that seemed to have blossomed overnight. "Yep," he told her.

"I *love* spring!" Katie gushed, throwing her head back, her arms wide. "It is *totally* my favorite season!"

"B . . . because you're in LOOoooove!" Buck crooned.

She gave him her look. "Okay. Your turn. I told you a secret. Now you have to tell me one."

"Why?"

Katie grinned. "Blackmail, what else? In case you tell mine."

"Have I ever?" He grabbed her arm. "Watch out. Pothole."

Katie turned back around and fell in beside him. "I never

42

had an important secret before. When Mom said no boy-friends till sixteen, she meant it."

Buck made a zipping motion across his lips with one finger. "Sealed," he said. "Thumbscrews? The r . . . rack? I'll deny it to the death."

They cut across the clearing, heading for the back porch. The Andersons still lived in the original house, which had been there since 1905. Now the barn was used for storing sawmill equipment, the family's livelihood for three generations.

Buck had just started up the steps, one hand on the screen, when suddenly Katie asked, "Buck, how come you don't stutter much when you talk to me? I mean, when there's just the two of us? Like now. Just wondering. . . ."

He was blindsided by the question. They'd never talked about it before. Not ever that he could remember. Of course, he'd wondered about it too in private. He tried to treat it as a joke.

"S . . . s . . . s . . . s . . . s . . . search m . . . m . . . m . . . me," he said.

Katie punched his arm and gave him a crazy cross-eyed smile.

But things would never be quite the same again.

Why had she brought it up now? He had always felt that with Katie, she didn't care. In second grade, he remembered, he'd been trying to tell some kids where he'd found his airplane, but couldn't say the word *radiator*.

"I f . . . found it on the r . . . r . . . r . . . ," he stuttered.

"Refrigerator?" someone guessed.

He shook his head.

"Road?"

"The roof?" said someone else.

"Just *wait*!" Katie had demanded, hands on her hips, and their playmates had dutifully waited Buck out.

But now, because of a boyfriend, maybe, she'd made it official: it wasn't just other people out there who were uncomfortable with his stuttering. Now it was Katie too.

And then there was that Sunday evening last month when he'd been reading the sports pages on the back porch until it got too dark to see. He'd leaned his head back, half dozing as night closed in, aware of his parents discussing supper options through the open doorway. Then Joel had come out in the kitchen.

"I found that website about a stuttering program in Norfolk," he had said, and Buck's eyes opened wide. "It's expensive, almost four thousand dollars for twelve days. . . ."

"What?" Mom's exclamation. "Is that for millionaires?"

"Norfolk's clear across the state!" Dad had said.

"Yeah. And Buck would have to stay in a hotel," Joel finished. "I'm just telling you what I found."

"Don, how would we ever afford that this summer, and which of us could stay with him for twelve days?" Buck remembered his mom saying.

"You know, if I thought it would cure the boy, I'd do it somehow" was Dad's reply. "Is that all you could find online, Joel?"

"Lots of other stuff—books on how to stop stuttering—I think he's got some of those. Then there are electronic devices, things you wear. . . ."

Buck had found he was gripping the glider armrests—

could remember that even now. Remembered how he had gotten to his feet and marched stiffly into the kitchen— surprising everyone there—and saying, "I'm not gggggoing to Norfolk. And I'm not going to wear any k . . . k . . . kind of electronic stuff either. Just ffforget it!" And he'd walked on through the kitchen and started upstairs.

But he had lingered long enough to hear his dad say, "Well, nothing's going to work if he's not willing to put in the effort. . . . "

And even now, just thinking about it, the familiar panic and heaviness rose up in Buck as he followed Katie inside. The feeling that if he *didn't stop stuttering* he was letting the family down, and they didn't realize—they just didn't know—that when he tried hard—really, really hard—to stop stuttering, the words clogged up his throat even more.

6

STAND OFF

Uncle Mel had only been home four days when he was off again, this time all the way to Idaho. He used to joke that there were places in the United States he could get to before he'd even started out. That was when Buck was five and didn't know about time zones.

Buck wished he were in a big semi with his uncle right now, going anywhere except down the road toward Jacob's. He'd rather be doing almost anything than this. He stopped at the mailbox, then wheeled his bike up the gravel driveway and leaned it against the grimy car. Uncle Mel had dropped by there on Tuesday before he left, so Buck was doing Friday solo.

A bumblebee was making slow irregular circles in the

air just outside the screen as Buck went up the concrete steps. He rang the bell and waved the bee off as he stood there in his cutoffs and a Ravens T-shirt. He waited ten or fifteen seconds, glancing out at the Volvo and wondering when Jacob had driven it last, then rang again and waited some more.

He hoped Jacob wouldn't have a long list of jobs to do. Hoped, in fact, that Jacob wouldn't want him today at all. He'd dropped his book bag home right after he'd gotten off the bus, grabbed a handful of Oreos, and wished now he'd had a soda too.

Buck rang the bell a third time, letting up on the button almost as soon as he'd pressed it as the door handle moved. And when Jacob Wall appeared at last, leaning heavily on his cane, he stared down at Buck as though he were a complete stranger. He was wearing a faded army-green T-shirt with two eagles facing each other on the front.

"Mr. Wall?" Buck said. "It's F . . . Friday, and my uncle's out of t . . . t . . . town." He hated the way the word stuck in his throat, as though the sharp edges of the *T* caught on the back of his tongue, and he felt his face redden as he tried to spit it out. The harder he tried, it seemed, the more he stuttered. It made him look as though he was afraid of the person in front of him, and that wasn't the case.

Jacob made no reply. His eyes, half hidden beneath his bushy white brows, continued to stare down at him, and Buck realized he was still holding the man's mail.

"I b . . . b . . . b . . . brought your m . . . mail," he said, opening the screen and handing over the clutch of envelopes and advertisements.

47

Mr. Wall accepted it wordlessly in his free hand, then turned away, leaving the door open behind him. Buck entered and stood just inside the screen.

"There's the garbage," Jacob called gruffly from the kitchen, pointing to an overflowing trash basket by the wall. "Goes out to the can by the side of the house." And when Buck started forward, Jacob said, "And there's an olive pit or something down the disposal. See if you can get it out, take it with the garbage."

In the kitchen, Buck warily thrust his hand through the slimy rubber opening in the sink and felt around. He couldn't help imagining the man with the piercing eyes putting his own hand on the switch and turning it on while Buck's fingers were probing the blades. But a few seconds later, he fished out the olive pit and a small piece of bone. "Pukeman Repairs a Garbage Disposal," he thought, and pictured digits flying through the air. He'd remember that when he drew his next comic strip.

He took the sack of garbage outside and, when he returned, surveyed the dirty dishes on the counter. It was Friday, and if he expected to be paid . . .

"I could do those d . . . d . . . d . . . dishes for you," he said.

Jacob gave an almost imperceptible nod and laboriously sat himself down at the small table, reaching for his coffee mug. Out of the corner of his eye, Buck saw that the man was watching him, and he began to resent the audience, the silence. Then suddenly:

"How old are you?"

The question shot through the air unexpectedly.

"Thirteen," Buck answered.

"Go to school?"

What did the guy think? That he was stupid or something? "Of c . . . course," Buck said.

"Public?"

"Yeah." Buck gave an impatient glance over his shoulder.

But Jacob looked irritated too. "Your uncle set this whole thing up, didn't he?"

This time Buck turned and stared at Jacob. "Yes! Like he t . . . told you, he'll be d . . . d . . . doing m . . . more long-d . . . distance hauls. Asked if I wanted to t . . . t . . . t . . . take over while he's g . . . gone." What he *wanted* to say was *Look, I don't want to be here any more than you want me. I'm doing this for Mel, not you. And for the five bucks, if you really want to know.*

There was a longer silence now in the kitchen when Buck turned back to the pots and pans. He focused on the grimy faucet handles of the sink, the grease spots on the wall above the stove top. Jacob's place had the kind of dirt that accumulated because there was simply too much for one person to do. Even when Jacob used his cane, he had to lean against something when he was standing, Buck noticed, but as far as accepting help, he sure didn't make a person feel welcome.

"You can go when you've finished up here," Jacob said.

"Fine," said Buck through clenched teeth. The guy was lucky Uncle Mel had ever stopped by at all. Lucky that anybody cared about him. Buck sure didn't.

He poured bacon grease from a skillet into a tin can on top of the stove, then wiped the skillet out.

"Okay, I'm off," he said.

49

Jacob made no move to stand up and didn't acknowledge Buck's leaving. Buck let the screen door slam behind him and got on his bike. He was already past the mailbox when he realized he hadn't been paid. A deal was a deal, and the old man had stiffed him. No way, however, *no way* was he going back.

Bealls' Country Store stood at a crossing, and the smaller room just off the entrance served as post office for the town. Mrs. Beall was the official postmistress, but most of the time she was helping out in the store.

Buck wheeled into the dirt lot and rested his bike against the porch. Then he stomped up the wood steps and lifted the lid of the giant cooler. Frosty cans of Pepsi and Mountain Dew, of 7UP and Orange Crush rested in disarray in the ice. He selected his drink, then stepped inside where Mrs. Beall was talking with two women at the cash register. He raised the can so she could see it, and when she nodded, placed his dollar bill on the counter and went back out to his bike.

He drank as he rode, one hand lightly on the handlebars. *Jacob should have paid me and I should have asked*. The chilly liquid cooled his mouth but not his temper. Finally, however, when the drink was almost gone, his feet moved more slowly on the pedals, and he let his shoulders relax, liking the feel of going in and out of shade.

He had just about concluded that maybe Jacob had been in the army once, and was used to bossing people around. But then he remembered the paperweight on his desk with an anchor imprinted on it. And the photograph of a ship in the hallway, with two signatures at the bottom. Maybe Jacob had been in the navy. Maybe the ship had gone down with his two best friends on board, and Jacob hadn't been the same since.

Oh, to heck with Jacob anyway, he decided. He had better things to think about. And the first one that came to mind was the Hole.

• • •

The sawmill sat in a clearing off the old county road among the oaks and poplars. The sign, back at the turnoff, read ANDERSON MILL AND LUMBER, and the *A*, the *M*, and the *L* were spelled out with little logs, Mom's idea, when the sign was changed seven years ago. It used to read simply SAWMILL in big black letters, and that was all anybody needed to know.

A high chain-link fence surrounded two acres bare of trees, where a thin layer of pine needles and sawdust covered the ground. A low cinderblock building was set back from the gate, with two carport-like additions, one on either side. Under the corrugated tin roof of one was a stack of four-by-eight plywood sheets, waiting for customers—contractors, hardware stores, and weekend carpenters. Next to the plywood was a pile of eight-foot pine planks. These had come from Gramps's own saw. And propped against one side of the addition were fence posts, also made on the premises.

Buck pedaled around to the other end of the building.

He was wrestling with not only *what* he would take with him the next time he went caving but *when* he would go. It had to be a day no one would miss him—when Mom was working and Mel was gone; when Joel and Gramps and Dad, all three, were here at the sawmill, preferably for the whole day. The old Wilmer place was eleven miles off, and Buck had to allow time to get there, pull on Mel's overalls, do his exploring, take off the overalls, hide them somewhere nearby, ride home again, shower, and put the rest of his clothes in the washing machine before anyone saw him. He didn't worry about Katie.

"What happened to *you*?" she might ask, staring at his muddy clothes. Buck would joke that he'd fallen off a cliff and was swept downriver and ended up in quicksand. "Haha," she'd say, and go on sketching or reading or watching TV, and forget about it.

A high-pitched whine split the air, meaning that someone was using the huge diesel-powered saw. Buck steered over to one of the posts holding up the tin roof of the second portico and parked his bike.

Grandpa Anderson—Art, to his friends—was leaning slightly forward, palms resting on a thick log he was splitting. At least an inch of sawdust covered the ground. Joel stood next to him, ready to reposition the log. The saw whined again.

When the old man saw Buck approach, he grinned and nodded a greeting, and Buck waited. Two log-slider tractors were parked some distance away next to a two-ton truck. Gramps had invested everything he had in the business, and somehow, after dozens of sawmills had stopped operation a decade or two ago, Anderson's kept going.

When the log was cut and Joel went off to get the forklift, Gramps reached for his water bottle and took a long drink. "Just one more week of school, huh?"

"Yeah," said Buck.

"Nothing to do at home today?"

Buck shrugged. He didn't know what it was, but Gramps always looked like a little old professor, even in his battered gray work cap and overalls. The way his glasses balanced on his nose, maybe.

"Just r . . . r . . . riding around. Dad going to be c . . . c . . . cutting timber anytime soon?"

"Why? You want to go along?"

That wasn't what Buck had in mind. If Dad and Joel went timber cutting, they were definitely gone all day, and Gramps was here at the sawmill. All Buck wanted to know was when. He shrugged.

"Well, a man's got a couple acres he wants thinned out west of here. You're on vacation. I 'spect you could go along."

"Just asking," said Buck.

He liked being in the woods with his dad and Joel all right, but he wouldn't go this time. With everyone gone all day, Buck could set out in the morning, not come home till afternoon, and no one would even know he was gone.

The biggest questions went unanswered: when he went into the Hole again, just how far would he go? Could he trust himself not to do something stupid?

7

THEFT

The talk was of tornadoes that evening. May was almost over, and there had been few of them around the country.

"Down in Texas, they're still remembering what happened in Saragosa that one time," Mrs. Anderson said, placing the scalloped potatoes, Gramps's favorite, directly in front of him. "My cousin said they always mention it in Sunday service—the thirty people who died."

"Didn't have any warning?" asked Joel.

"Town didn't have a siren. The warnings that came on the radio were in English, and most of the town speaks Spanish. Twenty-two of the people were in a church that collapsed on top of them."

Katie stopped chewing momentarily and shuddered.

"Well, if I had to choose, I'd take tornadoes over earthquakes. At least *someone* knows it's coming. With earthquakes, the ground just opens like a huge mouth. You're walking across the street and all at once you fall in this gaping hole and you're suffocated by dirt and mud. Like the earth swallowing the Israelites."

"What?" said Buck.

"Whoa," Dad said. "Not quite like . . ."

"One of the seven plagues," Katie continued. "You know— the frogs and grasshoppers and stuff."

"Locusts," said Gramps. "God sent locusts."

"The Israelites died in an earthquake?" asked Buck. "I thought they m . . . made it across the R . . . R . . . Red Sea."

Mrs. Anderson's face registered both shock and consternation. She'd lifted her fork, and now set it down again. "I can't believe that my children don't know their Bible any better than that. There were *ten* plagues, Katherine, but an earthquake wasn't one of them." She took a bite of turnip then, but her frown still rested on her daughter.

"I remember that God got angry and the earth swallowed somebody," Katie insisted.

"Just three of them, and they deserved it," said her mother. "Look it up in the Book of Numbers."

Down at their end of the table, Joel and his dad exchanged amused glances. It always got Mom going when someone forgot their Bible study. Buck's thoughts, however, were not on the Israelites, but on Katie's description of the earth caving in around you. He didn't much like the thought of that either.

"Never argue with a Sunday school teacher, Katie," Dad said, grinning, and reached across Buck for another roll.

"Well, I'd like to send a plague on whoever's stealing my plywood," Gramps said.

"You still going on about that, Pop?" Dad asked.

"I'm goin' on about it 'cause it's still going on," Gramps replied, "and don't tell me it's not, Don, 'cause I can count. We started with sixteen sheets of plywood on Monday when we restocked. I've checked off every sheet we sold since then, and two more's unaccounted for. Last time it was four went missing."

"You're telling me someone's come by at night, crawled over an eight-foot fence, pulled two four-by-eight sheets of plywood off the stack, and hauled 'em back over the fence?"

Gramps was getting hot under the collar now, Buck could tell.

"I'm not tellin' *how*, I'm tellin' *what*. Unless he walked out with it in broad daylight when we were open, the three of us blind as bats . . ."

"Yeah, we'd have seen him," said Joel. He ate with both forearms resting on the table, out of either weariness or habit. There was a new pimple blossoming on his forehead, and it looked as though he might have tried smearing something on it before dinner.

"That's what I'm saying." Gramps picked up his iced tea and looked around the table. Then he shook his head. "Things are sure different now from back in the fifties. Didn't even have to lock the fence at night. Nobody would dream of drivin' up to a lumberyard, going in, and taking things didn't belong to him. Not around here anyway."

"But you *do* padlock the fence at night, don't you, Art?" asked Mom.

"What do you think?" Gramps huffed. He seldom raised his voice to his daughter-in-law. "Now I got to get me a junkyard dog to guard the place? I just want to know who around here's doing a little remodeling—a little fixing up. That'll be my clue."

Dad wiped his napkin across his mouth and studied his father, bemused. Buck could tell by the look that passed between him and Joel that they weren't all that sure of Gramps's memory. "Heck, Dad, it could be anyone with a truck. From another county, even. A few sheets of plywood won't break us. Let it go."

"At twenty-six dollars a sheet? It's the way they're doing it, a little at a time so's we won't notice!" Gramps was fuming. "Well, I notice, and wonder what else they've taken we don't know about." His forehead was now as red as the plaid in his favorite shirt. "Anyone's kept a business going long as me, he's got to have an eye for detail. And I tell you, this thing upsets me."

For just a moment, Gramps's scowl reminded Buck of Jacob Wall's face when Buck had left him that afternoon. The difference was that Gramps only soured on the world now and then. With Jacob, it seemed, it was all the time.

● ● ●

The last week of school.

Uncle Mel had gotten home from his cross-country trip to Idaho the Sunday before, and left again on another run Monday morning to Michigan. As Buck rode to school on Tuesday, he wondered if wherever Uncle Mel was on the highway, it was raining as hard as it was here.

Stop! Stop! he begged, staring out at the dark sky. A downpour like this would make the Hole a waterfall, and he'd slip right down into it when he went in again. It could make the whole passageway a mudslide.

The huge rubber blades that swept across the windowpane with their rhythmic *swish, swash, swish, swash* provided the bus driver with only intermittent views of the road before the glass was covered again in wavy rivulets of water. Buck liked being in the seat at the very front, where the road rolled out before them like a movie set. Especially liked being away from Pete Ketterman and his friends, who were hooting it up in back.

Everyone talked excitedly about summer and how they were going to spend it. Not many went to camp in this part of Virginia—cost too much money, for one thing—but camp was all around them every day: the Appalachian foothills, the streams, the hiking trails. . . .

Thirteen and fourteen were too young for most jobs in town, but some of them, like Buck, would be working for their parents.

In the late afternoon or evenings, they gathered at the small grassy knoll outside the pharmacy on Center Street. It was just wide enough for two benches, facing each other, and a small dogwood tree that bloomed white about the middle of April.

Like the other kids, Buck and David used to ride their bikes along the popular two-block stretch of Center Street, past the Pizza Place, the shoe repair store, Jay's Optical, the Sweet Shop, and ended up parking their bikes at the rack outside the Palace Theater.

Friends would see how many of them could squeeze together on the two wood benches, and laugh at the tricks the guys were pulling on each other. Buck and David mostly watched, but all the kids wished they were old enough to hang out at the B&I across the street.

There was probably no other store in the United States named Billiards and Ice Cream, Doris Anderson had remarked once. Grandpa said it was started back in the forties because the man who owned it liked to play pool and his wife liked ice cream. And though a number of places along Center Street sold ice cream, including the Sweet Shop and the drugstore with its old marble soda fountain, the only one in the whole downtown with the word "ice cream" in its name out front was the B&I. It was a favorite hangout for anyone over sixteen, and even after it got its liquor license, the new owners kept the name and the ice cream.

The summer before, when Buck and David hadn't been exploring, they'd mostly sat straddling their bikes, providing an appreciative audience for Nat Waleski and his friends, who competed with each other to see who could balance a Snickers bar on end the longest, or juggle cellophane packs of jelly beans, three or four at a time. But as vacation approached this year, Buck wasn't thinking about Center Street or even the B&I. He had other plans.

At lunchtime in the school cafeteria, Buck always sat near the windows where he and David used to sit. Sometimes people joined him, sometimes not. Today, red-haired Nat, in one of his trademark black T-shirts with mythical beasts and Latin phrases on the front, sat down across from him, the obligatory apple provided by the school rolling around on his tray.

What Buck liked about Nat was the very thing he hadn't liked the first time they'd eaten together.

"What's the matter with your sandwich?" Nat had asked, looking at the Tuesday Special Buck had barely touched. Getting in his space already, and they hardly knew each other.

Buck had managed to shrug and mumble, "M . . . m . . . mayonnaise," sure that Nat was just trying to get him to stutter. Instead, he was surprised when Nat said matter-of-factly, "You care if I eat it, then?" and when Buck slid it toward him, he said, "Thanks," and ate the whole thing, even the half-circle imprint Buck had left in the bread.

After that, Buck was prepared for Nat's curiosity: "You like being a twin?" or "What's your shoe size?" he'd ask without sounding rude in the least. After a while, Buck even found it entertaining. Nat's whole face was interesting—the way his eyes, nose, and mouth were bunched together in the middle, with all that white space around the outside. His complete lack of self-consciousness made him popular with the other students.

"Whuzzup?" he was saying now, and took a huge bite of his cheesesteak sandwich, one finger poking a dangling grilled onion back into his mouth.

Buck smiled and shrugged. "N . . . nothing much."

Nat chewed, turning the cheesesteak around and around in his hands, studying it from every angle before he took his next bite. "I don't know why . . . they don't just let us out . . . a week early," he said as he chewed. "The teachers are only wasting time."

"Yeah."

"In Earth Science, we watched the same video we saw back in sixth."

"'The Ice Age'?" Buck asked, and they both laughed.

"Yeah. Were you in Rasmusson's class last year?"

Buck shook his head.

"You know what he did the last day of math?"

"Mmmmmade you do his income t . . . tax?"

Nat laughed, and Buck felt good about his joke.

"No, but almost as bad. He comes in with this big pile of newspapers, and wants us to circle all the ads for a used Honda. Says he's looking for another car. And when we'd finally finished, he said, 'Thanks, class. You've saved me a ton of work. Have a good summer.'"

That made them both laugh.

A girl came by—a pretty girl with braces on her teeth, a friend of Nat's, obviously. She sat down sideways on the chair next to him.

"I finally decided on my elective for next year," she said. "Speech and Drama. What did you choose?"

Eighth graders were allowed to choose one elective course—another reason to enjoy being in the top tier of middle school.

"Guitar," Nat told her.

"Cool!" The girl turned her green eyes on Buck. "What about you?"

All the self-confidence Buck had mustered in the conversation so far seemed to evaporate like steam on a mirror. The word he wanted—the only word possible—loomed up in front of him like a concrete wall, and he instantly felt the familiar shot of panic. Each syllable of pho-tog-ra-phy seemed to be imprinted there, one obstacle on top of another. The *ph* sound was tricky, and *T* and *G* were letters that usually felt like explosives to Buck, trying to get them out. For a moment he thought of substituting "camera" in its place, but a hard *C* was just as difficult.

He could feel his jaws turning rigid, his throat swelling. Air was escaping from his lips without a sound to go with it. Two people were waiting for him to speak—two normal people who could just open their mouths and say anything at all without a problem.

"Phhhhhh . . . phhhhhh . . . ," he began, blinking, then, "t . . . t . . . t . . ." He felt perspiration on his face and stopped to breathe, then began all over again. "Phhhhh . . . phhhh . . . t . . ."

"Photography?" Nat guessed.

No! Buck hated it when someone supplied the word for him—Buck, the simpleton who probably couldn't even tie his own shoes. Still, it ended the torture.

The heat of his face seemed to burn his lips, and Buck looked down at his tray, nodding without speaking.

"Well, that should be fun too," the girl said, in a tone someone's mother might use.

Buck didn't want a pat on the head. He didn't want pity. He waited while Nat and the girl talked a couple minutes longer, then he murmured a faint "See ya," got up, and returned his tray to the kitchen window.

What was wrong with him? Why hadn't he just stayed at the table? He and Nat had been hitting it off pretty good this last semester, and now he really had acted like a weirdo.

He knew by the way kids were looking at him that his

face was beet red. And as though life couldn't wait to pile it on, the moment he got out in the hall, he saw Katie and a guy he hadn't met coming toward him.

There was no way to avoid them. Nowhere to turn. Katie grabbed the boy's arm—a tall guy with eyebrows as blond as his hair—so blond it appeared he had no eyebrows at all.

"Buck!" she called. And then, turning to the guy beside her, said, "Colby, this is my brother."

Buck could tell by her face that she'd noticed the flush in his. Her eyes questioned him, but before she could say anymore, Colby said, "Hi. How ya doin'?" and smiled.

Buck didn't trust himself to say anything. And so he didn't. Just gave a feeble smile and kept walking, Katie staring helplessly after him.

8

THE UNEXPECTED

The problem with being mad at himself, Buck discovered, was that—short of riding his bike off a cliff—there was only so much he could do for punishment. The rain had stopped, so he used his anger to ride over to Jacob's house after school to get his five dollars.

He rehearsed his lines ahead of time. "You forgot to pay me on Friday," and then, when he got the money, "I won't be working here anymore. Sorry." He'd leave off the "sorry," maybe.

As soon as the door opened, however, and he stepped inside, Jacob surprised him by handing him the five-dollar bill.

"For last week," he said, and nodding toward the kitchen,

he added gruffly, "Want some lemonade? At least, that's what they call the yellow stuff at that bargain place."

What Buck wanted to do was to say no and leave, but in fact he was desperately thirsty. In his anger he had simply dropped his backpack at home, climbed on his bike, and taken off, without bothering to get a drink or a snack. How could he tell Uncle Mel that Jacob had paid him and offered him lemonade, and he'd still turned around and walked out? He'd already been rude once today.

"Okay," he murmured, and followed Jacob into the kitchen. But then, having said yes to the lemonade, he realized he could hardly say no to whatever jobs Jacob had lined up for him that afternoon, and he felt mad at himself all over again. He had been planning to finish the glass standing up, but when Jacob lowered himself to a chair and nodded toward the one across from him, Buck felt he had no choice. It was getting worse by the minute.

Jacob's voice was still deep and gravelly, but seemed to have lost some of its sharpness, and his bushy brows no longer met in the middle like a V. He picked up the plastic jug on the checkered oilcloth and filled two glasses. Pushing one toward Buck, he took a swallow of his own drink, his mouth puckering at the sourness. Then he asked, "How long have you been stuttering?"

One thing you could say about Jacob Wall, he didn't beat around the bush. What business was it of his? What was *with* this guy, anyway? It was all Buck could do not to say, or try to say, "What's it to you?"

What he said was "Why d . . . do you want t . . . t . . . to know?" He was surprised at his own boldness.

"I used to work in a military hospital with speech patients," Jacob said. "I figured your uncle found that out somehow and thought this whole thing up—you working here, and that annoyed me last week."

Buck lowered his glass. "You're a d . . . doctor?"

"Was. Not practicing anymore. A speech doctor, not an MD."

"We hardly know anyth . . . th . . . thing ab . . . b . . . b . . ." *Not here! Not now!* Buck thought, and started over. "Hardly know anything ab . . . b . . . bout you. J . . . just thought you n . . . n . . . needed some help."

For a long time, it seemed, Jacob sat without speaking, and Buck sensed that he too had to work not to be rude. Finally the man said, "Well, I was thinking the same about you. I worked with men who stuttered."

Try as he would, Buck could not picture this stern-looking man in this small cramped house as a professional in a white coat. Or maybe he hadn't worn a coat. Buck still couldn't imagine it.

"Wh . . . wh . . . what d . . . did you d . . . do for them?" he asked, unconvinced.

"It's what they did for themselves. But it's hard work, and I didn't accept just anyone into the program."

"Yeah, well . . ." Buck drained his glass and pushed it away. "I'm g . . . going to start th . . . th . . . the . . ." He took a deep breath and tried again, blinking his eyes and tightening his jaw. "I'm going to st . . . st . . . start th . . . therapy at school. Th . . . thanks." He was stuttering on practically every word!

"How often do they see you in therapy at school, Buck? Every day?" Jacob just wouldn't quit.

66

Buck almost laughed. If you saw the therapist every *week*, that was exceptional. "C . . . couple times a m . . . m . . . month," he said.

"And you think that's going to help?"

"I d . . . don't know," said Buck. "B . . . but it's all s . . . s . . . s . . . set up."

"Okay, then," Jacob said. "Just thought I'd offer."

Buck stood up. "G . . . got any jobs for m . . . me today?"

• • •

When Buck got home from school on Wednesday, Mel was there, showered and rummaging stocking footed through the refrigerator.

"Heeeey!" he said when Buck and Katie walked in. "What do you guys eat when I'm gone? Nothing much here but peas and carrots. You a bunch of bunnies or something?"

Katie laughed. "There's nothing in there you like, you mean. We didn't know you'd be home." She gave her uncle a quick hug. "Amy and Sara are coming over and we're making popcorn, if you want any."

"Take more'n popcorn to fill me up," Mel said, and sat down on a kitchen chair to put on his shoes while Katie took her stuff to her room. Soon music by her favorite band drifted down from upstairs.

Buck had just grabbed a couple of crackers when Mel gave him a mischievous look—first the squint in his brown eyes, then the smile that traveled sideways.

"Got an idea, Buck," he said. "Let's go pay your mom a visit at Holly's."

• • •

Whatever it was, Buck was ready—ready to forget this rotten, no-good day, and he was out the door even before Mel picked up his keys. He wished his uncle could drive the big semi he used for business home after each run, but he had to park it instead at the terminal in Roanoke, then drive his own car the rest of the way. It was fun the few times he'd let Buck sit up there in the passenger seat of the huge vehicle, though. Like riding around in a two-story building. Now he settled back in Mel's Ford and buckled his seat belt.

"Anything h . . . happen on this l . . . last trip?" Buck asked.

"Nothing much to speak of. Some crazy fool with a U-Haul trying to play musical chairs with me just this side of Chicago and almost got himself killed. I go to pass a Honda, see, travelin' along at sixty-five, and this guy's right behind me like he's riding my tailwind. I figure as soon as I pass the Honda and pull over, he'll pass me and go barreling on up the road."

"And what happened?"

"As soon as I see I'm clear, I start to pull over, but that's not soon enough for the U-Haul. Instead of waiting for my rig to move over, he tries to pass me on the right. I see him disappear from my side-view window, and I'm thinking, 'What the heck . . . ?' And then I hear the Honda blasting its horn and a squeal of brakes, and I realize the idiot with the U-Haul's between me and the Honda, 'bout to be squeezed like a tin can."

Uncle Mel reared back in his seat and wiped one hand on his thigh. "Makes me sweat just to think about it. I managed to pull back, just time enough that I didn't squash him like a june bug. Him and his U-Haul too. And you know what? When he *does* go around and I let him pass, does he thank me for saving his life? He gives me the finger!"

Mel shrugged it off then and let out his breath. Finally he glanced over at Buck. "So how are things back here? You stop by Jacob's while I was away?"

"Yeah. Put a p . . . patch on one of his s . . . screens. M . . . mopped the kitchen floor and stuff." Buck had already decided not to tell his uncle about his conversation with Jacob that day. Instead, he asked, "What k . . . kind of w . . . w . . . work did he d . . . do before? You know?"

Mel shook his head. "Haven't the slightest idea. I noticed one of his letters was addressed to a Dr. Jacob Wall, but there's all kinds of doctors out there. Could've been a dentist, for all I know. But you'll never get it out of him. Lucky he'll even give you the time of day."

Buck stared straight ahead and said nothing.

• • •

Fifteen minutes later they pulled off the highway onto a side road that brought them into the back lot of Holly's Homestyle Restaurant.

Buck tried to stop smiling as he went around and came through the front entrance, his Nationals cap backward on his head, as he usually wore it. Charlie, the short-order cook, raised a spatula in greeting and went on turning onion slices on the grill.

"How you doin', Buck?" he called.

Doris Anderson, who was cleaning tabletops in the booths, looked up as Buck sat down at the counter.

"Well, hi!" she called, stopping to wipe one arm across her forehead. "You come out here on your bike?" The white apron she wore over her green and gray uniform had a few spots on it from serving the breakfast and lunchtime crowd, and Buck knew she hadn't had a break yet because she always changed her apron at the break.

"G . . . got a ride," he said, and braced his hands against the counter, scanning the menu on the wall. It wasn't unusual for Buck to show up at the restaurant on a late afternoon when the place wasn't busy. Not unusual for him to get a ride with someone going this way, and then ride home with Mom if she had the car, or with Dad if he came to pick her up.

Sometimes, if there was food left over from the blue plate special, they gave it to him free. He was always hungry. "Anything you want t . . . to get r . . . rid of?" he asked.

"You," said Charlie, and they laughed.

"Well, now, aren't you something! Coming in here bold as brass, asking for handouts," said his mom with a grin. She picked up a tray on the counter. "Let me get these dishes in the machine and I'll see what we've got left in the fridge. Pork and sauerkraut, maybe. I'll sit down with you in a few minutes." She balanced one end of the tray on the palm of her hand, the other end on her shoulder, and moved through the double doors to the kitchen.

As soon as she was gone, Mel came through the front entrance, one finger to his lips. Charlie grinned and dumped another handful of onions on the grill where they spit and hissed, their savory scent filling the air. The small man looked something like an onion himself in his white shirt and pants, and an apron even more stained than Mom's. He

70

was sallow-complexioned, and what little hair he had stood up in one gray tuft on the top of his head.

It was several minutes before Buck's mom came back, wearing a clean apron and holding a dish of bread pudding.

"This is all we've got," she said, setting it down before Buck, and then, to Charlie, "My human garbage disposal." She nodded affectionately toward her son. As she straightened the salt and pepper shakers on the counter, she scanned the room, then fixed her eyes on a man who sat slumped at a booth in the corner. His head was buried in one arm on the table, the collar of his stained Windbreaker turned up around his ears.

"When'd he come in?" she asked Charlie.

Buck, perched on a stool, was glad he had a mouthful of bread pudding because it helped keep him from smiling.

"Couple minutes ago," Charlie replied, unsmiling.

"Is he drunk?"

"I don't know. Don't think so. But this is the last of the liver and onions, and if he don't want it, it's my supper," Charlie said.

At that moment a thin, straight-backed woman came through the kitchen door and looked over to where Uncle Mel sat sprawled at the table in the corner booth. *Holly*, the green embroidered letters on her uniform read. Her dyed black hair was scooped on top her head, held there with a comb, making her look even taller.

She turned to Buck's mom. "Who's he?"

"We don't know, but he's either drunk or asleep," said Mom. She pulled her order pad from the pocket of her butcher-style apron and walked over.

"You ready to order, sir?" she asked the man in the

71

rumpled Windbreaker, whose breathing was now loud enough for Buck to hear.

There was no answer.

Buck watched his mom try again.

"Good afternoon," she said loudly. She leaned a little farther over the table and took the menu out from behind the napkin holder. "Hello?" she added, nudging Mel's head with the menu. And when there was no response still, she said, "Sir? *Sir?*"

Holly stuck her head in the kitchen and called, "Pearl? Come out here a minute, would you?"

They were soon joined by a grandmotherly-looking woman whose blond hair didn't quite match her face.

"You know that man in the corner?" Holly asked.

"How do I know if I can't see him?" Pearl answered.

Buck had to drop his chin down to his chest and hold his shoulders rigid against the laughter swelling up inside him.

Pearl came out from around the counter and joined Buck's mom at the corner booth. The two women stood looking down on Mel, and then Pearl reached out and lightly shook his shoulder. "Excuse me," she said loudly, "but the kitchen's about to close. Won't be serving dinner for an hour. You want anything, you best tell us now."

Mel only grunted and Charlie rapped his spatula against the grill to disguise a chuckle. Buck wondered if Mel's watch wouldn't give him away, but perhaps the sleeve of the old Windbreaker kept it hidden.

Mrs. Anderson turned toward Charlie. "What am I supposed to do?" she asked.

"Tell him he can't sleep here, to move on," Charlie told her, deadpan.

Holly, watching from the kitchen doorway, agreed. "Not good for business, folks walk in, see that."

"You think we ought to pour some water on his head?" Pearl suggested.

And suddenly the rumpled jacket moved, the cap rose up, and two hands reached out, one to grab Doris Anderson's arm, the other, Pearl's.

The women screamed and stepped backward, and then the cap fell off.

"Mel!" Buck's mother cried, hitting at him, and she and Pearl both whacked him over the head with the menus while he roared with laughter, and Buck and Charlie joined in. Holly, trying to hide a smile, turned away with a shake of her head.

"You *tramp*, you!" Mom said, laughing too now. "Where'd you get that dirty old cap and jacket?"

"I keep 'em in the truck, case I have to change a tire in bad weather," Mel said, wiping his eyes, and guffawed some more.

"Well, I was about to call an exterminator to get rid of you," Holly told him. "But now that you're here, I suppose you'd like some coffee."

"If you please, ma'am," Mel said, making her smile. "I'll have that last piece of coconut cake too, and I'm paying."

Mom brought over the cake, the coffeepot, and some cups and sat down across from Mel. Buck took his bread pudding and joined them.

"I don't know how I tolerated a brother like you!" Mom said, reaching up to tuck a loose lock of hair under her small pleated cap. "Like to give me a heart attack, grabbing at us that way."

73

"Good for your reflexes," Mel said. "Keep you looking young."

"Why didn't you call and let us know you'd be home for dinner? I don't have a single thing on my mind to cook tonight. Figured I might buy something here to take with me."

"Don't you worry. Buck and I are going to pick up some ribs on the way back. We'll even have the table set. All you'll have to do when you get home is sit down."

"Now, that's the best news I've heard all day," said Mom. Then she looked at Buck and back to Mel again. "You guys!"

• • •

He was heading downstairs in his stockinged feet that evening when he heard Katie talking about him to Mom in the kitchen. Buck paused in the hallway, one shoulder against the wall.

"He just acts so strange sometimes, Mom. My friend Colby looked at me and said, 'What'd I *do*?' I had to explain it's because he stutters. Buck didn't even say hi. How can I introduce him to people if he acts so weird?"

His mom murmured something—Buck couldn't make it out—and then he heard her say, "I don't know, Katie. I really don't." She sounded tired.

Katie went on: "It didn't use to bother me, but . . . but I see how it's going to hold him back. What will happen to him when he gets to high school? Kids tease him on the bus—I hear it every day. I can't go around apologizing for him forever."

"Buck's going to see the therapist at school in September."

"Yeah? He's been through that before. I *worry* for him,

74

Mom. What kind of job is he going to get when he's grown up if he can't talk to anyone?"

"Now don't say he can't. You've heard him talk as good as anybody."

"But not when he really needs to!" There was exasperation in Katie's voice. Buck rarely heard it when she was talking with him, but he heard it now. "I want to help him, but I just don't know how."

"I don't know either, Katie. I don't know the answer to any of it," his mom replied wearily. "Each and every one of us will have a cross to bear before this life is over. Looks like Buck just got his a little early."

Buck turned and went back upstairs as softly as he had come. But when he sat down on the edge of his bed, he wheeled about suddenly and pounded the pillow. Again and again and again.

9

PUKEMAN
MAKES SPAGHETTI

Thursday after school, Buck rode out to check on the Hole. He couldn't keep away any longer. He told himself that all he wanted to do was make sure he could still find it.

Mel was sound asleep on the sofa, glad for some time off before his next run, and Katie had gotten off the bus a few stops earlier with one of her friends. Buck could get to the old Wilmer place and be home again well before dinner.

He left his backpack by the stairs so everyone would know he'd been there, and climbed on his bike.

Early June was a nice time in the valley, with the Blue Ridge Mountains beyond your backyard. Not yet too humid, the way it got in D.C., not as hot as North Carolina. The birds were going crazy, challenging each other's territory, and the air was sweet with their songs and the scent of honeysuckle.

As he neared the place, Buck had a momentary wave of panic because there were several fences that reached as far down as the road. Did he really remember which one he had followed before? But then he saw the edge of the woods coming closer and, more sure of himself now, he wheeled his bike off the shoulder, down into the gulley and up again, and left it beneath a gooseberry bush along the barbed wire fence that sagged in places and was completely down in others.

He tramped through the weeds, avoiding the nettles that sprang up here and there, and as he came close to the trees, he began counting the heaps of rock that spilled out into the pasture—the first, then the second, watching for the place where the ground dipped next to the tree line, the little heap of fox or dog bones. Yes, there they were, and his heart pounded with excitement when—there it was—just as before, the Hole, almost invisible.

Buck crouched on the rocks, feeling the cold draft coming up out of the earth, and pulled back the grass that hung heavy and wet over the entrance. Yes, the sides of the Hole inside were wet and sticky, and he knew that if he were to climb in there in the next few days, he would be covered with mud.

Now there was still another factor to consider. Not only would he need more equipment to go exploring again, not only did he need a full day, with everyone in the family gone so they wouldn't miss him, but it had to be a time the earth had a chance to dry out a little. An unexpected rain could ruin everything, no matter how well he planned the rest.

The important thing, though—it was still here. Still his. Once again he found himself smiling. Then he stood up and retraced his steps, back along the tree line to the road.

He was just wheeling his bike up out of the ditch when a car came around the curve ahead of him, and he stood there waiting till it passed.

There were two people in the front seat, and as it sped by, Buck saw that it was Ethan Holt and his dad. Ethan's face had a look of surprise as they passed, and then the car was gone.

• • •

Here it was: last day of seventh grade. And the worst.

In civics, Miss Gordon had a game. She was a young teacher in her second year, and near the end of class, she smiled as she handed a sheet of paper to each person in the front seats. Few teachers expected any serious learning to take place the day before summer vacation began, and often had something fun to do.

"There are six quotations on each sheet, and each sheet is different," she explained. "These are famous quotations on all sorts of subjects. Each person in the front seats will read their first quotation aloud and see who in the class can guess who said it. Then you'll pass the papers to the person behind you, and they'll do the same. We'll see how many we can guess before class is over."

Buck, in the third seat from the front, wished with all his heart that he had taken the back row when he came in.

Instead, he had followed Nat, taking a seat just behind him, and now he mentally calculated how long it would take before the sheet in their row got back to him. Each class was forty minutes long. Five rows, with four people per row . . .

He and Nat had eaten lunch together again today, and if Nat remembered his recent weirdness, he didn't show it. Now, Buck thought, if he could just get through this class without a major blockage . . .

"'Four score and seven years ago . . .'" came the first quotation, and almost everyone got it right: Lincoln.

"'One small step for man, one giant step for mankind,'" read the first person in the next row. Most of the class seemed to know it was said by the first astronaut who stepped on the moon, but only a few remembered that it was Neil Armstrong.

The quotes continued until the last person in the first row of seats had read his, and then all the sheets were passed to those behind them. Buck looked at the clock. This was going faster than he'd thought. He could feel perspiration trickling down his back.

For a long time the class was stumped on "'Ask not what your country can do for you; ask what you can do for your country.'" A debate broke out, and Buck watched the minute hand moving around and around.

"Well, let's move on, class," Miss Gordon said. "But I'm surprised you didn't know that was President John F. Kennedy."

"'Give me liberty or give me death,'" read the next girl, and several voices answered at once: "Patrick Henry!"

Buck's heart began to pound. There was a quote by Julius

Caesar that no one guessed, and it was six minutes before the bell. Two more students, and the papers would be passed along to the third row. Four minutes . . . Three minutes . . . Two . . .

Then the sheet of paper came gliding over Nat's shoulder and sailed onto the floor. Buck swallowed as he leaned down to pick it up in slow motion.

When he righted himself, his eyes traveled down the paper and settled on the next quote in the line. He felt his throat going tight: *To be or not to be; that is the question.*

Almost every single word began with a problem letter for Buck, a letter demanding explosive kinds of sounds: *T*s and *B*s were the worst—sharp sounds that even hurt his tongue to look at them, that stuck in his throat where they wouldn't come out. Choose another quote, he told himself, and he scanned the page. No, the next one began with a *D*. . . .

"Buck?" the teacher said.

He looked at the clock and down again. One minute left. One minute of absolute torture and humiliation. People were beginning to look his way.

"T . . . t . . . t . . . t . . . ," Buck began. The *T* was trying to get through, but his jaws were so rigid they even held his tongue prisoner.

He was running out of breath. He stopped, his shoulders sagging, took a monstrous breath, and tried again: "T . . . t . . . t . . ."

Someone giggled.

"Take your time," Miss Gordon said.

"He is!" someone said, and a few of the kids laughed.

"T . . . to b . . . b . . . be . . . be," Buck said, gasping, and

80

when he finally got to the last part of the quote, the part he could probably say, the bell rang.

Nobody stayed around to hear how perfectly he read the rest. And before Miss Gordon, with her sympathetic eyes, could make her way back to him, before even Nat could say anything, Buck scooped up his books with one hand, backpack with the other, and half walked, half galloped out the door.

• • •

On the bus, he sat four rows up from Pete Ketterman and his gang at the back. He positioned himself so that his body took up the whole seat, and neither Katie nor anyone else made a move to sit with him. He was glad, in fact, that Nat rode a different bus because he wouldn't have wanted to share the seat, even with him.

Buck wished more than ever that he was in the Hole right now, surrounded on all sides with rock and roots and earth, neither seen nor heard by anyone.

"Hey, Buck-o!" came Ethan Holt's voice over the rattle and chatter. "What were you doing out on old Bluestone Road?"

Buck almost stopped breathing. He refused to turn around.

"He was clear out there?" Rob asked.

"Yeah. Pushing his bike up out of the ditch. You ride off the road, Buck-o?"

"What do you *think* he was doing?" said Pete. "When you gotta go, you gotta go."

The four boys laughed, and a few girls ducked their heads and giggled too.

Except for the embarrassment, Buck was almost glad that this was what they thought. Just a brief pit stop down in the weeds.

"Hey, Buck-o, it's the last day of school," Pete called out. "Come September, Ethan and Isaac and me won't be on the bus anymore. Aren't you gonna miss us?"

That was *one* thing to be grateful for, Buck thought, except that Rob would still be here.

They tired of their heckling after a while, however, and talked about which bus they'd be catching in September, how early they'd have to get up to catch it. But it made Buck think about all the tricks they'd played on him the last two years—the embarrassment of knowing his face was Christmas red, that everyone was looking at him, whispering about him, and Pete Ketterman didn't care. Pukeman Ketterman just loved to watch him squirm. Boy, was Pukeman ever going to get it when Buck got home.

It was Isaac's stop, but Pete and Rob and Ethan usually got off with him. They always had something going, the four of them—they were just like Buck and David used to be—close.

As they passed Buck's seat, one of them whomped him on the head, and Pete said, "What *were* you doing down in the weeds, Buck-o? Wet your pants?"

"Shut up, Puke Face," Buck muttered, and felt his jaw freeze. *Had he said that?*

Pete came to a dead stop, Ethan bumping into him from behind.

"What's that? What's that?" Pete asked, leaning down, his face only inches from Buck's.

82

Buck didn't answer.

"You hear what he called me?" Pete said, turning to the others in mock horror. "The weirdo called me Puke Face. What d'you think we ought to do with him?"

"C'mon, fellas. Out! Out!" the driver yelled. "The rest of these kids want to get home too!"

Issac sent Buck's cap sailing toward the back window, and the four boys tumbled off the bus, laughing. Outside, however, Pete thumped hard on the window next to Buck, and he was only half grinning.

"Oh, Buck-o!" Isaac shouted. "You're in for it now!"

• • •

Now there was another thing to be careful about: not letting any of Pete's gang see him out on Bluestone Road again. Surely they'd be more than curious. If *they* found the Hole before he could explore it . . . That was the worst nightmare of all.

Buck was waiting for the day his dad and Joel would be out cutting down trees again, Gramps in charge of the sawmill; when Uncle Mel would be on another run, and Mom at work, Katie wherever . . . Maybe in the next week or two, if he was lucky.

On Saturday, his first day of vacation, he took the hoe to both the bean patch and the carrots, then lay on his bed, propped up on one elbow, and began a new Pukeman comic strip. "Pukeman Makes Spaghetti," he titled it in heavy black pencil.

In the first square, Pukeman was wearing a chef's apron and mixing the dough.

In the second square, he dropped the dough in the funnel of a big machine.

In the third square, with nothing coming out the other end, Pukeman stuck his head in the funnel to see what was wrong.

In the fourth square, his two feet were waving in the air as he was sucked down into the funnel, and in the final square, he was coming out the trough at the other end in ribbons, his body divided into noodles.

It was satisfying to draw, and now and then Buck found himself chuckling out loud. But in the end, it really didn't change anything, did it? Pete Ketterman was Pete Ketterman, no matter what happened to him on paper.

• • •

Mom had the day off. She came in Buck's room and sat on the edge of his bed, one hand resting on the green quilt, the other on her knee. Buck pretended to keep on drawing even though he'd finished the cartoon. He was glad she couldn't see it. He didn't want any questions.

"Buck," she said, "we need to talk about your stuttering."

He let a deep sigh serve as his answer.

"No, we really do," she continued, and Buck could see one finger nervously scratching at the quilt as she talked. "I want to know I've done everything I possibly could to help you. You understand that, don't you?" She waited.

"I g . . . guess so."

"It . . . really hurts me to see you hurting, Buck."

"I'm n . . . not hurting so b . . . ba . . . bad."

"Buck . . ." She touched his hand and kept it there. "You

would make me very happy if you'd go to a healing service with me over in Hillsdale on Sunday afternoon."

"Mom!" He jerked his head around and glared at her, then returned to his notebook.

"I read about a faith healer, Sister Pearson, coming all the way from Richmond to hold some healings in the area. The article said she's worked some real miracle cures for all kinds of problems. All I'm asking is for you to go with me."

"I'm n . . . not hurting that bad," Buck said again, without looking up from his paper.

"Well, I'm hurting for you." There was a catch in his mother's voice that Buck felt all the way down to the soles of his feet. "Please, Buck. If Jesus could cure the lepers and raise the dead, couldn't we show just a little faith in his power and see if it might help? It's just this one time."

"It's c . . . clear over in Hillsdale, Mom!"

"I know. But Sunday's the last day she'll be here, and then she's going on down to the Carolinas. We might never get another chance like this one."

Buck was trying to remember if Hillsdale sent their students to his school. No, they didn't, because they had their own basketball team.

Mom squeezed his hand and Buck swallowed.

"*Please*, Buck."

For thirty seconds or so, Buck didn't answer. As though if he didn't, she'd just get up and leave the room.

"Please . . . ," she said again.

He took a deep breath. "Just this one t . . . time."

10

SISTER PEARSON

Now that he had said yes, Buck wished he hadn't. He didn't mind going to church on Sunday mornings sometimes with Mom and Katie—even Dad, when he went along. He liked that he could sing every word of the hymns without stuttering once. He could even do the responsive readings, where everyone was reciting the same thing at the same time.

And Pastor Otis was okay. He'd taught Buck's Sunday school class once when Buck was nine, and one Sunday he told the kids that they could ask him any question at all about God or Jesus or sin. In fact, he had them write their questions down on slips of paper, fold them up, and put them in a box. Then he tossed them around a few times to mix them up, and read each one aloud, answering it in front of the class.

David had been here then, and his question was, "Who made God?" Four of the kids—and Buck suspected they were girls—had questions about sin: "Is it a sin to go to a movie with bad words in it?" Buck's question, though, was "Is heaven boring?"

"These are all good questions," Pastor Otis had said. "They show that you are thinking about your religious lives and what God has in store for you. Who made God? God simply was and is and always will be. How do we know he didn't make himself?"

And when David had given Buck the eye-rolling look, Pastor Otis had said, "If God is all-powerful, then why is that not possible?"

Finally, when he picked up Buck's question and read it aloud, he had smiled and said, "Is heaven *boring*? I want to ask you, is chocolate boring? Are roller coasters boring? I don't know what they've got in heaven, but think of all the pleasures of this earth and perhaps you can imagine what heaven is like. Everything you love multiplied by millions."

He made heaven sound like an amusement park, Buck had thought. And even those things could get boring if you did them long enough. Eternity was pretty long.

Out in the parking lot later, waiting for their parents, David had said, "I don't think he really knows any of it, do you? Did you notice how he always answered the question with a question?"

But the question Buck had thought a lot about but never asked was this: if God could do anything, even make himself, why hadn't he cured Buck of his stuttering? Buck had certainly asked him enough. In every prayer he'd ever prayed, that had been part of it.

Maybe Sister Pearson had the answer.

Still. He'd never been to a healing service, and life, to Buck Anderson, was something you always had to look out for, be ready for, and anticipate what was coming at you next. He pressed his head hard against the back of the seat as he watched the clear path the wiper blades made on the windshield, the way the rain simply drizzled back on it again. He'd rather be on the bus going to school, even with Pete Ketterman sitting behind him, than being here. His mother slowed the car as they entered the town of Hillsdale. This, he felt, was going to be a big mistake.

• • •

The first surprise was that the event took place in a tent, not a church. It was on a big grassy lot at the outskirts of town, beyond a Goodwill store. The words on the white banner stretched between two poles at the front of the lot were slightly blurred from the rain: FAITH HEALING, 4 P.M. ALL WELCOME. Still, the area was nearly filled with cars. Some people opened umbrellas as they got out; others simply made a dash for the tent, holding on to each other so as not to slip on the wet grass. A man in a wheelchair was covered top to bottom in a plastic raincoat.

It certainly wasn't a circus tent, but it could hold a fair number of people. There was sawdust on the ground to keep the feet dry, and maybe sixty or so folding chairs. Two wide aisles led to the platform in front, where only a chair and a table with a glass of water on it waited. And two middle-aged men were handing out song sheets, shaking folks' hands, asking where they were from, and helping them find seats.

Buck wanted to sit near the back, but his mom found two empty seats in the third row at the far left side, and Buck reluctantly sat down beside her, ducking his head and staring at the words of the hymns: *O, for a faith that will not shrink, tho' pressed by every foe, that will not tremble on the brink of any earthly woe!*

The first row was roped off, and the tent was filled with soft chatter and the squeak of folding chairs. Occasionally there would be a hearty hello of neighbor greeting neighbor, and finally Buck felt inconspicuous enough to look around. No one he recognized. Not even anyone his age. There were more walkers and wheelchairs than he'd ever seen in a service before. Seemed like every other person was sick or broken, and it frightened him.

Was that how other people saw him? Not just weird—he was used to that—but broken? Was that what his friends thought, all but David? Or Nat Waleski, maybe? What his family thought about him? Did Katie?

He stared down at the song sheet again: *There's not a friend like the lowly Jesus. . . . None else could heal all our soul's diseases. . . .* Was that what stuttering was—a disease? Something connected to sin? Something he had done? Or was it just that it rhymed with *Jesus*?

A sudden hush told Buck that the service was about to begin, and a gray-haired woman in a dark blue dress stepped up on the platform and sat down in the chair. She remained very still with her eyes closed, hands in her lap, her feet crossed at the ankles, and her face lifted toward the roof of the tent as though she were receiving telepathic messages from beyond, Buck thought.

At the same time, a gaunt-looking man took his place at the portable keyboard to one side, and the notes of "Take Time to Be Holy" came softly from the two speakers at each corner of the platform. Only his hands moved, his arms frozen above the elbows, and he sat bent over like a question mark, his shoulders were so stooped. In his black suit, he reminded Buck of a turkey buzzard that hung out near a yard full of chickens a few miles up the road back home. He would see it high in a tree looking down, or just making slow circles in the sky. These were not the kind of thoughts he should be having, he told himself. If he didn't believe that Jesus could heal him, he should have stayed home.

The music went on, one hymn running into another as late arrivals were seated, until finally, on some prearranged signal, it seemed, the music got so soft that it stopped, and Sister Pearson stood up. Her right hand moved to the little black microphone clipped to the collar of her dress, and she walked to the front of the platform.

She was not an especially large woman, but she had a large voice, low and clear, that carried well over the sound system. She gave a short talk about the importance of faith—how crucial it was to believe—really believe—that the Lord was able to heal through her.

"Doubt," said Sister Pearson, the gray hair across her forehead like the fringe on a lampshade, "is smoke, keeping the air from getting through. What you'll see at this service is not hypnosis or magic. It's the Lord's power—that's the sum of it. How many here will lift up your hand and say, 'Sister Pearson, I know it's not you doing the healing, it's God, and He's real'?"

Hands began to rise here and there until almost everyone's hand was in the air. Buck's mom raised her hand part-way and nudged him, but Buck sat like stone. How was he supposed to know for sure?

Then the rope in the front row was removed, and Sister Pearson asked those with a special need to come forward, down the left aisle, and sit down as space allowed. While the rest of the crowd was asked to sing the words on the song sheet, first one, then another person came forward and took one of the empty chairs while a few more stood in the aisle, waiting their turn.

Sister Pearson continued: "Friends, the Lord has been preparing me all my life for this work. If you want God to lift your spirits and heal your pain, you've got to believe He can do it. Sometimes you feel that relief right away. Sometimes you'll feel it by the time you get home. Sometimes it takes a day and sometimes it takes a week. But if His eye is on the sparrow, dear friends, it is certainly, most certainly, on you."

"Amen," said someone in the back row.

"Amen . . . Amen . . . ," came echoing voices from the crowd.

Buck's mind drifted again to the piano player, who was playing without music now, hymns Buck had heard played and sung in his own church with Pastor Otis doing the singing: "Love Lifted Me," "I Would Be True," "Open My Eyes," "Why Not Now?" He scanned the poles holding up the tent, the sag in the canvas at places where rainwater was probably collecting, then down to the electric cords that snaked from the speakers to some place under the side of the tent, and probably over to the Goodwill store.

Sister Pearson was stepping down off the platform now

and was standing over the first person in the front row of seats, placing her hands on his head. Her eyes were closed, and she looked upward again, her voice becoming a mighty wind as she called on God to heal this man of his sciatica—to straighten the disks in his spine that had given way, and heal him for the glory of the Kingdom of Heaven.

She grasped the sides of his face then, and it was hard for Buck to see what was happening next. But after thirty seconds, even forty, perhaps, with Sister Pearson continuing her prayer, the man slowly got to his feet, and the healer's hands went with him, so that she was reaching up now, and his back was erect, shoulders straight.

"Hallelujah!" someone said from the crowd.

"Yes, Hallelujah! God is good," said Sister Pearson, and the man began to smile.

As he moved on, one of the assistants helping him back to his seat, Sister Pearson bent over the next person in line, a woman in a pink jacket, whose hands clasped the handles of the walker that she had maneuvered jerkily down the aisle. There were murmurs between the two of them, and this time Sister Pearson kept her head down as she prayed loud and earnestly that God would relieve the woman of the pain in her hip and all the other internal problems that were plaguing her, for God knew our bodies more intimately than a surgeon ever could. . . .

One by one the people who had been prayed over rose and slowly took the right aisle back to their seats, some smiling, some not, and the empty chairs were soon filled by the next in line, then the next and the next. When Buck glanced cautiously around, he saw the line extending all the way to the back of the tent, and the stooped man at the keyboard played on.

"Mom, we're going to be here all night!" Buck whispered.

"What's a night compared to a lifetime of stuttering, Buck?" she said in answer, and Buck stretched his legs out in front of him as far as space would allow and settled in.

Sometimes Sister Pearson's voice was so faint it was only a murmur, not for the audience to hear, and other times she would let everyone in on the fact that this man or woman had been suffering with knee pain for eleven years, or headaches so severe it was impossible to get out of bed in the morning. There were people, Buck discovered, who had been in pain for more years than he was alive.

As rain pattered down on the roof of the tent, accompanied by a soft piano, Sister Pearson told the listeners that she could feel God's power surging through her shoulders, her arms, down into the palms of her hands and off the tips of her fingers. It was so strong, she said, it was like an electric shock, but she knew that she was taking the pain right out of the suffering creature before her. And then she would grasp the arm or the knee or the shoulder of that person, cover it with both hands, and once again plead with God to send his healing power. And suddenly she would jolt backward with the current and call out, "God is with you, brother!" or "Sister, you are healed!"

Sometimes the person she was touching would shout "Praise Jesus!" Sometimes he wouldn't say anything. Most looked somewhat stunned as they groped for their canes or their walkers again and made their way back to their seats.

Occasionally there was a distant rumble of thunder and a flicker of lights, but Sister Pearson carried on.

Buck wondered if he really belonged there. All the others seemed so willing, so eager, almost—to go down front with everyone watching, and tell Sister Pearson about their troubles. The thing he couldn't understand was why God had to wait for Sister Pearson to come to Hillsdale to do anything for them. God knew that Buck stuttered. If He didn't hear Buck's prayers, He surely heard Mom's. But it didn't seem right to ask *What are you waiting for?* of God.

Mom nudged him and gave him a quizzical look that meant *When are you going to go up?* and Buck just looked away.

Occasionally Sister Pearson would stop right in the middle of placing her hands on someone's head and call out something like, "God tells me there's a man here from Maryland who's had heart issues for seven years. Wherever he's sitting, God wants him to come up here where I can pass along God's healing grace." And once Buck heard a woman's voice say, "Howard, that's you! Go on! Go on up there!" And a man in a brown shirt and a bolo tie came down the aisle, surprise and wonder on his face.

How did Sister Pearson know that? Buck wondered. He wasn't sure when he should go up, though. He definitely didn't want her calling out his name, or the fact that he stuttered. He looked around and there were still a few people in the aisle, waiting their turn.

"Go *on!*" his mother urged.

He shook his head and folded his song sheet in halves, then in fourths, then folded it still again until it was just a hard lump inside his fist. His knee bobbed nervously up and down. What would Sister Pearson say to him? How much did she know? This was a hundred times worse than being on the school bus with Pete Ketterman kicking the back of the seat. This was a whole tent full of people watching.

"The service is going to be over, and you'll be the last one left," his mother whispered, nudging him again. "Is that what you want?"

Suddenly Buck propelled himself up out of his chair. He stumbled over the cane of the man sitting in the aisle seat and lurched down the aisle and onto one of the empty chairs in the first row. The two people sitting there turned and looked at him and so did Sister Pearson.

She closed her eyes again, however, and continued praying over the elderly man before her, willing God to cure his worsening eyesight.

Buck wished he were next. Wished it were over with and he was going back to his seat. Wished he and his mom were heading out to the car, and that on the way home he could talk a blue streak and the stuttering would be gone and finally he would be like everyone else. It could happen.

But there was still one more person between him and Sister Pearson, and the palms of his hands were so wet that he wiped them again on his jeans. The inside of his mouth felt like the dry fuzz on a tennis ball, and his jaws ached from the tension of holding them still. His whole body was trembling. Suddenly both the blind man and the man who had brought him down front were leaving, and the gray-haired woman with the piercing gray eyes was leaning over Buck.

"What do you ask of the Lord?" she said, and Buck tried to get his mouth open.

He jerked his head to one side, trying to fling the words

out, but his jaws were like a clamp. For a moment he felt as though something physical might have happened and he had lockjaw. His eyes were wild as he flung his head again and again, and the next thing he knew Sister Pearson had his head in both her hands, pressing her palms harder and harder against his cheeks until his lips puckered. She smelled of camphor and roses, and was so close that he could see all the lines of her face, even the faint fine mustache above her upper lip.

"I . . . I . . . uh . . . ," Buck stammered, but now he couldn't even shake the words out, and embarrassment was swallowing him alive. The two men who had started to walk away stopped and turned around.

Sister Pearson released his head and put both hands on his shoulders, pressing down, harder and harder to hold him still. Her eyes were closed, her face pointed upward, and everyone could hear her asking God to make this young man whole, dispel his troubled thoughts and heal his mind. "Give him the peace that passeth understanding, dear Jesus, because we know that in you, all things are possible. . . ."

11

RUNNING BACKWARD

Buck slammed the car door hard the moment he got inside.

"W . . . w . . . why'd you m . . . make me come, Mom?" he bellowed, writhing in the passenger seat as he clicked his seat belt buckle. "She th . . . th . . . thought I was c . . . crazy! Now every . . . b . . . body thinks it."

Mrs. Anderson was almost as upset as he was. "Buck, I'm *sorry*. I don't think she understood. Didn't you tell her you stuttered?"

Buck could only press his feet against the floorboards, his back stiff as a broom, then flopped himself against the door. "I t . . . tried b . . . but I couldn't s . . . say the w . . .

words!" he said miserably. "I hate myself! I h . . . hate b . . . being me."

"Buck, don't say that."

"You're not me!"

"There's so much about you to like. You know I love you just the way you are."

"That's a l . . . lie, Mom! If you d . . . did you w . . . wouldn't have t . . . t . . . t . . . tried to g . . . get that woman to p . . . p . . . p . . . pray over me."

"I only wanted to help! I want you to be happy in eighth grade, Buck! I want you to have a good time in high school. I want you to be able to get any job you want when you're grown. I don't want your stuttering to hold you back." She was crying, Buck could tell, and he hated himself all the more. Why *couldn't* he talk like other people when part of the time he could? Sometimes, he knew, teachers thought he didn't even try to control it. Or that he did it to annoy the other students and attract attention. He wished they could be him for just one day.

It was like a wall he couldn't climb over, he couldn't crawl under, and he couldn't get around. He didn't want to make his mother unhappy, always having to worry about him. And no, he didn't want to be teased or rejected either. He even imagined putting his mouth and jaws in some kind of primitive device all summer so his lips couldn't tremble, he couldn't make those awful sounds or stupid twisted faces when he stuttered that got people thinking he was weird or crazy. If there were such a device, he'd do it!

It just didn't seem fair. Not that he'd ever wish it on Katie, but they were twins. Why did he stutter and she didn't? He could remember back when he was four . . . maybe five . . .

thinking that someone must have taught her how to speak correctly but had forgotten to teach him. How desperately he had wished that, just as sometimes he'd go to bed with his leg hurting him, but wake up and the pain was gone, that some morning he'd discover he didn't stutter any longer. But that never happened.

• • •

It had been a quiet supper.

The tension between Buck and his mom was like vapor that had settled down over the table; every time people inhaled, their voices seemed higher, tighter, as though they might cough at any minute. When anyone spoke, it was about something trivial, with a lightness that belied the pink of Mrs. Anderson's face, the mechanical passage of Buck's fork from his plate to his mouth and back again.

He was the first one to leave the table. He rinsed off his plate and silverware in the sink, put them in the dishwasher, and went upstairs, closing the door to his room with a thud and flopping onto his bed. Buck lay staring up at the fine crack in the ceiling plaster that resembled, he'd often thought, the highway Mel took from Roanoke to Boston when he made the north/south run. Buck wished he were on that highway now, going almost anywhere, he didn't care where. Anywhere but here.

Downstairs, he knew, they were talking about him—Mom telling what had happened at the faith healing that afternoon. For several minutes there seemed to be no sound at all coming from below, and then, finally, an indignant cry from Katie—and he knew the story had been told about Sister Pearson praying to heal his mind.

Buck rolled off the side of the bed and noiselessly opened his bedroom door. Putting most of his weight on the banister, he maneuvered himself down the stairs, avoiding the step that creaked, and sat down near the bottom. He was good at eavesdropping these days. Would make a good spy. If anyone needed a spy who never talked . . .

Katie's voice: "But didn't he *tell* her?"

And Mom's anguished reply: "He tried to, but he couldn't get the words out, Katie! He simply couldn't tell her that he stuttered. I almost got up and came forward myself to explain it, but I knew that would embarrass him even more."

She was right about that, Buck thought. He remembered times people talked around him, even though he was standing right there!

Doctor to Mom: "Is he having any pain in the other ear?"

Neighbor to Dad: "Could Buck give me a hand with the trimming, do you think?"

Friend to Katie: "Does Buck want to come with us?"

There were murmurs in the kitchen that Buck couldn't make out. Then:

"Well, he's got to learn to stand up for himself." Dad's voice, a deep sigh in it. "Someone can't be following along after to explain him to other people."

"I know, Don, I know. And that's the last thing on earth Buck would want. But it's so hard to watch his face get all twisted, the way he tries to speak sometimes and can't."

Buck could actually feel the color rising in his neck.

Now Katie again: "He must have been so humiliated, Mom! Why did you ever take him there? Even if the woman realized he stuttered, how did you think it would help?"

Mom went on the defensive: "You can just get off your

100

high horse, missy! Who was it came out here in the kitchen on Friday saying why didn't we *do* something about that boy's stuttering? Well, now I did something, and everybody's jumping on me for it." Her voice wavered, and Buck swallowed.

"Look. Nobody's jumping on you, Mom," said Joel. "We read all that stuff I found online, and he's told you he won't go to Norfolk. . . ."

"Doris," said Mel, "let me tell you, if I thought Buck had something physically wrong with his mouth or throat, I'd drive him to the best specialist there was—the Cleveland clinic or over to Baltimore—that Johns Hopkins place. . . . I'd go in debt to do it. But if he doesn't want to go . . ."

No one spoke for a while. And then an exasperated burst from Gramps: "Let the boy alone, for heaven's sake. We know dang well there's nothing wrong with his mouth. He can talk right when he puts his mind to it. Don't drag him here, drag him there. He'll figure it out one of these days."

"And what if he doesn't, Gramps?" asked Katie. "He hasn't so far. None of us knows what it feels like to be Buck. We have no clue what he's going through."

More murmurings.

And finally, the squeak of chairs that meant the meal was over and so was the conversation. Everything was right back to where it had been, where it always was: nobody, including Buck, knew what to do, and even talking about it was painful.

Buck slipped out the front door before anyone left the kitchen. He climbed on his bike and took off, and when he reached the road, he didn't know whether to turn right or left. He didn't know where to go except back to the Hole, as deep and dark as he could get, but he wasn't stupid enough to do that. It would be night in another hour. Already the moon was out, faint over the poplars.

He was heading toward town, but he wasn't about to go to Center Street. A warm night like this, there would be a dozen or more kids hanging out in front of the B&I, going in and out of the Sweet Shop. The last thing he wanted to do was run into someone who had seen him over in Hillsdale that afternoon, unlikely as that was.

Everything he'd heard from outside the kitchen made him sick to his stomach. The pity in their voices, the way they predicted how the rest of his life would be. He hated his mouth, his throat, his tongue, his face. Hated himself for not being able to control anything, change anything, like there was a twin self inside him that took delight in every humiliation that came along.

He rode over a pothole on purpose and the bike skidded, almost knocking him off. He wished it had. Wished it had thrown him. Wished it had thrown him and landed on top of him, the chain cutting his stupid lips.

And then, because he didn't know what else to do, Buck turned a corner and rode straight to the driveway of Jacob Wall's house.

He wouldn't allow himself to just sit there. Even stopped himself when he started to turn and ride away. Leaving his bike by the Volvo, every step he took was full of disgust and embarrassment.

Finally the door opened, and there was Jacob. He didn't say anything. Just stood there looking at Buck. A dish towel was tucked into the belt of his pants, and Buck wondered if he'd interrupted a late night supper. He didn't care. It was now or never.

"W . . . what w . . . w . . . would I have t . . . to do?" Buck asked, and his throat hurt with the struggle.

The man's eyebrows twitched as they rose, and he stared intently down at Buck. He seemed on the verge of answering with a question, and then he checked himself, opened the screen, and said, "Come on in."

• • •

Inside, Buck sat stiffly on one of the leather chairs, and Jacob settled himself in the other, facing him, wiping his hands on the dish towel.

"About your stuttering, you mean?" Jacob said.

Buck nodded.

Jacob thought a minute, then said, "Listen, Buck, I'm not sure I want to take you on. I don't play around. Either you're in or you're not. I've never worked with someone as young as you. All my clients were in the military, and I'll treat you like I would any soldier or sailor. But it's hard work; I'll tell you that up front."

"I have to h . . . hold my b . . . breath or what?"

"You're doing enough of that already." Jacob studied Buck some more. "What made you change your mind?"

In halting phrases, Buck told him what had happened at the healing service when he was prayed over by Sister Pearson. How the guys on the bus mocked him, how he had embarrassed his sister when he met her boyfriend, how the whole family worried about him and tried not to show it.

"So you've spent most of your life trying not to stutter, is that it?" said Jacob.

Wasn't it obvious? Again Buck nodded.

"And how's that working?"

"It's n . . . not."

"Of course. The more you try to hold it back, the more your throat muscles tighten and the worse it gets. The worse it gets, the more you fight it, and this is something you worry about every time you open your mouth."

Exactly.

"S . . . so, can you cure m . . . me or n . . . not?"

Jacob shook his head. "That's what's causing all the trouble—trying so hard to stop stuttering that you tense up, choke up, tighten your jaw, grind your teeth, blink your eyes, shift your feet—do all manner of things to force the words out."

All true.

"If I work with you," Jacob went on, "—big if—I'm going to teach you how to stutter more, not less. I'm going to show you how to let it come out easily, naturally, letting go of all that tensing up and holding back. You are going to learn to stutter like nobody's business."

"But I d . . . don't want to do it at all!" Buck protested.

"You want to be normal, and normal people are disfluent sometimes. Everybody stammers occasionally, even presidents, and I have tapes to prove it. We just do it without thinking, and nobody notices. Nobody cares. It's when you start fighting it, making it a big deal, that the trouble begins."

It made sense and yet it didn't. Jacob pulled himself to

his feet to go to the kitchen and check on something he was heating for his supper, leaving Buck alone for a few minutes to figure it out. If most people stuttered occasionally and didn't even notice, Buck was thinking, what had made *him* start getting so upset about it? He couldn't even remember a time he didn't stutter. Couldn't remember a time he didn't feel different because he had this secret worry, this constant fear of stuttering.

What would it be like not to worry about a particular word? he wondered. How many times had he said *theater* because if he said *show* he'd probably stutter on the S sound? Or the other way around? How many times, because he had trouble with the M sound, he'd say *the day after tomorrow* instead of *Monday*?

Jacob came back with a calendar and a pair of eyeglasses. He lowered himself in the chair again and adjusted the glasses on his nose. "If you sign up with me, I want to see you three times a week, about forty minutes each time."

Three times a week! Buck stared at him, openmouthed. "How c . . . can I pay you for that?"

"All you have to do is show up. You don't show up, it's over."

"You wouldn't charge?"

"No, I wouldn't. I can't. I let my certification lapse when I retired. So I'm working with you as a friend, not a professional."

"H . . . how do you think it w . . . w . . . will help?"

"I want to get you to the place where you can glide in and out of a stutter easily, naturally, without all the drama that gets people's attention—the tongue twisting and jaw tightening and eye blinking and stuff. You're not getting anywhere doing that. The words don't come out any easier. All you're doing is running backward."

They sat for fifteen or twenty seconds staring at each other. Was this a game? Buck wondered. Was he supposed to believe in this guy any more than he could believe in Sister Pearson? What kind of therapy was this? Still . . .

"Think for a minute what your life would be like if you lost your *fear* of stuttering, Buck. Just the fear. Not have that sick-to-the-stomach feeling when the sergeant—I mean, teacher—asks you a question. Not have to change a sentence around to keep from saying a word that usually gives you trouble. To be able to tell your friends a joke without your mouth drying up . . ."

For a long minute, Buck didn't answer. He was thinking about that last day of school—*To be or not to be.* How he couldn't even read that out loud.

"I guess . . . I'd b . . . b . . . be like everyone else . . . except I st . . . st . . . stuttered." He *made* himself say the hated word.

"That's it, Buck. You've nailed it. Except that if you were like most other people you'd stumble right over a word and not even stop."

No. That was too easy, or too hard. Buck felt confused. It seemed as though Jacob was saying that the whole problem was being *afraid* to stutter. Wasn't it the stuttering that made him afraid in the first place? But what did he have to lose by trying Jacob's way? Correction: what *other* way did he have? School began again in three months. Did he want to go back the same way he was before?

"We'll work on things together here and you can work on some of it at home," Jacob said. And before Buck could ask, he added, "No one has to know we're doing this, but it's okay if you want to tell them. In fact, it might be a good idea to let your parents know."

Buck shook his head. The last thing he wanted was everybody watching to see if he was improving. And if he failed, why let his family in on it? Just another disappointment they could do without.

He realized that Jacob was waiting for his final decision. The shaggy-haired man was leaning forward, hands on his knees, signaling that it was time for Buck to leave. "You don't have to decide now," Jacob said. "Tell me when you come by on Tuesday. But here's the deal. . . ." He paused to make sure Buck was listening. "If you quit on me . . . even once . . . we're done. Just like in the military. You don't stop when the going gets tough. Once you say you've had it and walk out that door, it's over. Understood?"

"Yeah. I want to d . . . do it."

"Okay, then. I'm flexible about the day and time, as long as you get in three sessions a week. Name the day."

"Uh . . . Tuesday?" Buck said.

"What time?"

Buck thought. "One o'clock?"

"All right. Call me if we need to change it."

"I'll be here," Buck said.

• • •

He was amazed at Jacob's offer. Amazed at Jacob, period! A different personality than he'd seen so far.

What was he getting himself into? Buck wondered as he pedaled home—Jacob getting all military on him. How hard could it possibly be? He didn't have to do push-ups, did he? Slog through mud on his stomach? Still, he wished he were more enthused about it, not considering it a last resort.

At home, he could hear *60 Minutes* coming from the living room. He was getting ice from the fridge when his dad called to him. "Buck? That you?"

"Yeah?"

Don Anderson came to the doorway of the kitchen.

"Wondered where you went," he said cheerfully. "I've been meaning to tell you that Joel and I will probably be cutting some timber over near Coalsville next week—Thursday, maybe."

At last! A day when he could count on everyone being gone—Mom at work, Gramps at the sawmill . . . Mel had already said he had a run all the way to Kansas and back, and Katie was no problem. She was at Amy's so much it was a wonder she didn't pack a suitcase and move in with her. Buck liked Katie's best friend, mainly because she never said much to him. *Hi, Buck!* she'd say when she came over. *Hi,* he'd answer. But what kind of friendship was that— liking someone because she left you alone?

And then he heard his dad say, "You want to come along, we'll find something for you to do."

"What?" Buck said.

"Coalsville on Thursday. We'll be cutting timber."

"Uh . . . I don't know," Buck said.

"Come on! Be glad to have you." Now it was *Be Nice to*

108

Buck week. When he still didn't answer, his dad gave him a quizzical look. "Thought you were wanting a chance to see us down some trees. Dad said you were asking about it the other day."

"Yeah, well . . . maybe. Got a lot of things I w . . . want to do this summer."

"Glad to hear that," said his dad, and there was a gentleness to his voice. "Hope some of those things involve friends, not just going off by yourself all the time."

"D . . . don't worry. I got friends," said Buck.

The hardest part of going back into the Hole, he realized, was not the actual going, but keeping it secret from everyone except David.

12

DAVID TO BUCK,
BUCK TO DAVID

He didn't even tell David about Jacob, however. David texted him that night.

David: so school's out, and mom's already programmed the next 3 months

Buck: yeah? doing what

David: relatives, trip, relatives, science camp, relatives, survivor camp

Buck: whats that? u moving 2 the jungle?

David: learning 2 live without ur cell phone and stuff u should c the list of things they confiscate—electric toothbrushes, cameras, anything that has a charger

Buck: your mom hate u or something?

David: she says she wants me 2 see how clever i am on my

own she's going on a trip with her girlfriend then and wanted something special 4 me 2 do

Buck: tell her i can give u a job of caving assistant

David: don't i wish how was ur last day of school? somebody released all the frogs in the biology lab here

Buck: yay frogs

David: in the library principal NOT happy

Buck: LOL i called pete ketterman puke face

David: !!!!!?????!!!!!????

Buck: i know

David: he hear?

Buck: he heard

David: u want 2 die young?

Buck: guess i'm in 4 it now. . . .

13

A TASTE OF BUD

Monday, the first official day of summer vacation, and Buck smiled at the sunshine that fell across his pillow. Then he closed his eyes and slept a half hour more.

By the time he came down for breakfast, Katie had already taken over the kitchen table with her drawing. At the start of each year, Gramps gave her the old calendar at the sawmill when he hung the new, and she used the backside of each large sheet for her creations. She had collected quite a few calendars now, and sometimes, like today, she taped some of the pages together to make an even bigger canvas.

"Well, look who decided to get up," Katie teased, turning her pencil sideways to do some shading.

"Look who's showing off," said Buck as he set his bowl on the table. "What are you d . . . designing now?"

Katie quickly covered the paper with her hands. "I'll let you see it when I'm done."

Like Buck, Katie was barefoot, her flip-flops abandoned beneath the table. She waited until he was opening a box of cereal, then sat back and surveyed what she'd drawn so far, her uncombed ponytail dangling over the shoulder of her blue T-shirt.

"What are you g . . . going to do with all those? You've already c . . . covered half your walls," Buck said.

"I don't know. It's just fun." She nodded toward the fridge. "I saved you some strawberries."

"Sweet," Buck said, and got out the milk.

A cell phone buzzed from somewhere in the other room and Katie leaped up. "That's Amy," she said, and ran to answer.

Grinning, Buck stepped over to see her drawing, but suddenly leaned in a little closer, still holding the milk carton. It appeared to be a diagram of an outdoor area, a large bank of trees in the background. The lower part of the paper was shaded to indicate earth.

Hole, Katie had printed, an arrow pointing to a small opening at the surface, the start of a twisting underground passageway. . . .

Buck stared in disbelief. How did she know? How could she possibly have . . . ?

Katie came back in the kitchen. "Amy has an idea for . . ." She caught Buck studying her drawing. "I said *don't look!*" she cried, and ran over to shield the paper with her arms.

"What *is* this?" Buck asked.

"You *know* I don't let anyone see my stuff till it's finished," she scolded. "People start criticizing before it's done and it ruins everything!"

"Okay, so I looked. But I'm not c . . . criticizing. I just . . . wondered what this is . . . ," Buck said, pointing.

Katie gave him an exasperated glare and sat down again. "If you must know, I'm designing a fantastic park and playground. I want all kinds of different stuff for kids to do. This will be an underground tunnel they can crawl through, but it's got to have a roof over it or water would collect inside."

Buck's heartbeat began to slow and he could almost breathe again.

"And over here," Katie said, now that she had his attention, "at this end of the park, I've got this big pond that turns into an ice rink in winter. . . ."

Buck made sure that everything he said about the design was complimentary, and finally he sat down across from her to eat his breakfast.

Katie sighed and began drawing again. "I'm making a whole city. I've already got a layout of the town—the streets and the town center and parks and stuff. When you start something, you have to think of every little thing, you know?"

"Yeah," said Buck. "I sure do." There was an occasional clunk from the front of the house. "What's Uncle Mel up to?"

"I think he said he was going to scrub the porch or something," Katie answered. "Did you ever notice how he always does some nice thing for Mom before he leaves on a trip?"

"Just b . . . being part of the family, I g . . . guess," said Buck.

Katie got up to check the washing machine. "I'm going to start the last load. If you want anything washed, let me have it. That's all I have to do for Mom today."

So much activity! Buck thought. Didn't anybody just kick back and enjoy a June breeze while there still was one?

After he'd gathered up some socks and underwear for Katie, he went out onto the front porch to find his uncle in shorts, barefoot too, a large scrub brush in hand, bringing it down hard on one side of the doorframe. One half of the porch wall was a lighter shade of white than the other.

Seeing Buck, Mel said, "Can't for the life of me see how a doorframe can get so smudged." He wiped one thick arm across his face, the arm with the ship tattoo on it. "Come on. Pick up a rag there and help me out. Your mom might forget about painting this house again if the porch doesn't look so dirty."

Buck grinned and picked up a rag. Mom and Dad wouldn't take any rent from Mel—after all, they were lodgers too, since it was Gramps's big farmhouse to begin with—but they all paid back his kindness in other ways—this, for one.

"So what you up to today?" Mel asked as they scrubbed.

"W . . . weeding. The usual," Buck told him.

For a while they were working side by side. Then Mel climbed up the stepladder to wash the boards near the porch ceiling. The *swish* and *swash* of the rag and brush alternated sometimes with his grunts.

"Do you b . . . believe she can d . . . do it? Sister Pearson?"

Buck asked suddenly, the question that had consumed him the day before.

At first he thought his uncle wouldn't answer. The brush just kept swishing away.

Finally Mel said, "Well, you notice any difference?"

"No."

"Could be it takes a while. . . ."

They went on working and Buck said, "C . . . couple times she called out s . . . something about a p . . . person she didn't even know, and she was r . . . right about what was wrong with him."

"Huh." Mel came down off the stepladder and dipped his brush in the sudsy water, knocked it against the side of the pail, then climbed back up again.

"Mom believes in her, though. M . . . Mom thinks it's all m . . . me not believing enough."

"She say that?"

"N . . . not exactly, but I can tell."

"Well, the Lord works in mysterious ways, they say, but . . . I can't see him waiting to be begged to do something he already knows needs fixing. But don't you be telling your Ma how I feel, 'cause I don't have any business in it."

"But do you think Sister P . . . Pearson's a fake?"

Mel gave a loud sigh. "All I can tell you, Buck, is I travel all across the country, and I talk to different people and hear things on the radio when I'm doing a run. The local stations, my CB radio, public radio . . . I listen to 'em all. I hear country music and truckers crabbing to each other. I hear folks on talk shows and book writers and college professors, and I heard this one program telling how con-men preachers can fool folks into donating lots of money that never goes to what the preacher says it will."

"How?"

"By making them believe they have special powers. Sometimes the greeters out front find out things about folks when they show up for a healing service—like, the man in the blue shirt in the wheelchair, maybe, tells them he has kidney stones, and they'll get that fact to the preacher some way. And then the preacher will call it out during the evening like he's getting the message that very minute from God, and the man in the blue shirt can't figure how else he knows."

"B . . . but if he doesn't get better?"

"By then the preacher's gone. Or the man just keeps waiting. Or the preacher will say that the man didn't have enough faith in him. Or maybe the man does get better, but would have anyway without all that fussing over him. But what's to say that Sister Pearson really does have the gift of healing? I don't know. That's not my department."

Mel dropped the subject then, as Buck knew he would, because his uncle was never one to get in an argument with Mom or Dad, never forgetting for one minute that this wasn't his house and that Joel and Buck and Katie weren't his kids.

Katie came to the front door. "Could you guys do me a favor? The last load is sheets, and Mom likes them dried on the line. When the washer stops, could you hang them for me? Amy and Sarah and I want to see the first show at the Palace."

"We'll do it, Katie. You run along," said Mel.

Buck was glad when they'd finished the wall and windows—when they could pour the bucket of water over the porch and, sloshing around in their bare feet, mop the floorboards, pushing the water toward the edge where it ran off down into the azalea bushes.

"I'll take care of those sheets," Mel told him, "but unless you're planning to get to that weeding right away, think you could go to Bealls' and get me a package of Tums? I've got to pick up my rig at four this afternoon and head out, and the older I get, the less my stomach can take some of that truck stop chili." He reached in his pocket and handed Buck a few dollars. "Buy yourself a candy bar while you're at it."

• • •

Buck didn't want a candy bar as much as he wanted the feel of riding around on the first day of summer vacation with no destination other than the country store. And the bike was only six months old, a Christmas gift from his parents.

If all the land around was as flat as this little valley, he was thinking, he could explore on his bike for miles without ever having to get off and walk his bike to the top of the steepest hills. With this multispeed bike, though, he'd only had to do that once. Of course, if the land was all flat, and not the hilly countryside that surrounded him now, there probably wouldn't be many caves to explore.

He had only been in two caves other than Luray Caverns. Unless you counted a couple of so-called caves that charged five-dollar admissions, and then you discovered, after you went behind a curtain, that they only went back about fifteen feet. Mostly they were souvenir shops, with postcards showing the caves photographed in blue light, red light, and green light, plus fake emerald bracelets and even rosaries.

Mel had taken him and David once to a local cave called the Tube, because worming your way through it felt like crawling through a tube of toothpaste, and you came out covered with gray-white mud. After that, Mel said he wasn't cut out for cave crawling, but it only made Buck and David want to go exploring even more.

Just for the fun of it, Buck detoured onto Center Street where he entered the town limits and drove down beyond the B&I to see what was playing at the Palace. *Temptation Summer*, the marquee read, and the movie poster showed three young women in bathing suits, walking boldly along the boardwalk at the ocean. He'd pass, Buck decided.

He started to ride on when Nat came out of the drugstore.

"Buck!" Nat called, his eyes squinting against the sunlight, and Buck braked. "There's a spy movie showing at the Wednesday matinee. Want to go?"

"Sure!"

"Okay. See you," Nat said, and climbed in a car where his dad was waiting.

Just like that. He guessed they were still friends. He didn't know how much they had in common, but what was the hurry? In some ways even he and David were as different as . . . yes, a sheepdog and a Chihuahua, but so what?

Turning at the corner, he rode over to Fourth Street, passing the old Ambassador Hotel that had stood empty now for the past seven years. Buck remembered that it was shabby even when it was open for business, and now the missing window on the top floor had only pigeons for guests. The rumor had spread that because someone had died there in a top-floor fire, the hotel was haunted. Buck and David had both dared the other to crawl in a downstairs window some night and take the stairs all the way up to the third floor, but neither had ever tried it.

When he finally got to Bealls', Buck parked his bike beneath one of the sycamores out front and went up the planked steps, nodding to the two elderly women chatting in the rockers.

The minute he stepped inside, he saw them: Pete, Rod, Ethan, and Isaac, waiting in line at the cashier's counter.

He couldn't turn and leave; they'd already seen him. So he took the far aisle and headed to the back of the store, where the arrow pointed to *Paint, Garden, Housewares,* none of which were of any use to Buck.

The aisles at Bealls' were scarcely a yard wide, and the upper shelves were so high that if customers needed something from up there, they had to ask Mr. Beall for help. Soup bowls and saucepans were stacked helter-skelter next to two-gallon containers of glossy white paint.

Coming back here was a bad idea—a great place to be cornered, Buck thought. Pretending to look at paint samples, he could see Pete watching him from the other end of the long aisle. But Buck decided to wait them out, and finally, after two or three minutes, Pete and his buddies paid for their colas and cheese puffs and went out the door.

Still, Buck waited five minutes more before he paid for Mel's package of Tums and a Payday candy bar. Even then, he checked out the front window before he left, but the porch and yard were empty except for one of the elderly women, and she was asleep.

Buck opened the screen and stepped out. As he started to unwrap the Payday, he realized his bike was missing.

Pete! Then he saw it parked against the far sycamore. His forehead wrinkled in confusion as he replayed getting off the bike and parking it closer to the store. But there it was, almost as far as the road. He shrugged and went on down the steps, then set out across the bare dirt lot.

There were sudden footsteps behind him, and before he could turn around, he felt an arm around his shoulder from the left, another arm around him from the right, and then Ethan's voice saying, "Buck-o! Buddy! Whuzzup?" and the arms were moving him off toward the side, and into the woods that lined the edge of the Beallses' property.

"H . . . hi," Buck said, trying to steer them back toward his bike, but the other two boys were behind him now, hands against his back, and their fake cheery voices rang out across the lot.

"Long time no see!" said Pete. "How you doin', buddy?"

"H . . . hey!" Buck said, both feet coming to a dead stop. "I've g . . . got to g . . . get . . ."

But he was propelled forward whether his feet cooperated or not.

"Whuzza matter?" Pete said. "Good to see you! Got a little something for you."

They were half lifting him as they entered the trees. Buck turned his head, looking to see if anyone might be watching, if it would help to yell, but no other customers were coming out just then, and the lone driver who passed by on the road didn't even glance their way.

Maybe he should just play along, be a good sport, Buck thought. If he went totally limp, nothing would stop them from carrying him, and this was humiliating enough. Pete had never been known for beating anyone up, but there was always a first time. Was a big, overgrown guy like Pete, big man on campus, really so upset about what Buck had called him?

"Almost there," Rob said.

"Relax," Isaac told him. "Just doing you a favor, that's all."

Puzzled, Buck stopped resisting. They reached a spot where they were surrounded on all sides by pine trees, and the boys loosened their grip a little on his shoulders.

Pete moved around in front of him and looked down, a semi-serious expression on his face, though the other boys were grinning. Pete's face was so close to Buck's, in fact, that Buck could see the yellow specks in his hazel eyes, the little sore at one corner of his mouth, and definitely the gap between his two front teeth.

"Here's the deal, see," Pete began. "We've sort of noticed that our little Buck-o here has a speech problem. And we thought of a way we could help. Can you guess how?"

Buck didn't respond.

"No? Okay, here's what you do: open your mouth wide and repeat after me—slow-ly now—I . . . am . . . a . . . creep. Got it?" The other boys laughed aloud. "Come on. Just four words, Puke Face, I mean, Buck-o." And he exaggerated each one: "I . . . am . . . a . . . creep."

Buck knew he was in for it now. How could he ever have imagined that he could call Pete Ketterman a name—any name at all—and think that Pete would let it pass?

"What do you think, guys? He need a little lubrication first?" Pete asked the others.

"Yeah, that's it!" said Isaac. "His vocal cords are dry."

Pete reached into the paper bag he'd gotten at Bealls' and pulled out a can of Budweiser. Buck knew right away that the boys had shoplifted the can, because Mr. Beall wasn't about to sell beer to minors.

Ethan moved around behind Buck and grabbed his head in his hands, holding it like a vise, and it was Sister Pearson all over again, Buck thought. Rob and Isaac, on either side, pinned Buck's arms to his body.

Slowly Pete held the can in front of Buck and pulled the tab, making a *ssssspop* sound.

"Mmmm! Good!" said Pete, taking a swig. He held the can close to Buck's face as Ethan tipped Buck's head backward. "Now open your mouth and say, 'I'm sorry, Pete, for calling you Puke Face.'"

Buck tried to turn his face away, but he could scarcely move it at all. And no way was he sorry about Puke Face—just sorry he was where he was now. Maybe he *was* stubborn, like Dad said, but Pete would get no apology from him.

"C'mon," Pete said. "I'm . . . sorr . . . y. . . ."

Buck pressed his lips together even tighter.

"How you going to stop stuttering if you won't try?" said Pete, and he wasn't smiling anymore. And suddenly he tipped the open can against Buck's lips and the beer dribbled out onto his chin and down the front of his shirt.

"C . . . cut it . . . out . . . ," Buck stammered, but he'd opened his mouth just enough that Pete could press the can against his lips, hard enough to keep them apart, and the beer came pouring out in a steady stream.

123

It was filling Buck's mouth and throat and he had to swallow, swallow again, and still the beer kept coming. It ran down his cheeks and trickled into his ears. Isaac had tilted his head so that the beer had nowhere else to go, and then Buck was coughing and choking, and finally Isaac let go.

Pete stepped back and dropped the empty can on the ground. He looked down at Buck and shook his head in disgust.

"Anyone's gonna puke, weirdo, it's you," he said. "You just watch who you're calling names." And then, to his friends, "Let's go," and they pushed back through the pine branches and soon were out of sight.

Buck wiped his mouth on his sleeve. He reeked of beer, and there was a huge wet stain on the front of his tee. He ran his tongue over his upper lip and felt a cut from the edge of the Budweiser can. He blotted the blood on his arm, then made his way back to the parking lot.

At least his bike was still there. *The jerks!* Buck could almost taste the anger in his mouth. For a moment he thought he really might throw up, but then it passed.

• • •

He'd hoped to get upstairs to wash and change shirts. He went around the side of the house and zigzagged between the wet sheets hanging from the clothesline. But when he came in the back door, Mel was there at the table, eating a sandwich.

Buck laid the package of Tums and his change by Mel's plate and started toward the stairs, but Mel grabbed his arm. "Hey!"

Buck stood without turning around. "What?"

"Whaddya mean 'what'? You smell like a brewery."

Buck shrugged but still averted his face.

"You been drinking, Buck?"

"No. Some g . . . guys from school were h . . . h . . . horsing around and p . . . poured beer on me."

Mel still didn't let go of his arm. "Why?"

Buck gave another shrug. "F . . . first day of v . . . v . . . vacation. Just acting c . . . crazy."

Mel reached up and grasped Buck's chin in one hand, studied his face. "You been fighting?"

"*No!* Just cut my lip on the c . . . can when they p . . . poured it on me."

Mel frowned. "Well, go change before your dad comes home for lunch. You're not lying to me now, are you?"

"No," said Buck, and went on upstairs. He just wasn't telling the whole truth.

14

IN THE WOODS

"What I want you to do," Jacob said on Tuesday, sitting across from Buck in one of the two leather armchairs, so close that their knees almost touched, ". . . won't sound so hard as it sounds silly."

Here it comes, thought Buck. *Imagine yourself in a field of daisies with fluffy white clouds overhead* . . . something the first therapist had suggested.

"Find a comfortable position. . . ."

Yep.

Jacob waited while Buck made some adjustments. "Test each arm, each leg, to see if there is any tension at all. . . . Now imagine that someone is gently pouring thick, warm oil on the very top of your head."

"What?"

"Go on." Jacob was speaking slowly. "Close your eyes . . . and try to feel all the nerves and muscles in your scalp relax as the oil slowly . . . slowly . . . makes its way down. Can you feel your scalp relaxing? Try to feel that."

I feel that you are a nutcase and I know now why you live way out here by yourself, Buck thought.

Jacob was speaking more slowly still. "Now . . . it's sliding . . . down your forehead . . . feel those muscles relax . . . your temples . . . your eyelids . . . the length . . . of your nose . . . the space between your nose and mouth. . . ."

Buck sort of got it when the imaginary oil reached his eyelids. He was conscious of that almost imperceptible relaxing of fibers so small he didn't even know he had them. Good thing Jacob's air conditioner was working and the house was on the chilly side. Otherwise this would be torture.

"Now the upper lip . . . The warm oil is sliding down your top lip . . . the bottom lip . . . your chin. . . ."

This was just another version of relaxing the facial muscles, Buck thought—what the therapist had been talking about at school. But . . . if soldiers and sailors could do this, so could he. Didn't see the sense of it, though.

"Now let your shoulders relax as the warm oil slides down your back. . . ."

Finally, his legs and feet gave way and Jacob told him to open his eyes.

"Now . . . watch. I want you to flop your jaws like this. . . ." Jacob's lips parted and he let his mouth open and close, open and close, as though they were fastened with a loose hinge. They made a *ploh . . . ploh . . . ploh* sound.

"Go ahead," Jacob said. "So we both look stupid. Who's to see?"

Pla . . . pla . . . pla, went Buck, hating the session already.

"No! Unhinge your jaws. You're still holding them tight. Pretend your jaws are mops. Let them shake, let them flop."

Buck tried again. *Ploh . . . ploh. . . . ploh . . .*

"Okay," said Jacob. "N . . . nnnnnnow w . . . wwwwwatch mmmmmme ssssssssstutter."

Buck stared. "I d . . . didn't know you st . . . stuttered."

"I don't. But I can. Don't you see how easily I sssssslide into a wwwword? I don't fight it. I don't care."

But Buck cared. The only way he could imagine doing stuff like this was in his room with the door locked. They had talked awhile, he and Jacob, before the session began— about how long Buck had been stuttering (most of his life that he could remember). What kind of therapy he'd had, what were the most difficult sounds for him to say, what kinds of hobbies he enjoyed, what he did with friends (Buck never mentioned caving, and nothing at all about Pukeman and his gang).

He would have liked to ask some questions of his own: *Where did* you *come from? Why did you move clear out here with all this furniture? Why do you seem so grumpy all the time?* And, most of all, *Why do you want to help me?*

Jacob placed his elbows on the arms of his chair and leaned forward. "Now," he said, "letting your jaws stay as relaxed as possible, I want you to say, 'Now I'll let you watch me stutter.' And I want you to purposely stutter on as many of those words as you can."

"N . . . now I know you're c . . . crazy," Buck said instead, and for the first time since he'd met Jacob, he got a full smile from the man.

"Maybe so. That's what all the soldiers said at first," Jacob told him. "But they didn't say it quite as delicately. Come on. Let's hear it."

Odd how when he *tried* to stutter, he messed up all the more. "N . . . n . . . now I'll w . . . w . . . watch I m . . . mean I'll l . . . let y . . . ou see m . . . me stutter."

"Again," said Jacob.

Buck repeated the sentence.

"Again. This time, stutter on every word."

"N . . . now I'll l . . . let . . ."

"Stutter. Every word."

Over and over.

By the end of the session, Buck's jaws ached.

"They shouldn't," said Jacob. "If your jaws, your throat muscles, your tongue are relaxed, the stuttering should come as easily as the way you talk to yourself when no one's around."

Buck looked at Jacob in surprise.

"You do, you know," Jacob told him. "You test yourself sometimes. That's what the soldiers tell me. They think if they practice long enough—the way words come out smooth and easy when they're alone—it will carry over later. And then—just let one other person enter the room—and all bets are off."

"*Why?*" asked Buck. He'd always wondered about that. The very second he knew someone was listening, he stuttered.

"Anxiety. Fear of stuttering. That's all it takes to get the muscles tightening, the tongue stiff, the jaws rigid. And that's what we work on here. The fear." Jacob studied Buck intently. "You with me?"

"Okay," said Buck.

"One o'clock Thursday?"

Not Thursday! Dad and Joel would be out cutting timber, and Mel wasn't expected back till that night. Buck planned to go to the Hole.

"C . . . could I c . . . come Friday inst . . . st . . . stead?"

Jacob nodded. "That'll work, as long as you come here three times a week." As they stood up, Jacob handed him a clutch of envelopes. "Put these in the mailbox for me, would you? And stick up the red flag so the postman will stop."

"Sure," Buck told him.

Outside, he wheeled his bike down to the end of the gravel driveway, steering with one hand, envelopes in the other. But when he reached the mailbox and leaned forward, trying to open the flap and hold his bike up too, the envelopes scattered on the ground beneath, and Buck had to prop his bike against the post and pick them up. Electric bill, gas bill, telephone company, Speech and Hearing Association, and then, the last envelope, Buck discovered, was addressed to Jacob.

He paused, wondering if he should take it back to the house, but there, beside Jacob's name that someone had addressed in blue-inked handwriting, Jacob had printed in big black letters: *RETURN TO SENDER*.

• • •

Despite his careful planning, Buck did not go to the Hole on Thursday.

It rained the day before.

130

He had wakened to the sound of rain Wednesday morning, and he could tell by the look of the sky that it was not just a brief shower; it was a hard, steady, dreary rain with no intention of letting up anytime soon, and the Hole would be a mess the next day. Buck heaved himself over and faced the wall.

He realized now that it was useless to wait for the perfect day. There would never be a day he could count on, the Hole dry, and everyone in the family gone so that he could have a long time to explore without being missed.

To begin, it was about an hour's bike ride to the old Wilmer place by the main highway; and now that Ethan had seen him out there, Buck had decided he'd have to take a back route, which meant an hour and a half, at least.

He could always wash off his arms and legs in the creek when he was through, but he'd need to take a complete change of clothing and hide it somewhere in the bushes. Dad and Joel sometimes came home for lunch, and if they didn't see Buck around, it was no big deal. Same with Mel and Katie and Gramps. But he couldn't miss being on time for dinner. *That* was a big deal at the Andersons.

But . . . *if* Mom found his muddy clothes in the washing machine before he'd had a chance to turn it on, or *if* Mel wasn't on a run and didn't see him around all day, or *if* Mom got off work early and no one knew where Buck had gone—not even Katie—questions would be asked, and Buck had never been much good at lying.

One of these days he'd simply have to take a chance. He'd go with Dad and Joel to cut timber on Thursday, and maybe they wouldn't ask him for the rest of the summer. Maybe the rain now was a good thing.

131

And then he remembered the matinee at the Palace, so he still had something fun to look forward to. Nat called to say that his mom would drive them because of the rain, and all Buck had to say over the phone was "Hello" and "Okay."

They each got a tub of popcorn and a cola and settled down in the next to last row. There they watched an American spy jump from a helicopter, board a ship in the dead of night, steal a map, launch a speedboat, survive a collision, rappel up a cliff, and get to an embassy in time to stop a bombing, all in the space of twenty-four hours.

"Cool!" Nat said when it was over. "There's a Western on next week. Want to see it?"

So maybe, just like that, they were friends?

• • •

The sky was still gray on Thursday, but the thunderclouds were gone. Buck sat in the two-ton truck beside his dad, Joel to follow on the log-skidder tractor. The engine noise was loud, and the truck's large wheels made a smacking sound when they ran over wet places on the pavement.

Not many other dads did this kind of work anymore, Buck knew, and there was pride in it—that folks still called on him or Gramps when they had woods that needed thinning. The whole family knew that Dad would rather be out here cutting timber than hoeing potatoes in the field; Gramps would prefer sawing tree trunks into planks than standing behind a counter in the shop beside the sawmill, selling building supplies. Because it all started out here in the woods, felling the mature trees that needed to be harvested before they died, and that was what they seemed to love the most. But the family needed more money than cutting timber for the sawmill would provide, so the vegetable garden and the lumberyard store were necessary.

"You packed those lunch buckets, didn't you?" Dad asked as he steered with one hand, left arm resting on the open window, the faded blue cap low enough on his forehead to shield his eyes from the morning sun.

"Yep," said Buck. "And the thermos."

His dad nodded. "Hope the ground's not too wet to go in. Pretty thick bed of pine needles, if I remember. If it seems too wet, I'll not take the truck in very far."

"Where's the f . . . forklift?"

"I drove it over here yesterday after the rain quit—Joel picked me up. I think it's pretty safe back there in the trees. Though these days, never can tell. . . ."

At last they turned onto a dirt road and drove another few miles into a small clearing, leaving just enough room for Joel to park the tractor when he arrived. Buck climbed out and saw a patch of yellow off in the trees; the forklift was still there.

He had to admit that next to the muddy, moldy smell of underground, he liked the scent of a forest best. The woods had the same earthy wet smell, but this time there was the scent of pine and fresh leaf rot.

"How m . . . many acres are there?" Buck asked, waving away a cloud of gnats that greeted him and flew at his eyes.

"Only ten or twelve," his dad said. "Let's take a look."

There weren't any trails to speak of, but they tramped through the underbrush to where the pine needles and moss took over. Every now and then they came to a tree trunk circled with a white paint line—a mark the forester had left to indicate which trees had reached maturity and should be felled.

Both Buck and his father were counting as they went, but in some places the tangle of brush was so thick that they didn't go on, just scanned the trees ahead and tried to make an estimate.

"We've got to check for ticks when we get home tonight," Dad said as they started back to where they'd parked. "A lot of deer around here. A *lot*."

When they reached the clearing, Dad poured himself some coffee from the thermos, and they stood leaning against the truck, waiting for Joel. Buck tipped his head back as far as he could to see the tops of the trees. The poplars were the tallest around, maybe a hundred feet, Gramps had said, their branches starting far up the trunk, and they were ready to be cut in twenty-five or thirty years. But the oldest trees here were likely the hard red oaks that grew more slowly, only forty feet in eighty years.

Gramps liked figures like that, and knew dozens more, but these were the only ones Buck remembered.

"Got to cut out the old and let the young ones come along," he'd said, and Buck wondered if Gramps ever felt like an old red oak himself—he, and then Dad. . . .

Don Anderson must have been thinking the same thing.

"You know," he said, arms folded over his chest, his feet crossed at the ankles, "you and Joel and Katie could do a lot worse than taking over this business someday."

Sort of a strange way to put it, Buck thought.

"When Gramps and I are gone," Dad continued, "you're either going to have to run it or sell it, and being out in the woods all day with your brother just might be the ticket for you."

"T . . . to what?" Buck asked.

"To doing work you like. I tell you . . . there's something about seeing new trees coming along . . . cleaning out a woods so the sunlight gets through . . . you're giving 'em a chance. Same with a garden. I don't like hoeing any more than you do, but I get to the end of a row and see a long line of green coming along behind me, there's even satisfaction in that, the kind you don't get sitting in an office somewhere, shuffling papers."

And when Buck didn't respond, he added, "Just something to think on, Buck. You'd be working a lot by yourself . . . nobody else much to deal with. . . ." And then Dad said it again: "Could do a lot worse."

He could hardly have said it more directly: . . . *for a stutterer like you.*

Buck didn't have anything against logging or running a sawmill. But he wanted to choose a job because he liked it, not because he stuttered.

• • •

Buck was the first to hear the far-off grind of the tractor. Dad opened the tailgate and lifted out two chain saws, one at a time. He carried them to the base of the huge red oak just beyond the forklift and laid them down.

"Get the safety goggles, would you, Buck? There under the seat?" he called.

135

When the tractor pulled up and Joel got out, he called, "How many trees we got, Dad?"

"Buck and I figure around twenty. No more than two loads."

It wasn't long before a chain saw jerked to life in Don Anderson's big hands and, leaning over, he cut a notch a foot above the base of the first oak tree and angled the saw in. The whine grew louder the deeper it cut, and finally the heavy oak crashed to the ground, branches crackling, followed by a chorus of rustling leaves. Buck felt the thud in the soles of his feet as the earth vibrated, and then the woods were still.

He and Joel and their dad gathered around the fresh stump, a clean cut, and examined the butt ends for signs of rot, but this tree had no insect tunnels, no slivers. Buck began counting the rings as Dad and Joel moved along the trunk with their saws to cut it into logs.

". . . seventy-four, seventy-five . . . It's s . . . seventy-six years old, Dad," Buck called.

"A good long life," Dad said. And then the air was split with the buzzing shriek of first one, then two chain saws—Don Anderson cutting the heavy oak into sections just short enough to be hauled away, and Joel separating the branches from the trunk.

They moved on to the next marked tree, a poplar that seemed to tower above the rest of the woods, and when it began to topple, it seemed to fall in slow motion. Its high leafy branches were cushioned by the trees around it, snagging here and there, but ultimately ripping through the foliage and, once again, the earth shuddered as the poplar hit the ground with a thud.

Gramps had told stories of loggers who made sloppy cuts, or estimated the wrong direction the tree would fall. And as Buck followed along after his dad and older brother, making stacks of firewood from the smaller branches Joel had cut, he was already working up a new adventure for Pukeman. "Pukeman Fells a Tree"—and there he would be in the first square, cutting a notch in a tree with a hatchet. In the next square, Buck would draw him smiling broadly at the deep cut he had made, unaware that the tree was tilting in his direction, and in the third square, he's lying on the ground, Xs for eyes, the tree on top of him, and little birds, from a nest in the fallen branches, flying circles around his head and tweeting.

At noon, they stopped for lunch. Cutting the trees and sawing them into logs was the easy part. Using the tractor skidder to haul the wood through the forest and back to the clearing, then maneuvering the forklift to get the logs onto the truck, thicker ones first, was the hard part.

The three of them sat across from each other on two logs, eating the ham and cheese sandwiches Buck had packed that morning, and half an apple pie, plus the coffee and some lemonade.

Buck liked the weather of early summer. Not so insufferably hot the way it would get in July and August. That was when the Hole would feel the best. Fifty-six degrees all year round, the temperature of most caves.

"Gramps would have liked to c . . . come," he said, pausing between bites of his sandwich.

"I know, but somebody's got to keep shop, and the way his back's been acting up, he's got no business hauling a saw around out here," said Dad. "I think he figured that out for himself. Besides, he wants you guys to get a taste of the business. See how you measure up."

So it was still on Dad's mind. *Give it a rest*, Buck thought. He had a long time yet to think about that.

Joel, though, rubbed one shoulder and said, "Oh . . . I don't know. . . ."

"What? Your shoulder's hurting already?" Dad teased. "You getting to be an old man at the grand age of nineteen?"

"Naw. I just . . . maybe like to do something different, I guess," Joel said, and turned his face away as though waiting for another breeze to come through the stand of trees and cool it.

"*This* is different from being at the mill all day," Dad said.

Joel reached for the thermos and slowly poured some coffee into his plastic cup. Then he set it down carefully beside him on the log, pulled at his earlobe and said, "Been thinking of joining the navy. . . ."

Buck stopped chewing and stared at his older brother. Joel, the least talkative member of the family, next to Buck himself, had just said something so extraordinary that Buck could hardly believe it.

"The *navy*!" Dad was staring too, and then he snorted and put down his sandwich. "Where'd you get a cockamamie idea like that?"

"It's a job, like everything else," Joel said. "Learn a trade. They'd teach me one."

"You're learning a trade right here! What do you think we've been doing all morning? You're helping out at the mill, earning yourself some money. . . ."

"I don't want to spend my whole life just 'helping out,'" Joel said, and turned his face away again.

Dad sat shaking his head. "What makes you think the navy will even take you?"

Joel snapped around again. "What makes you think they won't?"

"Well, I don't know, son. What I mean is . . . this idea just come to you all of a sudden, or what?"

"I've been thinking on it a good long while," Joel answered, and bit into his sandwich again, jaws tight as he chewed.

Buck stayed so quiet he thought he could almost hear a beetle working its way up the bark on the log where he and Joel were sitting.

"Have you been talking about this with Mel?" Dad asked finally.

"Mel's got nothing to do with it. I've never mentioned it to anyone except my friends."

"So . . . some of them thinking of signing up too? Is this what's got you going? Or has some fast-talking recruiter come through?" There was a touch of anger in Dad's voice, like he needed to blame *somebody* for this idea.

"Jimmy . . . he's thinking on it. Can't swim, though. . . ."

"Can *you?*" Dad asked.

"*I* swim!" Joel retorted.

Don Anderson leaned forward, resting his big arms on his knees, and stared out toward the road. "Well, Joel, I'm not about to hold you back, you make up your mind on something. But just for your mother's sake, think on it awhile, will you? Don't go signing something you can't reverse."

They set to work again, a growing silence between them, only the skittering sound as a squirrel chased another around a tree trunk. But at some point in the afternoon,

139

Buck heard his dad say, "Let's do that big poplar next, Joel. Why don't you notch it this time, and I'll just watch. You lay it down, and Buck and I will chop it up."

Maybe it was the first time Joel had been allowed to fell a tree, Buck thought. It wasn't a clean cut—it splintered some when it fell—but it was a tall, straight tree, and it crashed exactly where it was supposed to fall.

"Good job!" Dad said as he inspected the end of the trunk.

But Buck doubted it would change anything.

15

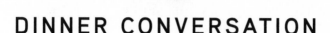

DINNER CONVERSATION

Everyone was ravenously hungry at dinner, and Mel had gotten home early, bringing a couple of cherry pies he'd picked up along the way. Katie, in shorts and a checkered top, hair in a French braid, had made a centerpiece for the table. She had used an assortment of wild flowers, greenery, and twigs she'd found in the field next to their property.

Uncle Mel eyed the bouquet with suspicion.

"Nothing in there about to erupt, is there?" he asked, and that brought a laugh from everyone, remembering the mass of praying mantis eggs that had come in two months before on one of Katie's bouquets; they had hatched right in the middle of dinner.

"Prepare to vacate!" Joel cried, and Buck jokingly grabbed

one corner of the tablecloth, the way they had back in April. They had carried it outside where dozens of tiny mantids rapidly scurried off into the grass, and they had to gather up all the silverware and put it back on the table.

"Lucky we hadn't put the plates and food on yet," Doris Anderson said. "I know they're a friend to man, but they'd got in my pork roast, I'd have smashed them flat."

Gramps wasn't his usual witty self, however. "Sure makes for a long day when I got to run the shop alone," he complained, resting one bony arm next to his plate. The frayed denim shirt he wore winter and summer alike was still buttoned at the wrist, and the sleeve opening seemed far too large for his wrinkled hand.

"Well, Joel and I have got to go back and finish that lot tomorrow, Pop. Figure one more day should do it," Dad said, passing the bowl of creamed peas around the table, "but we could let you have Buck tomorrow."

It wasn't the first time Buck noticed that his dad passed him around as easily as he'd loan out a ladder to a neighbor. He didn't mind especially, but it would have been nice to be asked first.

Gramps didn't respond one way or the other.

"Would that help?" Dad asked him.

Gramps dipped a bite of bread in his gravy and thrust it in his mouth. Chewed as though either his jaws were painful or the words he was about to say hurt them: "What would help is somebody taking it seriously, the thievin' at the shop."

"Oh, Dad, you going on about that again?" Don Anderson said, and gave his head a small shake.

Gramps caught it, though, and raised his voice: "All right now, you listen. While you were all at the woods today, I did some figuring." He took a minute to wipe the big blue napkin across his mouth and laid his fork across his plate. "Three weeks ago, see, I numbered every one of those plywood sheets—small numbers there on the edge. Wouldn't see 'em at all if you weren't looking for 'em. Did the same with my pine planks and my fence posts—every last thing we keep outside under cover, and whenever I sold a piece, I recorded that number."

Dad gave an astonished chuckle. "Heck, Dad, you'll give yourself a coronary, all that bending over."

Gramps waved it away. "The thing is, between three weeks ago and today, we've sold seven sheets of plywood, missing three. Sold fourteen planks, missing two. And a couple of fence posts."

It would be easy to blame the missing pieces on Gramps's arithmetic, Buck was thinking, except that the only thing Gramps was better at than running a log through a sawmill and turning out planks, was numbers. And every single purchase was itemized on the store receipt no matter who did the selling—Dad or Gramps or Joel.

"Hmm," Dad said. "Can't account for that. But you tell me how somebody's going to get that stuff out of there without opening the front gate."

"No, *you* tell me how it walks out on its own!" Gramps responded. "We don't find out pretty soon, they'll take the whole darn sawmill."

Buck and Joel exchanged amused glances.

"I'll say this for Gramps, he's one stubborn dude when it

comes to chasing down a penny," Joel laughed. "Talk about stubborn . . ."

Gramps was getting annoyed, and Dad said quickly, "Now look who's talking! Remember that argument you had with Mel, about what pitcher holds the record for most no-hitters in the major leagues?"

"And you were so sure it was Bob Feller you bet a whole day's pay at the mill?" Mel said.

"And was it?" asked Buck.

"Heck, no. It was Nolan Ryan," said Dad.

Katie turned to Mel wide-eyed. "Did you make Joel pay?"

"You betcha! Teach the kid not to gamble!"

Joel looked sheepish and gave Mel a pretend punch as the family hooted. All but Gramps, who silently continued eating.

"Okay, Pop, let's talk about it," Dad said. "Do you want to install some security cameras?"

"Never needed cameras before!" Gramps declared. "Been here sixty-two years, and my dad before me. Once we locked that gate at night, you could count on nobody even entertaining the thought of breaking in."

"Except nobody had to," Mom said, lifting her water glass. "All they have to do is climb over." She took a few sips and set it down again.

"You're telling me somebody hoisted all that over the top?" Dad asked.

"Why not?" said Mom. "Especially if there was more than one in on it."

But Buck had another idea. "There's a g . . . gap between the gate and the m . . . metal fence post," he said. "Someone c . . . could climb over the f . . . fence, then slide stuff through the g . . . gap. Especially the lumber and p . . . plywood sheets. I don't know about the fence posts."

"He's got a point," said Dad. "Not hard at all."

Gramps shook his head. "Can't get my mind around the thought of someone wanting to do me that way."

"Well, I can't either, Dad, but you say you don't want a security camera."

"How about putting barbed wire along the top of the fence?" said Mel.

Gramps straightened. "And make Anderson's Lumber look like a prison?" he declared. "All that says to customers is we don't trust 'em."

"But we don't!" Katie said innocently, and Gramps frowned at her. "Just saying . . . ," she murmured, sitting back in her chair.

"What do you want, Dad? You want a couple of us to stay overnight down there? Watch who comes by?" Joel asked.

"I'll d . . . do it," Buck offered. "Me and Joel."

Gramps ignored them both. "What I want is to find out who's doing some renovating around here . . . adding on a sunporch or carport, and is likely using my lumber."

Mom looked thoughtful. "Pearl mentioned the Iversons adding a room for her mother-in-law."

"Murphys are building a shed," said Joel, "but I can't imagine one of them stealing. What *about* Buck and me holing up in the shop Saturday night?"

"Yeah. I'll d . . . do it," said Buck. If he and Joel and Katie were going to own the sawmill some day, might as well take some responsibility.

"Could be any night at all," said Dad. "Could be *anybody* at all. Somebody with a truck. All he'd have to do is drive up around two in the morning—no traffic on the road—no one to see him coming in or out. Park it there in the trees, climb the fence, haul the stuff over the top or slide it through the gap. Then load it in the truck and take off. A few at a time. He's got away with it so far."

"So who do we know with a truck?" asked Katie.

"Just about everyone in the county!" said Gramps.

"Okay," Dad said. "Buck and Joel can sit watch at the sawmill on Saturday night. We'll see what happens."

Out in the kitchen, Katie and Buck filled the dishwasher.

"Whoever thought owning a sawmill had so many problems," Katie said.

"You wouldn't want it?" Buck asked.

"Never!"

"Really? What about the house?"

"*This* house?"

"Yeah. M . . . might be yours s . . . someday, you know."

Katie paused, a saucer in her hands, and looked around. "Oh, wow, if I owned *this* house, I'd take out the wall between the kitchen and dining room, and have one big space, and I'd put a skylight in the front hallway and extend the porch all the way around both sides. . . ."

Buck laughed. "S . . . sorry I asked."

Katie slid the saucer onto the stack in the cupboard. "Why would it be just *my* house? Why wouldn't it belong to all three of us?"

"It w . . . would, I suppose. Any of us who stayed."

"Maybe we'd decide to sell it and all of us just go and do what we wanted."

"Well, that too," said Buck. "It's a l . . . l . . . long way off."

16

BUCK TO DAVID,
DAVID TO BUCK

Buck: just call me private eye

David: yeah? who u spying on? male or female?

Buck: don't know yet someone stealing stuff from the sawmill

David: he walk away with a saw or what?

Buck: lumber and plywood mostly. gramps been keeping a record. joel and i are on watch saturday night. 2 bad ur not here

David: yeah. i'd rather b caving though

Buck: me 2

David: i want to discover something i want something named after me

Buck: get a dog and name him david II

David: ha ha i want a cave

Buck: david's den?

David: how about weinstein caverns?

Buck: or not

David: they'll probably name a weed after me my allergies are awful since we moved

Buck: so tell your mom pennsylvania's bad 4 your health

David: its good for hers tho she loves her new job, but not her boss

Buck: u could always join the navy that's what joel wants 2 do

David: we could both join navy seals underwater caves and stuff

Buck: im 2 short 4 the navy

David: and sharks freak me out

Buck: bummer

17

SURVEILLANCE

On Friday, Buck went looking for all the numbers that Gramps had penciled on the edges of the plywood sheets, the pine boards . . . everything he kept stored outside under tarps. He found the numbers, faint and shaky—never noticed, perhaps, by a customer, but distinct enough for Buck to catch.

At noon, halfway through the sandwich he had brought, he remembered his appointment with Jacob. He'd already changed it from Thursday to Friday, because he'd been in the woods with Dad and Joel. Jacob was expecting him at one o'clock, and Buck had ridden in with Dad, who let him off with Gramps. He had no bike this time.

His heart thumping, Buck looked Jacob's number up in

the directory. He waited until Gramps had gone to the back of the shop to measure a cut for a baseboard, then picked up the phone and punched in Jacob's number.

It rang three times, and then Jacob picked it up. "Jacob here."

Buck tried, but all he got out was a puff of air.

There was a pause. "Jacob Wall," the voice said. "Whom am I speaking with?"

"B . . . Buck." The answer came in a struggle. "I c . . . c . . . c . . . can't . . ." He stopped, breathing hard, and tried again. "I c . . . can't g . . . g . . . get . . ." It was impossible. The words wouldn't come.

"Buck? Where are you?"

"The m . . . m . . . m . . . m . . . mill. I h . . . have to w . . . w . . . w . . . work. . . ." Buck's heart was pounding so hard it hurt, and his hand was wet with perspiration.

Jacob's voice was stern, unforgiving: "We had an agreement, Buck."

"I know, b . . . b . . . but my d . . . dad . . ."

"See me tomorrow, Buck. Excuses won't work." The phone clicked.

Buck wiped the sweat off the handset and put it back. Maybe it was time to tell Mom and Dad. But even as he thought it, he shook his head. He could already hear the questions:

Why is Jacob offering this, Buck?
I don't know.
Why isn't he charging?
I'm not sure.
Is the therapy working?

150

I can't tell yet.

What kind is it?

He used it on soldiers and sailors, that's all I know.

It wouldn't be enough. They'd keep asking. And asking. They'd listen to him stuttering more and ask if it wasn't getting worse. And what if it was?

• • •

He explained as best he could on Saturday. But all Jacob said was "If you want to feel better about yourself by the time school starts again, then you come here three times a week. You'll have to make up your third session tomorrow. Will that be a problem?"

"I'll b . . . be here," Buck said. There was something challenging in knowing that he was being treated like a military man; the urge to see if he could take it.

The session that followed was more of the same, but this time Buck found himself facing the big mirror that Jacob had propped against the wall. Jacob asked him to recite something from memory—anything—the Pledge of Allegiance, even—and to watch himself in the mirror.

Already the *P*s and the *F*s and the *S*s loomed up before him. Buck made it through the first *P* by crashing forward, bulldozing his way in with explosions of spittle, but by the first *T*, he saw his face transformed, as though it were made of modeling clay. Something, it appeared, was pressing down on his forehead. His teeth were clamped tightly together, his lips stretched into a hard tight line, and he was straining so hard that the sinews on his neck were visible.

". . . t . . . t . . . t . . . t . . . t . . . to the United St . . . St . . .

151

St . . . States of America, and t . . . to the r . . . r . . . r . . . r . . .
r . . ."

It was hideous. *He* was hideous. It was like he was changing into Wolfman, right there in front of his eyes. Was this the way he looked to other people when he stuttered? What friends saw when he tried to tell a joke or a story? What teachers saw when he recited in class?

As before, Jacob worked with him to relax the forehead, the jaws, the lips, the tongue, and when they went through the jaw flapping exercises together, both making the *ploh, ploh* sound, Buck looked so ridiculous that he laughed out loud and this time Jacob actually smiled.

But when Buck tried to recite the Pledge a second time, Jacob stopped him on almost every word.

"Stutter!" he commanded. "Slide right into it, easy like, and stutter as long as I hold my finger in the air. Watch yourself in the mirror."

Buck took a deep breath and faced the mirror again, Jacob's raised finger very visible off to one side.

"I p . . . p . . . p . . . pledge . . ."

"I didn't put my finger down. Stutter and keep stuttering, Buck."

"I p . . . p . . . p . . . ppppppppppppppppppp . . ."

"Good!"

"Pledge allegiance t . . . t . . . ttttttttttttttttto the flag of the United St . . . St . . . Sssssssssssssss . . ."

He got used to it after a while. It was only Jacob, after all. If Jacob could sit in that armchair across from him and listen to this all day, what did it matter?

". . . and to the Republic fffffffffffffffffffffffor which it stands . . ."

152

It was still embarrassing, whether he kept repeating the first sound or simply holding it for a long time, but it did seem as though he wasn't fighting it quite so much.

Maybe he was doing so well that he could skip Sunday, Buck thought as Jacob said another "Good! Keep it up!"

But when the session was over, Jacob said, "Tomorrow. Whenever you finish your Sunday dinner."

As Buck headed for the door, he joked, "So when do I g . . . get the speech about all the famous pppppppeople who've st . . . st . . . st . . . stuttered? Moses and Isaac Newton and K . . . King George and M . . . Marilyn M . . . Monroe?"

Jacob's eyes too had a twinkle. "You want a speech?"

"Nnnnnot particularly. It's just that anyone who www-wwrites about stuttering always tttttells about the f . . . famous people who stuttered."

"Well, I don't think King George or Moses are going to do you any good. When you're standing in front of the class and your jaws tighten, the fact that King George did it isn't much help. You're you. The sooner we can get you to accept that you are not a stutterer, just a guy who happens to stutter—one of the many things you do—when you can concentrate on the rest of you and the things you have to offer, the better your speech will be."

And Buck had to believe it, because there wasn't anything else.

• • •

Around eleven that night, Dad drove Joel and Buck to the sawmill. The Buick moved slowly around the bends in the road, their wanting to take any truck by surprise that might be parked near the mill. A quarter of a mile away, the two

brothers climbed out with sleeping bags to sit on and sandwiches and went the rest of the way on foot.

At the sawmill, the only light came from a bulb just inside the entrance. It illuminated a square patch of concrete
beyond the door and window, but the fence and gate were
largely in shadow, lit only by an erratic moon that slid in
and out of the clouds.

Joel put the key in the lock at the gate, closing it again
after them, and went across the clearing to the shop. Once
inside, they placed their sleeping bags in the shadows on
either side of the entrance, then sat across from each other
so they were facing in two directions.

The shop smelled of fresh-cut wood, old oil and new
paper, of metal and printer toner.

When the first hour had gone by, Joel said, "This. Is. The.
Slowest. Hour. I. Ever. Spent. In. My. Life."

Buck laughed. "W . . . which would you r . . . rather be?
T . . . tired or bored?"

"Tired," said Joel.

"Cold or b . . . bored?"

"Cold," said Joel. "Shoot, I'd rather be almost anything
than bored. That's why I want to join the navy."

His brother was serious about it, Buck realized. He silently stretched one leg, then the other, and tried to make
out Joel's face in the darkness, but all he got was a faint pale
blur.

"Wh . . . what would you d . . . do in the navy?"

"Whatever they tell me to do. Eat when they say eat. Sleep
when they say sleep. Heck, I'll bet you even spit when they
say spit."

"Not m . . . me. I'd hate for s . . . somebody to always be telling me what to d . . . do."

"Well, that's what you've got here, isn't it? Dad and Gramps always calling the shots? Work in the shop: I'm in the shop. Cut timber: that's where I'm at. Trees and sawdust. That's all I see. At least in the navy you learn new things, go new places—see the world. We've been looking at the same darn hills since we learned to walk. . . ."

"Shhhh." Buck suddenly learned forward. "Something's out b . . . by the fence."

Joel crawled over on his hands and knees. "Where?"

"To the l . . . left of the gate."

"Don't see it. How high up?"

Buck gave a disgusted sigh. "Aw, j . . . just an old fox. What's she think she's g . . . going to find to eat around here?"

Joel leaned back against the wall and put his hands behind his head. "Didn't you ever want to do something different, Buck? I mean, I'm not knocking it, if you like to hang around home. It's pretty here, I'll grant you that. But me? I just want to get away."

It was all Buck could do to keep his secret. Yes, he wanted to do something different too. He wanted to see what was down *under* the earth they'd grown up on. Go somewhere that nobody—not even the United States Navy—had ever been.

"Yeah, I think about it sometimes," he said. "Have to w . . . w . . . wait and see what happens."

18

BUCK TO DAVID,
DAVID TO BUCK

Buck: all night and nobody came

David: figures

Buck: going in the hole again next week there will always b a reason not to go so i won't wait 4 the perfect time

David: yeah if ur mom finds out tho that's the end of it. where do u say u've been all day?

Buck: remember nat waleski? i hang out with him sometimes i say i'm with him

David: u won't tell him about the hole will u?

Buck: u crazy?

David: just don't get urself stuck tho. U don't have me 2 pull your butt out when u get in those tight squeezes

Buck: i'm careful so what do u do all day when u don't have me 2 entertain u?

David: i joined a canoeing club

Buck: u?

David: something wrong with that?

Buck: canoe didn't sink or anything?

The minute Buck thumbed the last response, he wished he hadn't. Knew he shouldn't have, when David didn't answer. The thing about texting was that you couldn't slap someone on the back or make a funny face or squeak out "just kidding" in a Mickey Mouse voice or anything. He tried, though.

Buck: kidding! kidding!

Finally, an answer from David:

David: actually i'm pretty good at it. i'll paddle all the way down the shenandoah someday and say hello

Buck started to say, "Yeah, right!" but thought better of it.

Buck: sure wish u could

David: me 2

19

IN THE HOLE

Buck's chance in the Hole came sooner than he thought.

It hadn't rained for at least a week and there was no talk of more timber cutting soon. Logs from the last cut were still piled on the two-ton truck; Gramps and Dad hadn't had time to run them through the saw yet, since summer was also a season for remodeling, and both Dad and Joel were hired occasionally for carpentry work in town. Gramps told them to keep an eye out for any job using his plywood, but it wasn't likely that any person stealing from Anderson's Mill would want Dad or Joel on the job.

On one of his days home, Uncle Mel had taken Buck to a baseball game to watch their local team get creamed. And Buck and Nat had gone to a few matinees at the Palace, so no one got alarmed, it seemed, when Buck wasn't around at lunchtime.

His pack was ready. He kept it that way now. It was a cheap, flimsy backpack that held Mel's old overalls, cut to a shorter length, extra flashlight batteries and electrical tape for sticking on rock walls to mark his route. Also duct tape, peanut butter crackers, water, Band-Aids, mini boxes of raisins, and a box of Skittles. Shin guards, jacket, knee guards, and a clean T-shirt.

On this particular morning, Dad and Joel were working at the sawmill with Gramps, Mom was at Holly's, and Mel was on a truck run. Buck had risen early, hoed one long row of peas, and picked another of lima beans. Then he had come inside, finished a bowl of cereal and a banana, and had just slipped his backpack over his shoulders when he heard Katie's voice saying, "Everyone's got somewhere to go but me."

He turned to see her standing in the kitchen doorway, blond hair uncombed and dangling in her face. He tried to sound casual:

"Where's C . . . C . . . Colby these days?"

"Working for his stepdad. And Amy's in Iowa visiting her grandparents." Katie plopped down on a chair and pushed back the stray lock from her eyes. "So where are *you* going?"

"Just l . . . looking for some good b . . . bike trails for me and Nat," Buck said, which was about four percent true.

"I like to ride too, you know," Katie said.

"Well, if I f . . . find any new ones, you c . . . can go with us sometime," Buck said. He gave her a quick grin and was out the door, climbing on his bike, the pack on his back shifting slightly as he rode.

He hated lying to Katie. Hated to see the look of disappointment on her face when he went off without her. She was still in her pajamas, though, and hadn't had breakfast. She couldn't have expected him to hang around waiting.

• • •

He'd only been riding ten minutes when the first obstacle came to mind. Though he knew a back route to the Wilmer property, he would be coming in from an entirely different angle. He wasn't at all sure he could find the same field, the same woods and fence posts to get his bearings and locate the Hole.

He *had* to take the old route, and would have to rely on luck that Ethan and his dad—or any of the other boys— would not be on that same road at the same time, to see him get off his bike and head out through the tall grass. The sun was already hot on the back of his neck, and this made him all the more eager to slide down into the cool damp darkness of underground.

Buck was dismayed when he rounded a bend after forty minutes to see a maintenance crew working about a mile from the old Wilmer place. A large slab of concrete seemed to have buckled along one edge of the roadway and separated from the rest. He slowed when he came to a flag man.

"What happened?" Buck called.

"Sink hole," the man answered, and waved him on around.

And once again, the thought came to mind that someday Buck might bike all the way out here to find that the shallow dip in the earth he had encountered close to the Hole had become a wide crater, and that all the secrets of its underground passageways were open for everyone to see. Not likely. But still. . . . He *had* to be the *first*.

There was no more construction, no more workers, and Buck rode around the last bend to see the long curving ribbon of roadway ahead of him. He counted the number of fence posts and slowed as a dump truck went past, finally disappearing around the far bend. Then all was quiet, and the road was empty.

Buck quickly dismounted, then pulled his bike down into the gulley and into a thicket that covered it completely. He crept unseen to where the line of trees began, the tall, jagged outline of Eagles Cliff beyond them, and made his way to the Hole.

Yes, here was the shallow recess in the earth, and Buck checked that he was no longer visible from either the road or the faraway windows of the abandoned farmhouse. And here was the little pile of fox bones—what was left of them anyway.

He reached the third outcropping of rock and stopped, taking off his backpack. He put on his old brown jacket, then stepped into Mel's overalls, and probably could have fit in them twice. The shin guards he strapped to his forearms protected both his skin and the jacket. He put the knee pads on top of the overalls and used duct tape to bind the legs of the overalls and his jeans snugly around each ankle. Next, the pair of gloves he'd worn all last winter, the ones with the fake leather palms. And finally, the bicycle helmet still on his head, flashlight in hand, Buck lowered himself into the Hole.

For the first fifteen minutes he was in familiar territory as he crawled or slithered along on his knees or belly, pushing his backpack ahead of him. Unfortunately, of course, it blocked out much of his light. There were times he thought he'd known the passage's contours better than he did and lifted his head a little too high, too quickly, and felt not just a gentle tap of rock above, but a sharp *whang* against his helmet that resounded in his ears.

It was difficult to gauge how far he had traveled or how fast he was moving. A foot in ten seconds? Fifteen? The rocks beneath him were sharp in places, and at times he struggled to find room for a knee, an elbow, and wondered when he would get to the place in the passageway—if it was a passage—where it turned. Other times he wondered if he was making much progress, or just rearranging himself in the same small space.

But finally, there it was, the turn. He took a minute to rest, pointing his flashlight in all directions. Mostly he saw only rock and mud and fungus. Crickets with no eyes scurried to get out of the flashlight's beam. But then, something else he had not noticed before. Behind the boulder on his left, what at first glance was a shadow, was actually an opening, so that he had a choice of going to his left, up over rock, or to his right, which slanted downward.

His heart thumped so hard with excitement it almost hurt. So which would it be? If he chose left and started to climb, he imagined that he would be entering the wooded hillside next to Wilmer's pasture, the narrow sliver of Blue Ridge Mountains that crossed the county.

If he went right and started downward, he might well come to water. And possibly the end of the passage.

Decision time. He figured he had about four hours and twenty minutes before he had to head for home. The passage on the left was larger—here at least—the opening on the right, a little smaller. He decided to save the mud for another day, and see where he got by going up. He could wear his backpack now, at least for a while, instead of pushing it.

So with one final look at the faint glimpse of daylight coming far back from the Hole, he maneuvered his body into a sitting position and took out the bright yellow electrical tape. Tearing off each piece he would need, he made two arrows on the rock—the upper arrow to show the way he had chosen to go forward, the lower arrow to show the way back to the Hole.

And then, after slipping his arms through the straps of the backpack, he started crawling left up the rock. It was difficult, because he had the use of only one hand, his other holding the flashlight. On all sides, there were holes and cracks and crevices that made him aware of how important it was not to drop the flashlight. All the more reason he needed a headlamp.

The rock beneath him was slippery, and he chose to crawl rather than crouch, even when the passage widened and he had more room. He needed the added traction of his knee pads. Each time he stopped to reconnoiter, he checked to see if there were any rocks that looked as though they might be ready to fall, any drop-off ahead, any opening too small to even try to get through. He had read enough caving manuals to know that you never made the next move

163

until you knew exactly where each foot, each hand, was going.

Now and then his heart gave an extra thump in the knowledge that he *should not be here,* attempting this alone. No excuses. He should NOT. He had written the note he'd promised David he would write and leave on his pillow: *Mom and Dad, if I don't come back, call David. He'll know where I am.*

He had given David the most specific directions he could. But he had placed the note on the far slope of his pillow. You wouldn't see it just by glancing in his room. You'd have to go in and start searching the covers before you'd find it. Which, David explained, would be after the police had been called and were searching his room for clues.

The ceiling above him suddenly expanded, and he found he could actually stand up, relieve his aching back muscles. Ahead of him, however, was a jumble of rocks he'd have to climb over to go forward. When he rested a minute or two, he slowly began hoisting himself up, rock by rock, checking each one to see if it moved at all, wanting to take no chance that the whole pile would give way under him. If only he'd get a sign that this was the right way to go—the draft of air getting stronger, for example. Maybe a far-off pinpoint of light.

All he got was this rock slide he couldn't see over. Man, he really needed a light on his helmet—a stronger beam that would light up everything around him. Already the beam in his flashlight seemed to be getting weaker. He might have to change batteries. He'd found headlamps advertised on the Internet for as little as nineteen dollars, plus shipping, but he wanted a really good one. And how was he supposed to talk Mom or Dad into ordering one for him without a zillion questions?

He turned the flashlight off when he could to save the battery, but each time he did, the blackness was so total, so complete, that it took his breath away. And when it took his breath away, there was no sound at all, not even the gentle *whuff* of his own breathing.

Once over the rock slide, the surface under his feet turned to clay again. The ceiling got lower and lower, until he was on his belly as before, and again, he took off his backpack and pushed it ahead of him as he crawled. Thirty more minutes and he had to start back. He realized that all it would take was another rock slide, or even one big rock to roll out of place, blocking his path back, and . . . Buck took a shaky breath and went on.

He moved as fast as he could, the shin guards on his arms making soft grating sounds as he set one arm down, then the next, followed by the soft scrape of each leg as it dragged along after. He ached from his cramped position and his neck had a crick in it that wouldn't go away. He tried lying down on his side so he could raise his chin off his chest, and reached out his left arm. His fingers closed around something loose, something light. He tried to make out what it was—smooth, with a ridge, and . . .

Carefully Buck positioned his flashlight so that he could turn it on.

"Oh!" he said aloud, and dropped the skull in his hand.

For a moment he remained perfectly still, staring at it. Not a human skull, but that of an animal he couldn't quite

165

make out. A possum, he decided finally. A lamb falling into the Hole would never make it back this far, and most certainly would never find its way out again. The very thought sent pinpricks down his spine. Buck may have been the first human to explore this place, but animals had been here, and journeyed to . . . where? He gently pushed the skull to one side and kept going.

• • •

It was tedious work and Buck would allow himself only one real rest stop. He ate a small box of raisins and half a box of Skittles and drank some water. That gave him a new burst of energy. He felt like some kind of insect, scrambling along, up and down and over the bumpy path, sometimes on his feet and hands, butt in the air, conscious always of whether he would get confused finding his way back, and taking time to mark the rock wall with taped arrows, pointing the way he should go.

He struggled to make the next turn, curving his body like a question mark, wriggling and pushing and pulling, and saw in the beam of the flashlight that the channel was narrowing, smaller and smaller still, until it was only as wide as his own body. Inch by inch, he made the turn on his belly. Trying to keep his head up so he could see, his legs completed the maneuver and he scanned the passage ahead.

There wasn't any. He was facing solid rock except for a football-size hole between boulders in which a strong draft of air chilled his face. He directed the light into the hole and saw only rock, but it was some distance away, meaning there was a larger cavity somewhere beyond. Buck knew what his aching muscles already told him, however—this was the end of the passage he had chosen, and his bumps and bruises were all for nothing.

Well, not quite. It was all part of exploring. He'd never know unless he tried, and he'd make notes when he got back home as he mapped out his underground maze.

And then he faced a second problem. There was no way to turn around.

20

ALL THAT WAY . . .

He had to concentrate on getting out, but he couldn't even pull up a knee. No way in the world he could try to sit up and twist himself around so as to get his legs behind him and start the crawl back again.

Think, he told himself. How far back was that space where he had stood up and climbed over the rock pile? Twenty minutes back? Forty minutes? An hour? How wide was his helmet? Nine inches . . . ten? Maybe . . . if he took his helmet off, just for now, he could edge himself sideways. . . .

Just thinking about it made sweat trickle down his face. This was the way cavers died sometimes, getting wedged between rocks. And this was the worst place of all to be trapped because he was at a dead end. Rescuers, if anyone found his note at home, could only come from one direction—behind him. If he couldn't even bring a leg up past his body—well, perhaps they could drag him off by his feet, but what if his head got stuck?

No, he would have to crawl backward, which would probably take twice as long, and he hoped he wouldn't miss the arrows he had placed along the way.

His chin scraping the rock beneath him, Buck turned his head in the other direction and, with the hand that was holding the flashlight, took one final look around, as much as he could see beyond his backpack. Definitely a second rock slide here, jamming the passageway in front of him, but he knew for sure that there was more on the other side.

Now, instead of pulling himself forward on his forearms and elbows, he had no choice but to slowly, awkwardly, dig his arms, his hands, into the rock and clay beneath him and push himself backward, dragging his backpack in one hand, flashlight in the other. And rather than focusing on keeping his head and shoulders down to fit in the space before him, he had to concentrate on keeping his bottom low enough with each push that it wouldn't scrape the roof of the passage.

With no light to guide his way back, his blind feet had to kick out at each side to determine which direction the passage was winding, but a heavy boot could not detect each sharp angle of rock, and now and then in the slow progression, Buck felt a stab on his leg, a prick on his arm, a long scrape against his shoulder. What he did *not* want to do was to kick off a loose rock and block his way out.

The light was getting dimmer, and he quickly switched

off the flashlight. No use studying the way he had come, but he didn't want to miss any arrows he might have left along the way, either.

STUPID, STUPID, STUPID, David would tell him. Buck used to jokingly call David Mother sometimes, when he worried too much about safety. David even had one of those cheap survival blankets in his backpack that had been there unused for so long that once, when they were caught in a cold rainstorm, he pulled it out to cover themselves, and it tore along its middle fold. They had each wrapped themselves in half of the Mylar blanket, and Buck had joked that all they needed were a couple of pacifiers.

David didn't seem so foolish now, Buck was thinking. If he ever got out of here . . . His heart pounded again, and he stopped crawling and took several deep breaths. *When* he got out of here, he would never come back without a headlamp. He had almost nine dollars saved from the money his dad was paying him to hoe, and with the money Jacob was giving him, he could afford one of the best.

Crawling blind this way, Buck worried he may have missed a turn, and was taking a route he hadn't seen before. But when he turned the flashlight on again, the faint beam showed that he had just passed a slight indentation that he remembered in the rocky wall—not the little closet-size space he'd been in once before, but enough, he felt, to turn himself around.

Carefully, carefully, testing the rock around him to see if there was room enough for his helmet, his shoulders, his butt, his knees . . . he began the slow twist, inch by inch. And finally, finally . . . he was facing forward—his head and shoulders where his feet had been. He opened his backpack and took out fresh batteries.

Another thing he was doing wrong. David would really get on him about it. You should never enter a cave without three different sources of light. Not three batteries for the same flashlight, but three flashlights, in case you dropped one in a crevasse. Or one flashlight, one headlamp, and some glow sticks.

He changed the battery and put the old one in the bag. Then, after another drink of water, and after devouring the cheese crackers he'd brought along, he put the water bottle back and started off.

He looked at his watch. Two-forty-six. He still had a little time left.

When he reached the place the passage divided, the yellow arrows on the wall, he could see the welcoming faint light of the Hole's entrance far off in the distance. He decided to use the remaining time he had to explore the passage on his right. When the time was up, he promised himself, no matter what he found—even the skeleton of a Stone Age man!—he had to save the rest for another day, and start home.

He took out his tape and placed an X over the two arrows on the left so he wouldn't take that route again. And then he started his descent.

For a while the scrambling, though difficult, at least allowed him to wear his backpack, freeing his hands. But the path was up one rock and down the next, like a marine obstacle course, and he was dismayed at how soon his back ached miserably from being stooped, so that he almost welcomed crawling on his knees again.

171

From somewhere in the distance he heard a faint but steady *plip, plip . . . aplop. Plip, plip . . . aplop.* Fascinated, he paused and gave it his full attention. *Plip, plip . . . aplop. Plip, plip . . . aplop.* Maybe there was an underground spring. His mind raced with possibilities. Wherever it was, it was still a long way off. There seemed to be an echo along with it.

Now he was climbing again; the passage curved and was going up, not down. He was able to stand but desperately needed both hands to steady himself as he crawled over boulders. He paused once to place an arrow, then chose the direction of the dropping water, sensing that the cavern was opening up the farther he went. But then, around the next boulder, he faced it again: a solid wall of rock, as if to say, *End of the line, Buck. You shouldn't be here. How many times do we have to tell you?*

He leaned one hand against the rocky surface on his left, panting, huffing out his disappointment. But he could hear . . . He could *feel* . . . Yes! The draft was stronger here, much stronger, so it must be coming from someplace!

He sank to his knees, giving his thighs a rest, and trained the flashlight on the wall to his left, foot by foot, inch by inch. Then the right. There was a ripple in the rock on this side, he discovered, so he began crawling forward, dragging one hand along the rock, looking for any hole large enough to channel the draft through.

And then, just beyond the ripple, the wall seemed to disappear. When Buck trained the flashlight on it, he discovered an opening the size of a closet door—a narrow, vertical drop-off, but how far down it led, he didn't know.

I knew there was more! he told himself, even as the realization hit that if he had used up his last battery and been wandering here in the dark, he could have walked right off into the space.

His mouth dry, heart pounding, Buck lay down on his stomach and inched his way to the edge of the shaft. A rush of air met his cheek, and a musty scent assaulted his nostrils. Carefully, leaning over as far as he dared, he directed the beam of light straight down. Perhaps fifteen feet below, there was a shelf of rock, but beyond that, the channel went down even farther, and the *plip, plip . . . aplop* was loudest of all.

"Yes!" he said softly, as if his discovery might scare it away. He *had* to explore it. If only David could come down for a weekend and do it with him!

He felt something move in the breast pocket of the overalls, and suddenly he realized that the Skittles were falling out of the box and into the hole below.

Buck jerked himself upright, slapping one hand over the box to preserve what were left. He couldn't quite believe his carelessness. What if those had been batteries? What if they had been glow sticks, or an extra flashlight? Water? He couldn't afford mistakes like this when he came again. He just couldn't.

He took another look around him, then glanced at his watch.

Four-fifty-two. *No!* How could this be? It seemed only a half hour or so that he had started on this second journey. How could he possibly get home now before five-thirty? Six, even. He was filthy! He turned around and plunged back into the passageway.

WHONK!

Ouch! His head again. That one probably put a dent in his helmet. He had to pay attention now. If he was late, he was late. But he couldn't be lost.

It was almost five-fifteen when he came to the arrow he had placed on the rock. From here on, the passageway was familiar territory, and when he finally saw his first glimpse of daylight, and better yet, when he popped up out of the hole at ten of six, his eyes could not take the brightness. The sky was overcast, but still it took a while for his eyes to adjust.

He took a minute to see the world through his spread fingers, squinting, as the sweet smell of grass seemed to saturate the air.

Buck looked himself over. It wasn't just the overalls that were muddy; his legs and arms were streaked with dirt and clay. He took off the overalls and hid them in a plastic bag he had brought, tucked it under one of the rocks. Then he put on the clean T-shirt, headed back through the meadow to his bike, and stopped at a creek several miles away to wash off what he could. All the while he thought of the excuses he'd make. Nobody would want him at the table looking as he did.

• • •

He was right about that.

It was almost six-forty-five when he walked in the back door.

"Will ya look at *that!*" Gramps exclaimed, lowering the sparerib in his hand.

174

"What on God's green earth happened to *you*?" his mom said. "You look like you went down a mudslide."

Buck tried smiling a little. "S . . . something like that," he said.

"You find a good bike trail?" asked Katie.

"N . . . no, but I tried. Just t . . . took a mean s . . . s . . . skid."

"Break any bones?" asked Dad.

"Don't think so. . . ."

"Well, go shower, then," his dad said, more gruffly this time. "You can't come to the table like that. You know what time it is, don't you?"

"Yeah. I'm sorry. Had to rescue my b . . . bike."

"Why didn't you call? You've got yourself a cell phone now," Mom said.

"Didn't think to t . . . take it," Buck told her, and realized that from now on, he had to, even though the Hole was a no-service area, for sure.

Joel didn't say anything, just gave him a puzzled look, and Buck went on upstairs before anyone could think of something else to ask him.

21

BUCK TO DAVID, DAVID TO BUCK

Buck: dude, i went back

David: in the hole? how far you get?

Buck: don't know was in it 5 hours

David: jeez, buck!!!!!

Buck: i know all that way and i come 2 a dead end but then i went another place that led to a drop-off and i could see far down there's water dripping

David: buck listen u leave a note like i said?

Buck: yes

David: man what i'd give to b back there right now

Buck: any chance?

David: zilch next week mom and i are going 2 my uncle's up in vermont. i've been accepted as a junior counselor in a day camp the first 2 weeks of august then grandma's coming to visit and after that i've got survival camp don't u get stuck in there while i'm away

Buck: i don't want 2 get stuck either. i'm careful. i had 2 go 20 minutes crawling backwards at that dead end because there wasn't room 2 turn around. i'm not taking any chances like that

David: so what's it like? what do u see?

Buck: a possum's skull, mud, clay, mold came home all filthy tonight and they thought my bike rolled down a ravine

David: and how many more times can that happen before they suspect?

Buck: none

22

TORTURE

A carnival was coming to town the middle of August. Fergus Brothers Fabulous promised fourteen different rides, as well as the Human Scarecrow, Fortunes of Fate, cotton candy, strawberry slushies, and more.

It came every year, and always in the same place—the large field behind the Super G market that had been closed for over a decade. There were Fergus Brothers Fabulous posters, however, plastered all over the store's grimy windows, and on a sweltering seventh of July, Buck and Nat stood in front of one of them trying to decide if the most distant ride in the background was part of a Ferris wheel or a roller coaster.

"I like bumper cars. They always have those," Nat said.

His dark red hair clung to his forehead. The back of his neck was sunburned, and he shielded it with one hand. He and Buck both were sweaty from a bike ride in the afternoon heat.

"There's n . . . never been a roller coaster," Buck said. "But I hope they s . . . s . . . still have the Loop-the-loop."

"Not me!" said Nat. "Any time I go upside down I get sick."

"Remind me n . . . never to sit below you," Buck told him. "You going opening night?"

"Sure. G . . . go with us, if you want," Buck said. "My brother will d . . . drive."

• • •

The next evening, when Buck plunked down beside Katie on the porch, she put her magazine aside and, placing her hands on each of her thighs, spread her fingers wide. "Look," she said, grinning.

He looked at her brightly painted nails, each one a different color, and saw that—beginning with the pinkie on one hand, thumb on the other—every nail had an elaborate letter painted on it: *C-O-L-B-Y, C-O-L-B-Y.*

Buck rolled his eyes and she giggled.

"So, C . . . Colby got your name tattooed on his backside?"

She swatted his arm. "How would *I* know?"

"Mom notice?"

"No. And she just thinks he's a friend." Katie dug her heels into the floorboards and the glider slid back and forth, a high squeak with each forward movement, and Buck helped a little.

"It's not fair, you know?" Katie said, folding her hands

over her stomach, fingers interlaced. "What's so magical about sixteen that I can't have a boyfriend till then?"

Buck shrugged. "Search me."

"Is there anything *you* have to wait until sixteen to do?"

Probably couldn't have a girlfriend till then, not that he wanted one. They both had to wait until they were sixteen to drive, but he'd known a few boys of fifteen or even fourteen who drove their dads' cars or pickups on short errands around town, and nobody stopped them. "N . . . nothing I can think of," he said.

"That's because you already have an older brother," said Katie.

"What's that g . . . got to do with it?"

"If I had an older sister, she'd pave the way for me. She'd fight all the battles about when she could have a boyfriend or wear makeup, and how late she could stay out. Then when I came along, it would be a done deal. Instead, I've got to fight them all myself."

Buck laughed and pointed to her fingernails. "That's a start." And when she didn't respond, he said, "You'll see Colby at the c . . . carnival, right? You can be with him then."

"Yes! And I'm going on every single ride that he does. I'll tell Mom I'm with Amy and Sara. They'll be there too, so it's not a real lie. Okay?"

"Don't need to ask m . . . my permission," said Buck. What he was hoping was that he could be hired at the carnival as one of the helpers—set up bottles at the ball toss, wipe off the horses on the merry-go-round. . . . There were a number of two-dollar-a-day jobs the carnival offered kids twelve

180

and over, just to make a community happy and get the folks coming.

He actually hoped he'd have the money to buy the head-lamp soon, long before summer was over, but if he wanted a good one—and he didn't want to waste his money on something cheap that didn't work right—it would be around forty dollars, counting postage and handling. He'd already found the one he wanted online, with LED lights and night vision. It might take a few more weeks, a few more rows to hoe, a few more Friday five-dollar bills from Jacob, before he'd have enough—he'd been spending too much on soda and snacks and movies at the Palace. The real problem was how he could order it, since he'd need something he didn't have—a credit card.

• • •

The next day there was another letter in Jacob's box from the woman who had written before. Buck recognized the handwriting when he pulled the envelope, along with bills and catalogs, from the box: *Karen Wall Schuster,* read the sticker in the upper left-hand corner. Beside Jacob's name in the address, she had written *Personal* and underlined it.

Buck tried not to look at it as he shuffled the envelope into the small clutch of mail he carried to the house and gave to Jacob when he went in.

Jacob glanced at the envelope and laid it aside without comment. "Let's get to work" was all he said.

So far, the hardest part of Jacob's therapy was getting over here three times a week without anyone asking where he was going. They understood he liked to ride around on his bike, though—the only form of transportation for anyone who couldn't drive—and summer was the time to be with your friends, always something going on at the grassy median in the middle of Center Street.

"That boy sure does like to be out and about," Gramps said of him once to Mom. "One way to catch a breeze."

If there was improvement in his speech, Buck couldn't tell yet. Jacob never praised him for reading a sentence through without stuttering, only when he "stuttered well," as Jacob put it, meaning easily, effortlessly, without all the facial contortions and jaw clenching, the shoulder shifting and eye blinking, or any of the other little mannerisms Buck had used unconsciously to take the attention off his lips and tongue. The only way he was able to tell what he was doing was to watch himself in a mirror while he read, and then, only if someone else was listening. As Jacob said, "It takes two to stutter—one to talk and one to listen."

He also found that he could dispense with the warm-oil-sliding-over-the-head-bit and get right to the *ploh, ploh, ploh*. When he knew what to look for—what to *feel*—it was easier to relax the right muscles. The big leather armchair across from Jacob was beginning to look more friendly. Welcoming, even.

And today, he was an exceptionally good student. Jacob asked him to say, "I'll be returning to school on September third," and, as always, to begin stuttering on a word when Jacob raised a finger, and to continue to stutter until the finger went down. Buck referred to it as the "giving me the finger" game.

He sat in front of the big mirror, his eyes on Jacob right behind it.

"I'll b . . . be returning . . ."—the finger went up—". . . t . . . t . . . t . . . t . . ."

"Don't fight it," Jacob reminded him. "Loosen your jaw and let it come out easy, Buck."

". . . t . . . t . . . t . . . tttttttttt . . ."

"Good!" The finger went down.

". . . to"—finger up—". . . sssssssssss . . ."—finger down—"school on"—finger up—"SSSSSSSSSSSSSSS"—finger down—"SSSSeptember third."

For the first half hour, they worked on stuttering more easily, as they usually did. Then Jacob reached around behind him, picked up the phone, and set it on the stool beside Buck.

Instantly Buck tensed. It was only a simple telephone with black numbers on white buttons. But Buck would have preferred a snake coiled there beside him. He watched as Jacob adjusted his glasses and fumbled with the phone directory.

"I want you to dial this number—it's a pizza place—and ask the price of a large cheese pizza. But I want you to stutter and hold it whenever I raise my finger, no matter how long I keep it up."

Was he insane? Buck wondered. Just asking the question was torture enough, without purposely stuttering and holding it forever.

"Nice and easy," Jacob said. "Just give me that slow, effortless stutter you were doing a while ago before I lowered my finger and you could go on."

Buck felt himself bending stiffly toward the phone, felt

his hand grip it, his index finger punching out the numbers as Jacob read them off. Saliva gathered in his mouth, making him swallow in a sudden frantic gulp, when a loud voice on the other end of the line said, "Mario's. Help you?"

Buck's mouth felt like a steel trap and he worked to unclench his jaws. His teeth rattled. He could hear them clicking against each other. Jacob was nodding at him.

"Mario's!" the voice on the phone said more loudly. "Can I help you?"

"Y . . . yes. H . . . how much is a large . . ."—the finger went up—". . . ch . . . ch . . . ch . . . ch . . . chchchchchchchch . . ."

"You want a pizza?"

"Keep stuttering," Jacob commanded.

". . . chchchchchch . . ."

"Look. Call me when you know what kind you want, okay?" the man said, and hung up.

Buck slammed down the phone and glared at Jacob.

"This is stupid!"

"Actually, it's real life, Buck. Call them back."

"What? They hung up on mmmme."

"Call them back. Sitting here talking with me is one thing. Stuttering freely . . . easily . . . without fighting it when you're out in public is the real world, and that's what this is all about."

"In the r . . . real world . . . I don't order p . . . pizza over the phone," Buck said hotly.

"And why is that?"

Buck slumped against the back of the chair without answering. Jacob pushed the phone toward him again and gave him the number.

"Mario's. Can I help you?"

"How mmmmuch is a ch . . . cheese . . ."—the finger—". . . pppppppppppp"—the finger went down—"pizza?"

"Large, medium, or small?"

"Large."

"Six eighty-five, six bucks with a coupon."

"Th . . . th . . . thhhanks," said Buck, and put the phone down.

Buck was through with this assignment, but Jacob wasn't. "Here's another. It's a dry cleaner's. Just ask what time they close."

Annoyed, Buck punched in the number Jacob gave him and took a deep breath.

"Don't hold your breath. It's not an execution."

"Not to you, mmmmaybe," Buck said.

The phone rang twice and a cheerful woman answered. "Valley Dry Cleaners."

"W . . . what t . . . t . . . time do you . . . ?" He'd almost made it when Jacob held up his finger. "Cl . . . cl . . . cl . . . ?"

The woman made it easy for him. Too easy. "Close? Six o'clock," she said.

"Thanks," Buck told her, and pressed *Off.*

"Wasn't so hard, was it?" Jacob thumbed through the yellow pages of the short directory again. "Here's a service station."

"Aw, come on!" Buck said irritably.

"You don't have a choice, sailor," Jacob said.

Glowering, Buck picked up the handset.

"Ask the price of super unleaded," said Jacob. He read the number and Buck punched the keys.

The phone rang several times, which probably meant someone was super busy. But finally, "Ed's Gulf," came a familiar voice. "Can I help you?"

It was Ed Ketterman's service station, and this was the unmistakable voice of Pukeman Pete himself. Probably there helping his dad.

"W . . . w . . . what's the p . . . p . . . price of . . ." The finger. "S . . . s . . . s . . . s . . . s . . . s . . . s . . . s . . . super."

"Who's this? *Buck?*"

Buck looked helplessly at Jacob, but Jacob thrust his finger forward, meaning to keep at it.

"Sssssssss . . ."

"Quit playing around, creep," Pete said, and hung up.

Buck put down the phone. "He hung up on me."

"Call again."

Buck shook his head.

"You can't back out of life, Buck. This happens. People don't understand. Call back." He repeated the number and Buck slowly punched it in again, fury in his chest.

This time the phone rang twice, and again Pete's voice resounded at the other end:

"Ed's Gulf Station."

"What's the . . ." The finger. "P . . . p . . . p . . . p . . ."

"Will you stay off the line, you moron? What do you want? Super gas for your bike? Quit calling! I mean it!"

Again he hung up, and again Buck dropped the phone.

"Call again," said Jacob.

Buck sprang to his feet. "No! It's n . . . not enough that I have t . . . to call somebody. I have to have a f . . . freakin' f . . . f . . . fit while I'm doing it! Pete already said n . . . not to call back."

"Call," said Jacob.

Buck whirled around, almost stumbling over a magazine rack, and headed for the door.

"Buck," Jacob said, "this is life we're getting you ready for. This is eighth grade and more. It's hard, I know. Stronger men than you . . . marines, even . . . have walked before. But I'm telling you now the same thing I told them—if you walk out that door, we're through. You can't come back. I'm not wasting my time on you."

Buck stomped on across the rug and put his hand on the doorknob. He swung it open and pushed open the screen. And then he paused, his heart beating fiercely against the wall of his chest.

If he left . . . what did he have to look forward to in the fall? Being called out of class a half hour every two weeks, maybe, to meet with a speech therapist who may or may not help? Spending his lunch period with her? There were only five more weeks left of summer. . . .

He leaned one forearm on the doorframe and rested his head against it, staring down at the toe of his shoe. He still had the Hole, but he couldn't live his life down there. He turned back and closed the screen. Then walked over to Jacob.

"I'll stay, but I won't ccccccall that n . . . number. It's . . . s . . . somebody I know, and I h . . . hate his guts."

Jacob exchanged a long unblinking look with him. "All right," he said finally. "Have a seat." And then he added, "It's okay to be mad at me, Buck, even when you're really mad at yourself. And believe me, I know what it's like to be mad at myself. . . ."

23

PUKEMAN
GOES EXPLORING

Propped against the pillows on his bed, knees bent, his heavy notebook resting on his thighs, Buck bore down with his number two pencil, his jaw clenched as he worked. This would be a five-panel strip, and he'd worked it all out in his head on the way home.

First panel: *Pukeman, with a huge backpack over his shoulders, wearing shorts and flip-flops, stands at the mouth of a cave:* "Hey! Think I'll go exploring today."

Second panel: *Pukeman, on hands and knees, one flip-flop missing, his shorts torn, says:* "Man, sure is dark in here. These rocks hurt my knees."

Third panel: *Pukeman starts to climb up a pile of rocks.* "Glad I got this penlight. Wonder what's on the other side of these rocks."

Fourth panel: *A huge rock from the top of the pile tumbles down, smashing Pukeman flat.* Bearing down hard with the pencil, Buck drew two Xs for Pukeman's eyes and made a long tongue hang out one side of his mouth.

Fifth panel: *Three men, dressed as park police, are rolling a huge rock in front of the entrance to the cave. One of them says,* "Might as well close this cave up. Nobody's come here in years." *And another one says,* "Yeah. Besides, it smells too bad in there."

24

THE SUSPECT

"Well, I was robbed again."

Gramps tucked his napkin under his chin and looked around as though he expected everyone to rush to the phone and call the police.

Buck saw Joel roll his eyes toward his dad, but Gramps saw it too. "And more than that," he continued, "I can tell you when the last three four-by-eights were taken: each one on a Sunday night."

Buck tried to imagine somebody sliding that big sheet of plywood through the space between the gate and the fence post, then climbing over the top and carrying it away. He could imagine it very well. But his dad paused with a forkful of cabbage halfway to his mouth and said, "Now, Dad, how would you know that?"

Gramps was only too glad to tell.

"I told you that when I began to suspect that stack of plywood was giving out faster than we were selling it, I numbered each sheet that was left. Every morning, first thing, I checked the pile. And each time that a sheet was missing, I wrote the number down and the date. The last three were all taken on a Sunday. Must have, 'cause Sunday the numbers were all there; Monday morning, each time, one was gone."

Now the family was paying attention.

"Did you check the receipts? Sure we didn't sell them?" Joel asked.

"Checked and checked again. Every single thing sold from Anderson's Mill and Lumber has been listed on a receipt. Those plywood sheets were not. And one more thing: you know the tarp we keep on top? It was getting mighty ratty—couple holes in it, so last Saturday I put a new one over the old. It's gone too."

Dad shook his head. "I don't know what to think, Dad. How much work do you want to do to stop it?"

"Well, you can't just let it slide, Don," Mom put in. Her cheeks were that faint pink they got when she was the least bit upset. "If they think they can get away with this, who knows? They could break in the shop next, if nobody seems to care."

Mel reached across Buck's plate for the bread and then in the other direction for the butter. His faded tan shirtsleeves were rolled up almost to the shoulder, and his ship tattoo appeared all the darker in contrast. "I'll go on watch this next Sunday," he said. "Haven't got a run till Thursday, so might as well make myself useful."

"I'll go too," said Buck.

"Okay. Deal. Buck and me will team up this time and see what happens."

• • •

After dinner, Buck and Katie went out to the net they'd strung up between the maple and the beech trees, and hit a volleyball back and forth, smacking it hard to make the other miss when they could.

"Let me show you how it's done!" said Joel, who'd been watching from the steps. Grinning, he swaggered across the grass, swiping the ball from Katie's hands. "Me against the two of you."

"Wow! Listen to Mr. Big Mouth!" Katie jeered, ducking under the net. "C'mon, Buck. Let's slaughter him!"

The air was soon filled with the hollow thumps of fists against ball—grunts and groans and occasional cheers as the ball sailed over an opponent's head and made him chase it across the yard.

Fifteen minutes later, with no apparent winner, the three sprawled under the maple, tugging their shirts away from their bodies to cool themselves.

"Whew! Long time since I played that," said Joel.

"We weren't even playing a real game. You're getting to be an old man," Katie teased.

Buck went inside and returned with three cans of Mountain Dew. He held one can against his forehead before he opened the tab and took a drink.

Katie jostled Joel's foot with her own, mischief in her eyes. "Hey, old man, Amy and I found a girlfriend for you."

Joel gave her foot a shove. "Who said I was looking?"

"You don't have to be. She's Sarah's cousin—about five inches shorter than you, with long brown hair and a really deep dimple in one cheek. She sings country. Amy heard her at that karaoke place and showed me her picture."

"What's that got to do with me?" Joel said, taking another long drink of his soda.

"She saw you at the bowling alley last week and asked who you were," Katie said.

Buck was surprised to see color rising up his brother's neck, into his face. He was thinking that he had never heard Joel either mention a girl at the dinner table or heard him call one that he could remember, though he'd seen Joel leafing through a country singer magazine and lingering over photos of some of the female singers. And he realized for the first time that even people who didn't stutter could be shy. Weird that he had never thought of this before now.

"Too bad," Joel was saying. "I'll be in the navy."

"You serious about that?" Katie said.

"Why not?" said Joel. "Doesn't mean I'll make a career of it. Don't you guys want to see more of the world than this?"

"I want at least to see New York," said Katie.

It was hard for Buck to keep his own secret. So he changed the subject. "What do you b . . . bet nobody shows on Sunday n . . . n . . . night?" he said.

"At the mill?" said Joel. "If he gets wind that Gramps is on to him, he probably won't. Can't have a guard there all the time."

"I wish somebody *would* show when Mel's there. He'd take 'em apart!" said Katie.

"With a llllllittle help from me!" said Buck.

• • •

Sunday night, Buck and Mel were ready to go. Joel was happy to drive them over, glad that he could spend the evening with his buddies, and let them out a quarter mile from the mill.

It was not quite dark—past that point at dusk where everything looked extraordinarily clear. This time of evening you had to stare hard at something to make it out.

They made their way quietly across the dirt parking area and Mel unlocked the gate. Once they were inside, he locked it after them and Buck followed his uncle up the cinderblock walkway to the door.

Just as Mel swung it open, however, Buck said, "Mel, look!" and pointed.

The big man turned, following Buck's outstretched hand, just as a figure jumped down from the top of the fence at the far end of the lumberyard.

"Hey!" Mel yelled, dropping his pack.

He and Buck turned in tandem and raced back to the gate.

By the time they unlocked it, however, and ran along the fence, the hooded figure had disappeared into the woods beyond the sawmill.

Mel crashed through the underbrush to the place where the intruder had entered the trees. There the forest became black and there was no point in going on. He and Buck had left their flashlights in their packs inside the door.

Mel turned to Buck, still panting. "Was it just the one?"

"Far as I could see."

"You get a good look at him? Any idea who it was?"

Buck shook his head. "Could have been anyone. Dddddark jacket . . . pants."

"A man? A teenager?" All Buck could do was shrug.

Mel let out his breath. "Well, I'm not about to go searching these woods without a flashlight. And meanwhile we've left the gate and the shop wide open. . . ."

They started back.

"What are we going to do?" asked Buck.

"Might as well stick it out in case he comes back later, though I doubt it. Not tonight. He didn't seem to be carrying anything, did he?"

"Don't think so. Hard to t . . . tell in the dark. Not a big sheet of plywood, anyway."

"Did you hear anything at all?" Mel asked.

"Seemed like . . . when he was running toward the trees . . . maybe there were voices, I dddddddon't know."

"Yeah. I thought so too. Like there were more waiting for him. Or waiting to jump me if I was stupid enough to follow him in there."

Back inside the low building, Mel made a quick inspection of the place to see if anyone had broken in. But no window was opened, the rear door still bolted, cash register untouched. Still, someone had been on the property, and it was another Sunday night, just like Gramps had predicted. The only day of the week the mill was closed, no one about at all.

On Monday, when Gramps checked his supply, two more four-by-eight plywood sheets were missing. Buck and his uncle had arrived shortly after the wood had been carried off. The last of the culprits must have heard or seen them coming and, instead of climbing over the fence by the gate, had headed for the back of the lot nearest the woods where he might escape unseen. It was anyone's guess if this would happen again.

• • •

As July drew to a close, the vegetable garden was giving all that it had. Dad took time away from the mill to tend to it. Buck was needed more at home, especially on Fridays, to crate things up for his dad to drive to the farm markets on Saturdays.

That made it more complicated to go to Jacob's three times a week without the family getting suspicious, and Buck still wasn't ready to tell anyone about their sessions. But the fact that he was sticking it out—doing something even marines had walked out on occasionally—gave him pride in doing something really difficult, and "difficult" wasn't even the word for it. Going down in a hole where he might possibly be trapped was scary, but this was a different kind of dark.

Three times a week, after he'd practiced relaxing his tongue and jaw, Buck dialed the numbers Jacob read off to him and asked the pertinent question: *How much does it cost? What time do you close? Are you open on Sundays?*

Lately it wasn't just a single question that Jacob insisted on—more a conversation: "How old do I have to be to work there?" and "What kind of work would I be expected to do?" and "Is experience necessary?" Whenever Jacob held up a finger, Buck started a stutter and kept it going until the finger went down.

Sometimes . . . a very few times . . . he got to the end and was able to say, "Thank you very much." Half the time the other person hung up on him. And sometimes they said, "What's the matter with you?" or "Don't call back." And when that happened, Jacob made him do just that.

On better days, however, Buck and Jacob made a game of it. When Buck called back, Jacob would pump his fist in the air to urge him on, and once in a while, when Buck was able to explain to the other person that he stuttered and was learning to speak over the phone, the person he'd called would suddenly turn human and wait patiently as Buck stuttered his way to the end of a sentence.

They couldn't see him—he had to remind himself of that. He sat safely here in one of Jacob's chairs, and would probably never meet them in his whole life or talk to them again on the phone. Just knowing that, and doing it over and over, made him bolder. Funnier, even.

"Who are you? Some kind of wise guy?" one man said, to which Buck replied, "N . . . no, I'm DDDDDDonald Duck," and laughed along with Jacob when the man hung up.

The stuttering was coming out more gently, sometimes in a whisper, effortlessly, like a puff of air. Maybe it was like one of the therapists had told him—a free ride. Only with them, the goal was to stop stuttering. With Jacob, it was not. A huge difference. There were times Buck didn't stutter at all, but Jacob never praised him for that. Only when he kept his face and jaw relaxed—didn't struggle, didn't fight it. Let it come and breezed right on.

One sticky afternoon, the first week of August, when Buck was giving himself over to stuttering, his mind more on the Hole and when he could go again, there were footsteps outside the door, and suddenly, without ringing the bell first or even knocking, Mel stepped boldly into Jacob's living room.

Buck turned and stared at his uncle, and Jacob stopped midsentence. All three stayed frozen in place, like actors caught in a strobe light.

"Mel?" Jacob said.

"Buck, I just want to know what's going on," Mel said a bit uncertainly.

It was hard to explain, because Buck, at the time, was sitting in front of the long framed mirror propped against the wall, and Jacob was sitting beside it, a telephone directory in his lap. And when neither Buck nor Jacob answered right away, Mel got right to the point:

"Been noticing that you pretty regularly get on your bike and go somewhere once your folks are out of the house," he said to Buck. "Today I just decided to follow you over here, and seeing as how you don't appear to be doing any work at the moment, I want to know what the heck this is all about."

Buck turned and looked at Jacob, and the older man said, "I think it's time you told them, Buck."

Mel took a few steps farther into the room. "Told me what?"

"He's helping me with my sssssstuttering," Buck said. "He's a speech ddddoctor."

"Pathologist. I was a speech pathologist in the military, Mel, and I offered to help Buck over the summer. I really saw no reason to keep it secret, but Buck seems to feel otherwise."

Mel sat down on the arm of the couch. "Well, for the lu'va'mike, why, Buck?"

"I just . . ." Buck shrugged. "Everybody wwwould always be asking, was I getting better and what did it c . . . cccost, and . . ."

Mel sat speechless for a few moments, then lifted his palms in the air. "I don't get it. What do we owe you, Jacob?"

Jacob shook his head. "No charge, Mel. I'm just doing this as a friend."

"Well . . . that's really great, but . . ." Mel turned to his nephew. "How do *you* feel about it, Buck? *Is* it helping?"

"I guess I feel bbbbbetter about . . . about me."

For a long moment Mel studied his nephew. "So . . . you still don't want your folks to know . . . ?"

"Not really," Buck said. "Later."

Mel nodded and thought some more. Then he slapped his leg and stood up. "Well, I've got no quarrel with that. Sorry I barged in like this, Jacob. Hope you understand."

"Indeed I do," Jacob said.

• • •

Buck rode his bike occasionally out to the old Wilmer place just to make sure no one was surveying the land, that it wasn't for sale. And it wasn't. Stood there as abandoned and forgotten as many of the trees on the place. Buck worried it might not be until late fall, when the vegetables were all harvested and the farm markets closed, that he'd have a chance to sneak away to the Hole again, but that was too far off. There wasn't a day he wasn't thinking about it—the new passage he'd take the next time he was down there; the arrows he'd leave on the walls, what he might find. . . .

He finally decided he would ask Joel to order the headlamp for him. If Joel wouldn't order it, no one would. He

199

approached his brother one evening when Joel was on the back porch clipping his nails over a wastebasket. Buck sat down on the glider beside him.

"What's up?" Joel asked.

"You have a cccccccredit card, don't you?"

"Yeah, why?"

Buck handed him six fives and ten one-dollar bills. "Bbbbbig favor," he said.

"What's this for?"

"I wwwwwant you to b . . . buy something online for me."

"Must be pretty darn secret, you coming to me."

"Sorta. I know for sure DDDDDad and M . . . Mom wouldn't get it for me."

"What the heck is it?"

"A headlamp. T . . . to wear in the dddddark." He showed him the picture he'd printed out on Joel's computer.

Joel pulled away from him a little and looked him over.

Before he could ask any more, Buck said quickly, "So I d . . . don't have to hold a flashlight . . . you know . . . rrrrrriding my bike at night."

"Wouldn't it be cheaper just to buy a light for your bike?"

"Yeah, but . . . if it was on my head, I ccccccccould use it other t . . . times too."

Joel shrugged. "Well, I don't see why Dad or Mom would care."

Buck nudged his brother's arm. "D . . . do they understand why you wwwwant to join the navy?"

This time Joel grinned. "Okay. Right. I'll send for it. It'll come addressed to me, but you can open it when it gets here."

Later that night, however, when Buck was working on another Pukeman comic strip in his room, Joel stopped in the doorway.

"Hey, Buck. I started to place that order for you, and that model's discontinued. You want to choose another one?"

Buck spent the next fifteen minutes in Joel's room, looking at other headlamps on the computer, and finally chose a less expensive model. With the money he saved, maybe he'd get some really good knee pads later on, with Velcro fasteners.

He sat on the edge of Joel's bed as Joel typed in the new model number.

"Okay," Joel said finally, when *Order received* came on the screen. "They say it's on back order, but that we should receive it in ten days to two weeks. Okay?"

No, but Buck was learning patience. He would have liked it to come tomorrow. He would have liked it to come tomorrow with everyone out of the house, Katie included—nobody to see him ride off with his backpack and everything he could possibly need in the Hole. And he would like tomorrow to be one of those incredible days where things went exactly the way they should.

25

QUESTIONS

"Tomorrow" was not that kind of day. In fact, it rained for the next two days. Both mornings Buck woke not to a blazing August sun, but to a gray sky, with air so heavy with moisture he could almost drink it. He was sweating before he even got out of bed. Finally, like it happened every year when summer was almost over, Gramps consented to turning on the air conditioner and leaving it on for the rest of the month.

"Never needed it when I was a boy, and you can't tell me the weather's changed all that much," he'd say.

They humored him because it was, after all, his house, his land, and when you came right down to it, they were his tenants, even though they were family.

Buck had been spending more time with Nat, not only because his parents might think he was off with Nat the next time he disappeared for a day, but because he really liked him. Not as much as David, maybe, but for different reasons. David made him laugh. Nat kept him guessing about what he'd come up with next.

Now, with the water high after the rains were over, the boys decided to hike beside the swollen river that ran through the forest behind the sawmill and disappeared again into the mountain. They left their bikes in a thicket and teetered along the bank, trying not to fall in. Nat carried a sturdy stick for balance and used it to poke and prod at debris trapped among tree roots or washed up between the rocks.

As Buck watched him jam the long stick into the ground between himself and the water, and use it as a vaulting pole to leap across a crevice in the bank, he looked for a stick of his own. When he found one, Nat took out a pocketknife and carved one end of it smooth for a handle. Buck was impressed.

"You always cccccccarry that in a pocket?" he asked.

Nat rubbed his thumb over the handle and whittled a bit more. "Just stuff that's useful. That and my cell phone."

"Yeah?" Buck pulled out his own cell phone and flipped it open so Nat could see it. *No service*, it read, and they both laughed. Not surprising, here in the forest.

They continued tramping, Nat in the lead, one or the other stopping now and then to prod a toad or flip over a rock or study a branch with berries.

"You g . . . going to tttttry for a job at the carnival?" Buck asked him, wiping one arm across his forehead.

"I'd like to," Nat said over his shoulder, "but I'm helping

my cousin finish his basement. We've got it mostly done except for the walls."

Buck plodded along, following the blue jeans in front of him. "Yeah? When d . . . do you think he'll gggggggget it done?"

"I dunno. Needs more plywood, then some paneling. Depends when he gets enough money."

For just a moment, Buck's foot hovered above the ground before he slowly put it down. He didn't want to think what he was thinking. Didn't even want to imagine that he and Nat could be having this much fun, and then . . . he might find out. . . . Not that Nat was in on it. He was trying to figure a way to phrase his next question without sounding suspicious. And perhaps, because they went so long in silence, Nat finally broke it with, as always, a question Buck didn't expect: "Have you always stuttered?"

"Ummm, yeah. I guess."

"Do you care when people ask about it?"

Did he? It happened so seldom he wasn't sure. Generally, people just looked away. *Talk* about it, Jacob had ordered.

"Naw. Nnnnot really."

"'Cause I don't care if you do," Nat continued. "Stutter, I mean. I just . . . sometimes . . . when you're trying to say a word, and I know what it is, I want to help you along." He was still talking with his back to Buck, but he slowed a little.

"Huh-uh."

Nat glanced over his shoulder. "No?"

"Wait and mmmake me s . . . say it."

"Really?" Nat started to grin. "But that could take all day."

Buck grinned too. "So . . . tough," he said, and poked Nat

with his stick. For a minute or two, they had a mock sword fight with first one stick, then the other breaking in half, and they had to look for others.

Buck wasn't offended by what Nat had said. In fact, it felt good to talk about it, even that little bit. There was so much more he could tell him. What he was really thinking about, though, was Nat's cousin and his basement and the plywood he didn't have. He didn't want to suspect, but he did.

• • •

Buck recognized the handwriting even before he turned the card over.

Standing at Jacob's mailbox, he saw the postcard on top of the little pile of bills and circulars, and the blue ink and the large J and W of Jacob's name gave it away.

Dad, it read, in big letters. *Please! Jim and I are so sorry, but we're hurting too. Johnny misses his grandpa. Please let us try to make this up to you in any way we can. . . .*

Buck stopped reading because he was almost up the driveway to the house, and he shouldn't have been reading it in the first place. Only ten days ago, Jacob had handed him another unopened envelope, which he'd marked *Return to Sender* and had asked Buck to put it in the mailbox for him.

When the door opened, Buck thrust the mail into Jacob's hand as he went inside, and if Jacob saw the postcard, he gave no sign.

"New assignment," he said as they took their usual places in the living room. "Homework. Every day, you are to go up to somebody—anyone but family—and start a conversation.

Someone on the street, someone at Bealls'. Even if it's just to say, 'What do you think about the weather?'"

"Sssssssome days the only p . . . people I see is family," Buck told him.

"Then you make a phone call you wouldn't have made before. But I want to know about each one—how it went. And don't make something up or I'll work you twice as hard."

Buck believed him.

When the session was over, Buck did his usual chores for Jacob. This time he changed the sheets, put one set in the washing machine, took out the trash, and washed the dishes in the sink.

"Anything else?" he asked when he'd finished.

"That's about it," Jacob said, and then, as Buck headed toward the door, he handed him the postcard, and Buck couldn't help but see that in red marker, Jacob had printed *REFUSED* over the handwriting. "Drop this in the box for me," he said, and turned away.

• • •

When Buck got home, he pulled out a container of potato salad from the fridge and dug around some more until he found the coleslaw. Then a bagel from off the counter.

He'd just sat down to eat his lunch when Katie came into the kitchen, a puzzled look on her face. She was holding something in one hand, but he couldn't tell what it was.

She sat down across from him. "Buck," she said. "If I asked you a question, would you tell me the truth?"

He wasn't sure he could promise that. "I'll try," he said.

Her green eyes on him all the while, Katie unfolded her fingers and gave him the slip of paper in her hand.

Mom and Dad, if I don't come back, call David. He'll know where I am.

"What does this mean?" she asked.

26

DISCOVERY

When is a lie not a lie? What if every word is true one way, but in another, it's not?

"Wh . . . where did you find this?" Buck asked.

"In your room. Mom asked me to run the vacuum over the upstairs today, and this was under your bed. Did you mean to give it to Mom? To Dad?"

"Oh, that," Buck said, laughing a little. "It's old." His mind was racing on ahead of him. Was it possible he'd forgotten to hide that note again after he'd used it once?

"Yeah?" Katie waited.

"You know that Ambassador Hotel?"

She stared at him with squinting eyes. "What does *that* have to do with anything?"

"David and I once made a bbbbbbbet with each other, that we wouldn't dare go in that hotel at nnnnnight alone. All the way up to the third floor—where that man died— back again. And I decided that if I ever did, I'd leave this nnnnnnnote on my bed so if I never came b . . . back, David could tell them about our bet."

There was a flash of hurt in her eyes, and he realized he was admitting he'd trust David with a secret before he'd tell her, but it passed. Still, the way she was studying him . . .

"Honest! We really did dddddddare each other. You can call David yourself."

She dropped the note on the table beside him and sat down. "Okay, but that doesn't explain the other stuff."

"What other stuff?" Buck started to take a bite of bagel, but Katie's eyes stopped him.

"Buck, you've been sort of strange lately, you know it? I see you riding off on your bike every day and you're gone at least an hour. Where are you going?"

"N . . . not every day . . ." And then Buck realized that was already a confession.

"Several times a week, then. And that one time you came home late to dinner, all muddy. And you said your bike went down a ravine? But I went out after dinner and saw your bike and it wasn't banged up or scratched or anything."

"You tell Mom?"

"Of course not." Katie was loyal. "But now . . ."

Buck pushed his plate away. "Katie, if I ttttttold you something, you've absolutely got to pppppromise not to tell anyone."

Now her eyes were wide and she had that same trusting

look she used to get when Buck confided in her. It made his chest hurt.

"I promise," she said.

"Really?"

"Totally."

"Okay. Jacob Wall is a . . . speech d . . . doctor. Used to be. And he's helping me with my sssstuttering."

Slowly her forehead wrinkled into the puzzled look he knew so well. "That old man in the yellow house?"

Buck nodded.

"The one you and Mel do jobs for?"

"Yeah . . . He offered to help me, and I've bbbbbbeen going over there three t . . . times a week."

Katie raised both hands, then let them drop. "But . . . why are you keeping it secret? Why can't Mom and Dad know? They'd be grateful."

"You know how they are, Katie. Mom would be all the t . . . time on me asking if I was gggggetting better. And Dad would be embarrassed Jacob wasn't charging us anything, like we couldn't afford it or something. They'd have a mmmillion questions, like why he's doing it at all, you know?"

Katie thought about it. "I guess so. But . . . it still doesn't make sense."

"Why not? Jacob used to work for the navy, and it's a tttttt-tough course. He said some of the marines couldn't handle it . . . that they . . . walked out."

"You mean, like boot camp or something?"

"Sort of."

"It sounds hard . . . the course, Buck. What does it have to do with stuttering? *Is* it helping?"

"I just feel different, Katie. Do I ssssound any different to you?"

She thought about it a moment. "You don't get tensed up so much like you used to. What I mean is, when you stutter, I hardly notice it anymore."

When you stutter, I hardly notice it anymore.

It was the first time anyone had ever said that to him. In the past, people only wanted him to stop stuttering. But now, if nobody noticed . . . Well, why should he care whether he stuttered or not?

The thought was so new to him it was like a fragile piece of china he had to protect. As though, if he examined it, it might slip from his hands and crack. Like a dream that after you'd dreamed it, you had to quickly remember or it would just disappear.

• • •

The tomatoes hung heavy on vines that had already begun to wilt. Pole beans were picked every week to keep them producing, and the last of the beets and potatoes, the carrots and onions, called to be dug out of the hot soil.

Whenever Mel wasn't on a run in his semi, he pitched in to help with the digging or crating, while Buck, and sometimes Katie, did the back-breaking job of straddling the rows of lima beans, the sun beating down on their heads, fingers sore from grasping the spiny pods and dropping them in the bucket.

For the last two weeks Buck had consoled himself with the thought that any day his headlamp would arrive. The longer he had to wait, the more desperately he wanted it, and the more he worried that it would be one big disappointment.

Nat stopped by on his bike that Thursday. He stood at the head of the lima bean row, waiting to see if Buck could join him, his Eagles cap low on his forehead.

Dad came out of the house just then from answering the phone.

"Buck," he called. "Your mom left her glasses here this morning and decided she really needs them. You and Nat want to ride out to Holly's and take them to her? You can take a couple hours off if you want."

This must be what every convict feels when he goes on parole, Buck decided as he headed inside to wash up, Nat following behind.

"The carnival's generator truck was in the lot behind Bealls' this morning," Nat told him. "That means the rest will be here soon. Heard they've got a new ride, the Wildcat."

Buck reached the kitchen sink and turned on the faucet. "Yeah? What's it d . . . do?"

"You sit at the end of those long poles, two to a cage, and it jerks you in and spins you around, then shoots you back out again, all the while it's whirling around in a circle. Something like that."

"Cool." Buck leaned over, burying his face in a two-hand pool of cold water, then another, till his hair was plastered to his forehead in front. He followed it with a long drink.

"I've earned enough in the gggggarden to ride everything they've got this year, I'll b . . . bet," he said. He picked up his mother's glasses case from off the counter, put them in one pocket, and they went back outside and around to his bike by the shed.

"I'll come help you pick beans if I run low on cash," Nat joked.

Buck had been thinking all morning of a way to ask Nat about his cousin and the basement he was paneling—where he'd gotten the plywood they were using. But how could he ask that? Nat would wonder why he was so curious about plywood.

The boys were hot again by the time they got to Holly's Homestyle, and found there were four other bikes in the rack out front. And before Buck could wonder whose they were, the glass doors opened and Pete and Isaac, Rod and Ethan, spilled out onto the steps, kidding around with plastic straws and their wrappers. Then they saw Buck.

"Well, look who's here!" Pete said. "El Creepo himself." He turned to the others. "Did you know he called my dad's station the other day and wanted to know the price of super premium for his bike?"

The other three boys guffawed.

And then, mimicking Buck, Pete said, "'Wh . . . wh . . . wh . . . what's the p . . . p . . . p . . . p . . . price of s . . . s . . . s . . . s . . . super p . . . p . . . p . . . premium . . . ?' And when I told him to shove it, and hung up on him, the little creep called back." He turned to Buck. "You know what? I think you just do it to bug the heck out of people, that's all."

Another customer was coming out of the door just then, so Pete and his buddies went on down the steps and Buck and Nat went in. They stayed inside the entrance, though, to make sure Pete didn't do something with their bikes. He didn't. The foursome pedaled away.

Nat didn't believe any of it. "What a moron," he murmured. "Aren't you glad he'll be in high school in the fall?"

"Rod won't, though," said Buck. He looked around for his mom and saw her at the far end of the counter, listening to a middle-aged woman in a straw hat loudly complaining about something. Mom glanced over at the boys, her eyes saying it all, and they slid onto stools near the pie display.

". . . and another thing," the woman said, both elbows on the counter, one hand holding half a sandwich, the other delicately pulling out pieces of bacon. "I've been getting my BLTs here for the last seven years, and if the bacon doesn't crumble in my mouth, it's not cooked enough. I shouldn't have to tear it with my teeth. And the tomato . . . was that homegrown?"

"Indeed it was," Mom said patiently. "It was out of our very own vegetable garden."

"Well, it was picked too soon," said the woman.

"Oh, spare me!" murmured Pearl, who was wiping off a table next to the counter, and Buck and Nat ducked their heads to hide their laughter.

"If you'll excuse me," Mom said to the woman. She made her getaway while she could, and turned her attention to the boys. "Thanks, Buck. Your dad and Mel out in the field?"

"Yeah. He asked mmmme to ride over."

"Well, I thought maybe I could get through the day without them, but when it got to the point where I couldn't read my own handwriting, I knew I had to have them. How you doing, Nat?"

214

"Okay," he said. "First carnival truck's here."

"That's good news for Holly's," Mom said.

When the straw-hat woman realized Mom wasn't coming back, she gave a loud sigh and climbed down off the stool, taking her check to the cash register.

Pearl sidled up to Mom behind the counter. "That woman!" she declared. "She'd blame sugar for being sweet."

Buck and Nat laughed out loud.

Holly came out of the kitchen then with a tray of apple and blueberry pie slices to put in the pie safe. "You boys want some ice cream?" she said. "First dip's on the house. Second dip's on you. Sprinkles are free."

The first dips of Holly's ice cream, however, were always huge, and with sprinkles, they were enough.

"Nat says a carnival truck is here," Mom told her.

"Ah!" Holly wiped her hands on her apron. "Let's hope the carnival workers get tired of eating carnival food and want some honest-to-goodness home-style cooking."

"They usually do," said Mom.

• • •

On their way home, Nat said, "Let's go back to the river. We went almost as far as the bend last time, so let's start hiking from there."

"For a while, maybe," said Buck. "I should probably help Dad a little more before dinner."

It was cool in the woods—perhaps ten degrees cooler—and just looking at the water seemed to help dry the skin. That and a breeze blowing in from the north. Buck figured the sawmill couldn't be more than a half mile off. The woods

215

was a real tangle the farther they went, the trees so close together it was hard to find a way through them. Walking along the riverbank itself was impossible at points, forcing them back into the underbrush.

"What's that?" Nat said, stopping and wiping one arm across his face. His hair was a mess, with leaves and twigs stuck every which way.

"Whhhhere?" Buck asked, almost bumping into him from behind.

"There." Nat pointed. "That . . . shack."

Buck moved up beside him and looked in the direction he was pointing. "S . . . somebody's house? A homeless person?"

"Could be. Should we look?"

In answer, Buck began making his way through the trees and vines, each step breaking a net of leaves and branches.

It was a strange put-together structure about eight feet square, with a flat roof half-covered with tarp.

"Hello?" Buck called, and waited, listening.

"Anyone there?" yelled Nat.

They moved closer.

There was no sound from inside. No scuttling or scraping.

"Hello!" Buck yelled again, and reached out to rap on the side of the plywood frame.

Suddenly his hand froze motionless in the air, and he stepped a little closer. Along one edge of the plywood sheet was a number, scribbled in Gramps's shaky handwriting.

27

CONFRONTATION

Buck stared at the sheet of plywood in front of him, then at Nat. He started to say something, then stopped. Dad had told him to keep the robberies quiet—better chance of finding the thief if he didn't know they were looking for him. So he simply knocked on the side of the shack.

Still no answer. No sound of movement from inside.

"There's got to be a door," said Nat, moving in closer.

They tramped around a huge bush on one side and found a narrow doorway facing the river.

Buck leaned down and looked in. It was too dark to make out much. The little light from the doorway showed the corner of a rumpled sleeping bag, a plastic milk crate turned upside down with some magazines on it, some empty beer bottles on the plywood floor.

"W . . . wish we had a flashlight," Buck said.

"You going to crawl in?" asked Nat.

"Are *you*?"

Nat shook his head. "Like invading someone's house, man. But next time we come, we'll bring a flashlight."

Buck straightened up. "Listen. I nnnnneed to get home. Dad didn't say I could have the whole afternoon off."

"Okay," Nat conceded. "Let's remember where this is, though—that we've hiked this far, about a hundred yards beyond the bend in the river."

"Yeah," said Buck, but as Nat started back with his big stick, whacking at weeds as he went, Buck examined a second panel of plywood. And yes, along its edge, another of Gramps's shaky scrawls. Wow!

"Hey, Nat!" he said, unable to hold back a grin. "Here's some plywood for your cousin's basement."

Nat laughed. "Yeah, right. And when whoever lives here comes back, he'll know somebody's been around." He pointed to the trampled weeds making a path to the door. "Do we care?"

"*He* might. Whoever lives here."

• • •

At the crossroads, they separated, and Buck pedaled furiously on home. He dropped his bike at the porch and raced through the house, out the back door to the vegetable field.

Breathless, he ran over to Dad and Mel, who were dumping buckets of beans into a bushel.

"*Wondered* where you'd gone off to," Dad said.

"We found it! The ppppplywood!" Buck cried. "In the woods."

Dad lowered the bushel basket and stared at him. "*What* woods? All we've got around here is woods."

"That runs in bbbbback of the sawmill, down by the river."

"How do you know it's ours?" asked Mel.

"It's g . . . g . . . got Gramps's writing on the edge. The numbers."

"How many panels?" asked Dad.

"I don't know. Somebody built a shack."

Uncle Mel turned to Dad. "I'll go, Don. You've got enough on your plate."

"Could be it's legitimate, Mel. That it's bought lumber. Dad numbered them all, remember, so even the paid-for plywood has numbers."

Buck hadn't considered that.

"Then Gramps should know, him and his ledger book." Mel set the bucket down and started for the house.

"Go with him, Buck," Dad said.

As though he wouldn't! Mel wouldn't be able to find the shack without him.

Buck ran upstairs to use the bathroom and get a long drink of water, and when he came down and went outside, Mel was throwing a hammer and shovel and a large canvas tarp into the trunk of his car.

As they started down the driveway, Buck asked, "What are you g . . . going to do?"

Mel's big, muscular arms swung the steering wheel around when they reached the dirt road. The tattoo of a ship beneath his sleeve tipped sideways and righted itself again.

"First we're going to the sawmill to get a list of the plywood sheets that are missing, not sold. Then, I want you to take me to that shack," Mel said.

"And then what? What if someone's in there?"

"Well . . . I guess we'll have a conversation."

• • •

Buck could hear the whine of the saw blade even before he saw the mill itself—the high whine, which changed note and volume depending on the thickness of the wood and the knots it encountered.

They got out and walked around to the side portico where Joel was holding on to one end of an eight-foot tree trunk, while Gramps, at the blade, guided the smooth plank that was slowly appearing at the other end.

Mel waved one big arm, and Gramps looked up, nodded to show he'd seen him, then waited until the log was all the way through and the plank fell sideways before he turned the switch.

"What you doing, loafin' around down here?" Gramps said, grinning.

"Need to borrow Joel's pickup," Mel said. "Could be we've found that stolen plywood, so might have to do some hauling."

Gramps pushed his safety goggles up on his forehead. "Who took it?" he asked.

"Don't know yet. Buck found a shack off in the woods made out of plywood with some dates on the side, but we've got to be sure these weren't bought fair and square. I need to see your sales ledger."

Joel gave a little whistle. "Hey, Buck! Nice going!"

And Mel added, "Good thing you numbered all the plywood, Art!"

Gramps walked with his head high as he led them all inside the shop. "You darn betcha!" he said.

As he read off the numbers of the plywood sheets that had not appeared on any sales ticket—twelve in all—Buck wrote them down on a piece of paper. Then he copied down the numbers of the missing pine boards and studs as well.

"If we bring some back, Art, what can you do with used lumber?" asked Mel.

"Somebody will always be able to use it at half price," Gramps told them, which made Buck think of Nat's cousin and his rec room.

• • •

Mel transferred the hammer and shovel and canvas into the back of Joel's pickup, and drove slowly along the old mill road. It was difficult to see the river's bend from here, but finally Mel backed the pickup into a bare spot along the side of the road. Then, carrying the tools while Buck carried the canvas, they set out through the trees.

It took about ten minutes to reach something that looked familiar to Buck, and when they came to the berry bush, with one branch broken the way Buck had left it, he knew they were going in the wrong direction. They turned and hiked for fifteen minutes in the other.

At last they saw traces of the trail he and Nat had made earlier, the tramped-on weeds and underbrush, and finally, the tan color of the plywood through the trees.

"That it?" Mel asked.

"Yeah."

Whoever lived inside must have used a flashlight, Buck decided, and he could have kicked himself for not bringing one along this second time.

Mel knocked on the wall, the same as Buck had done, and called out a greeting. But once again there was no answer.

"Don't want to stick my head in there and get a shotgun blast in the face," Mel murmured to Buck. "Okay. I'll read some dates as I find them, and you see if they're on the list." Mel squatted down to read the first of Gramps's shaky handwriting.

"June thirtieth . . ."

"It's here," said Buck.

Mel went a few steps farther in the underbrush and leaned in close. He gave a whistle. "May twenty-sixth . . . Guess Gramps was right, all that complaining. . . ."

"Yeah. That one tttttoo," said Buck.

Mel came around the corner and examined an exposed edge of another sheet.

"July seventh."

Buck ran his finger down the page. "Yep."

"Well, that's enough for me. Have to take this thing apart to find the other numbers, but if there's any here not on the list, I'll leave 'em." Mel lifted the hammer and, using the claw end, gently pried up one corner of the plywood roof. Then the other side. And finally, he lifted the sheet of plywood on its side so that daylight streamed in.

"Nobody here."

Buck went around to the low doorway and looked in.

A couple of sleeping bags, an old gray and white sneaker, sports magazines, beer bottles, pop bottles, empty pretzel bags, a dirty T-shirt . . .

"You recognize any of this stuff?" Mel asked him.

Buck shook his head. "Could belong to anybody."

There were eight plywood sheets altogether, counting the roof and floor—a few more than there were numbers for, but that was because Gramps didn't start numbering until he'd suspected some were missing. One of the four fence posts at the corners was not on the list, the other three were.

"And this has got to be the new tarp Gramps put over the pile," Mel said. "Let's see if we can make it in one trip. We've got to take the posts too—Art said those are missing as well—but I think we'll leave the floorboards. One has been stepped through, probably rotting beneath."

One by one the plywood sheets came loose and were placed on the canvas Buck had spread on the ground. Then the four posts. Mel looked at the four eight-foot pine planks that had supported the roof and decided to leave those. They were undoubtedly stolen too but had no numbers, and whoever had done the nailing had split some of the ends—a pretty messy job.

"Don't know where these men got their building know-how, but it sure wasn't from a carpenter. I'd give this shanty about a year . . . ," Mel said.

"What if it's somebody homeless?" Buck wondered.

"Somebody this desperate, I'd have built it for him if he'd asked," Mel said. "But stealing's not the way to go about it."

They placed the last sturdy fence post on top of the pile, and Buck wiped one arm across his face. Mel took out a big blue handkerchief and mopped his own neck and ears. They took one final look at the floor of the shack, littered with the two sleeping bags and other refuse, the four long planks they'd laid neatly in a square around them, and grinned at each other.

"Hope it dddddoesn't rain," Buck said, and they laughed.

It was slow going, trying to maneuver a path through the trees wide enough to take their load, and they'd only gone about fifteen feet when they heard voices coming from the trees along the river. Laughter. A yelp, and more laughter.

Buck froze, and almost dropped his corner of the canvas.

Mel glanced over, then turned to look behind them.

There was another yell—this time a loud one. Then another, and a string of curses as Pete Ketterman, Isaac, Ethan, and Rod came into view.

The four boys stopped about twenty yards from Mel and Buck and simply stared, first at them, then at the sight of their demolished hideaway.

"Hey!" yelled Pete.

Mel looked over at them. "Hello."

"What the heck . . . ?"

"I could ask you the same thing," Mel said.

"You friggin' out of your mind?" Pete bellowed. "You took down our duck blind!"

"Oh, is that what this was?" said Mel.

"Well, what do you think you're doing?" demanded Isaac, moving closer, looking menacingly first at Mel, then Buck.

"Just returning some stolen property, that's all," said Mel. "You have something to say about that?"

"How do you know it was stolen?" said Ethan.

"You show your receipt from the sawmill and I'll be glad to build it back up for you. Better than how you built it, that's for sure," Mel said. "We left the two sheets for the floor, though, so you still owe Mr. Anderson for those." And then, to Buck, "Let's move."

Buck lifted up his corner again and started to pull, but Pete came forward and stepped on the end of the canvas, jerking them to a stop.

"You've got no proof, and you better put our stuff back."

Mel turned around. "Mr. Anderson has all the proof he needs in his record book, and you can see the numbers on the ends of that plywood yourself. You want the sheriff in on this, we'll be glad to get him. You boys have better things to do, and you *ought* to have more sense than to go doing something like this. Now get the heck off this canvas." And giving it a mighty jerk, he threw Pete momentarily off balance so that the canvas was free again, and, with his hammer in his other big hand, he motioned to Buck. "Come on, let's go."

With the four boys gaping after them, Buck and Mel continued pulling their cargo until they were back to the old mill road and the waiting pickup.

• • •

It was the main topic of conversation at dinner that night.

"I don't know," said Mom. "Do you think that was the best way to handle it? Maybe you should have gone to Pete's dad instead and let him deal with it."

"And let him beat the stuffing out of his kid? I've seen

enough of Ed Ketterman to know the kind of discipline he'd use."

"But maybe Pete will tell him you tore down his duck blind, and his dad will come after you," said Katie.

Mel chuckled. "If that was a duck blind, I'm a fried dough-nut. Nope. Won't happen. Pete would have to explain how he got the plywood in the first place. I don't think one of those boys is about to tell his parents."

Buck thought he was right, but wished that Mel had not told Pukeman he could build the duck blind better than Pete had. Just stuck to the facts.

"I suppose you could have let it stand and made the boys pay for it," said Dad, helping himself to the turnips and on-ions.

Mel was getting a little tired of defending himself. "We didn't know who it belonged to, Don, and I wasn't about to sit around there waiting for the owner to come back. I'm on another truck run tomorrow, so what's done is done. Art wanted that lumber back and he's got it. Wanted to know who was doing the thieving, and now he does."

Gramps nodded. "Topic closed."

Buck sure hoped so.

28

WILDCAT

They could hear the calliope music pumping out each bright note into the night air even before they reached the crossroads at Bealls' Junction.

"Look at the way it lights up the sky!" Katie said, her cheek pressed against the passenger window in the back-seat of their dad's car, Buck crammed in beside her, and Nat at the far window. Joel was driving, his friend Kyle beside him. "They've got one of those searchlights or something to show people the way."

As though folks the whole county over didn't know where to find it. Mr. Beall said that what he got for renting out the land to be mowed and the wire fencing dismantled and put back up again was almost as much as he'd get if he tried to farm the "dad-gum place."

"I heard that the Ferris wheel guy will keep it going a ride or two after midnight if you give him a dollar," said Nat.

"*I* heard he'll stop the wheel when you get to the top if you want to propose to your girl," said Kyle, and Katie whooped.

"Don't look at me," said Joel. "I'm not even *thinking* about getting hitched till I'm thirty."

Buck grinned, and let all the talk swirl about him as he tried to pick out the Wildcat over the head of his brother. The only time you saw this much traffic on the road was at carnival time, and there was a slow line of cars funneling in through the gate, as drivers handed over their five dollars for parking.

As soon as Nat opened the door, he and Buck spilled out on one side, Katie on the other, all staring up at the Ferris wheel, the small lights of the frame a circle of blue and yellow against the night sky as the bucket seats rocked back and forth, and yelps of laughter greeted their ears.

The carnival covered an area as big as two football fields. Looking down one long grassy strip, Buck could see the Tilt-a-Wheel just visible beyond the huge orange and red letters of the Cliff Hanger ride, and farther still, Zero Gravity and Freak Out.

"Hey!" Joel called as Katie started off, and Nat almost bumped into her when she stopped. "Everybody back here by eleven, you got that? Kyle and I want to play a few games at the B&I before it closes at twelve."

"See you!" Katie said, and she headed for the ticket booth where Colby, Buck was sure, was waiting for her.

Buck turned to Nat. "What's first?"

Nat grinned. "What else?" he said, and they raced for the Wildcat.

228

They were hemmed in on both sides by booths selling huge purple hippos, orange teddy bears—anything to buy for a child or even a girlfriend if you weren't lucky enough to win a prize at the ring toss. Every ride, every booth had a brightly colored skirt around the bottom to hide its wheeled carrier, so that the whole carnival looked as though it had been solidly built in that very place, not towed in a week ago, to be wheeled out again just as quickly.

It was difficult, though, not to stop first at the other rides, for there were lines at the Dragon, at Pharaoh's Fury, and Fire Storm, each one seemingly guaranteed to make your heart race, your head swim, or your stomach lurch. But Buck could see the line growing longer at the Wildcat, and he and Nat took their places beneath the crazed look of the giant feline's eyes, which rolled up and down and left and right as the huge head twisted and turned.

There were eight paws extending outward like the spokes of a wheel, each ending in a clawlike cage holding two seats each. When it was their turn at last, Buck and Nat slid into the neon yellow seats, pulled the bar shut, and watched the sharp metal claws clamp around their cage, as though to squeeze them in tighter.

Then the ride started up with a catlike hiss. The paws began to lift into the air, and soon the boys were whirling around and around, rising up so high they would almost fall out, it seemed, then suddenly they plunged downward with an earsplitting yowl. At some unexpected moment, each arm would telescope, jerking a cage inward and spinning it this way and that, like a cat playing with a mouse, then thrust it outward again.

Buck and Nat tumbled out when the ride was over,

counting the times they had bumped heads, uncertain whether they wanted to ride again or try something new. But the other rides lured them on, and they headed for the Death Drop, and after that, they tried Soar, each lying on their stomachs, strapped to small platforms no bigger than a child's sled, with nothing else around them, arms outstretched. When the ride took off, they found themselves flying in wide circles around and around, the wind blowing their hair.

"Hey, look," Nat said as they waited in line at Vertigo, and Buck turned to see Katie and her boyfriend slowly coming to a stop on the Ferris wheel, holding hands.

The four of them met up at the funnel cake booth. Colby was holding the paper dish and laughing, as Katie tried to navigate a piece of the powdery stuff into his mouth. Her own cheeks and chin were christened with powdered sugar.

Buck and Nat bought cakes and went over to stand beside them. Buck took a deep breath and faced Colby. "How do you llllllike the rides?" he asked.

Colby gave a surprised grin and motioned to his mouth, and they all laughed.

"You gggggotta try the Wildcat," Buck told them. "It's fantastic!"

"I know! I heard!" Katie said. "We're doing that next."

Buck nodded toward Nat, who was holding both their drinks. "Colby, you know Nat WWWWaleski?"

Colby wiped one arm across his lips. "Hi. I've seen you at school."

"I've seen you on the court," Nat said.

"Yeah, when I finally get a chance to play," Colby said. But

Katie gave him a proud smile, and they wandered off after a bit, heading for the Wildcat.

• • •

After they'd finished their cola, Nat wanted to find the toilets, so Buck said he'd be at the ring toss. They had gone on most of the big rides, but still had about thirty minutes left before Joel wanted them back at the car.

He had just taken his empty cup to the trash can when he saw the bumper cars stopping across the grassy thoroughfare. Stepping out of the black-and-red car were Pete and Isaac, with Rod and Ethan in the car behind.

For a fraction of a second, Buck and Isaac locked eyes, then he saw Isaac nudge Pete, and Pete looked in his direction. His heart thumping, Buck dropped his cup inside the trash container and as nonchalantly as possible joined the passing crowd. Still remembering the afternoon that Pete and his buddies had come up behind him in Bealls' parking lot and edged him over into the woods—he knew that no one would pay much attention if it happened now unless he began to cry or yell, and he wasn't about to do that.

He ducked between the merry-go-round with its painted ceiling of old-fashioned ladies riding white spotted horses, and the movie-set front of the haunted house. It pictured an openmouthed Dracula with bats flying around him, as though daring customers to come inside. But the fake front was like a giant postcard propped against a trailer that was only half its width. Screams and rattles came from the electronics somewhere inside.

Without thinking twice, Buck lifted the canvas skirt around the base of the trailer and crawled beneath, knowing that if Pete's gang had seen him come back here they would be after him like bloodhounds after a fox. He breathed through his mouth so he could listen more acutely.

He didn't just hear them coming; he saw their feet.

"I *know* he came back here." Ethan's voice.

"Yeah, I saw him too." Isaac's.

"You think he got on the merry-go-round?" Ethan's again.

"And be a sitting duck?" Pete's voice. "He's hiding somewhere."

"What are we going to do if we find him?" asked Rod.

"Give him a scare he'll never forget," said Pete. They were walking right beside the trailer.

"What you fellas doing?" A man's gruff voice.

"Just hanging out," said Pete.

"Well, the public's not allowed back here. There's machinery and stuff. Now scram."

"We're leaving," said Isaac, and Buck watched their feet head back to the grassy aisle between the rows of rides.

He also heard Pete murmur, "The heck we are."

29

DUCK AND COVER

Buck realized he had made a mistake when the footsteps came back, though he'd known they would. He should have stayed with the crowd, no matter how embarrassing it might have been.

He could have just yelled at them, "Leave me alone!" if they'd tried to edge him behind the rides. At least *someone* would have stopped them. Here in the darkness beneath the trailer, wheels turned and rods moved back and forth only inches above his head. Screams and laughter came from inside when the whole trailer shuddered and shook, and little bits of loose rust and dirt came raining down on him. If they found him here, no way could he escape.

He wondered what time it was. The last time he'd looked

at the clock there in the belly of the mechanical clown, it had been twenty-five of eleven. He had to get back to the car.

His best chance, he figured, was to get to the trailers parked in a long row at one side of the field, homes of the workers who traveled year-round with the carnival. If he could make it over there, he would dart behind one, then another, until he reached the end of the field and the row of portable toilets. And if he could make it all the way past them and into the swarm of parked cars blanketing the entire left half of Bealls' lot, he was home free.

He laid his cheek on the ground to see through the two-inch space between the earth and the trailer skirt. He could see the red stripes on Rod's white sneakers, and lay stone still.

"Not behind here," Ethan called, probably inspecting the trash cans back by the fence.

Then the man's voice again. "I told you guys to clear out. Now *do* it!" A large boot appeared only inches from Buck's face, but he didn't move an inch until both the man and the boys had left.

When several minutes had passed and there were no more noises, Buck peeked tentatively out and saw no one. Carefully, he worked his way out on his elbows, crouched like a runner on his mark, then tore across the short open stretch to the row of house trailers, around a picnic table squeezed between an old Ford and a silver Citation and lurched behind it, as a dog began a frantic barking.

He'd cut his hand on the green-and-black license plate

of the Ford, and he crept over to a large Fleetwood Prowler, making the dog inside it bark all the louder. A woman came to the door and peered out, then told her dog to hush. Buck pressed himself flat against the back of the Prowler, and finally the woman went inside again and shut the door.

Buck thought about Nat, hoping he'd simply gone on some rides without him. He heard a gong, and a loud speaker announcing a prize from the fish tank, another contest. "We have a winner, ladies and gentlemen," the voice said. "Every fifteen minutes, another prize!" *Eleven o' clock,* Buck guessed.

How much farther to the end of the row? Five trailers? Six? Some of the spaces between them were only a couple yards wide, others room enough for a table, a grill, and some folding chairs. If Pete or any of the others were looking this way, they'd see him make the run.

They were searching, all right. They had moved away from the haunted house to the snow cone stand and the fortune-telling machine, each looking in all directions.

Buck made another run, crouching low. As he darted behind a gray-and-white Palomino, an old man, sitting on a box and smoking, eyed him without expression and took another drag on his cigarette. But above the calliope music, Buck heard Ethan yell, "Pete! I saw him!"

There was nothing left to do now but run. He tore past the row of toilets—no use hiding now—and plunged into the sea of parked cars on the far side of the field, trying to remember how far in Joel had parked.

With four boys spreading out in all directions, however, he knew he was going to be caught. Pete was up ahead between an SUV and a convertible, shouting at Rod to grab him. Ethan had hold of his shirt, and then Buck heard another voice:

"Buck? C'mon! We're ready to go!" Joel was standing on the hood of his car, yelling at him.

Pete emerged from behind the SUV and punched his arm—hard—before he disappeared, and Ethan let go of his shirt. As David had once said, the other boys followed Pete like ducks, and they all disappeared into the shadows.

"What was *that* all about?" Joel asked, jumping down. "Were those the guys who . . . ?"

"Just horsing around," Buck said, panting, and collapsed against the car.

"Well, get in. We're ready to leave," Joel told him.

The others were inside and waiting.

"Where *were* you?" Nat said. "You didn't show up, so I went on the Whiplash without you. Man, I liked that better than the Wildcat."

"I ddddon't know what happened. Goofed up, I guess," Buck told him. His arm ached where Pete had punched him, but he was sort of glad in a way that it had happened. Did that mean they were even now, for his tearing down their shack?

As the car moved toward the exit, there was a loud *whang* as a stone hit the fender.

"Somebody throw a rock?" said Nat, half turning in the seat.

"Just Pete's goons acting up," said Buck. He wasn't too

afraid. What else could they do? They were lucky Dad and Gramps hadn't reported the stealing, or they'd really be in trouble. The car reached the end of the lot and turned onto the main road, leaving the lights and the music far behind.

30

BUCK TO DAVID, DAVID TO BUCK

He told David about every ride at the carnival before he told him about Pete and his gang chasing him down. Told him about the Wildcat, in fact, before he told him about the robberies at the sawmill and how he and Nat had discovered Pete's shack in the woods.

David: **man, buck! u should have hung out with someone at the carnival the whole time!!!!**

Buck: **i know i was by myself when they spotted me**

David: **they're going to b gunning for u**

Buck: **pete socked me hard before he left he'd get in trouble if he did much more**

David: **glad they'll b in high school when u go back**

Buck: **yes to that! how was the counseling job?**

David: i don't ever want 2 b a teacher, that's 4 sure gram's here now baking up a storm fattening me up 4 survival camp I guess i'm going 2 hate it

Buck: maybe not can never tell when u might be trapped in a submarine or something

31

JACOB'S STORY

Any day now.

Any day the headlamp should be arriving, and Buck checked the Anderson's box several times each afternoon to see if the mail had come. The weather had turned unusually cool for the end of summer. He was used to autumn coming early here in the foothills, but couldn't remember ever needing a jacket quite this early.

"See?" Gramps told them, buttoning up his sweater. "Hardly had the air conditioner on before we turned it off again."

The carnival had packed up and moved on, and Buck wished more than ever he could have one last trip to the Hole before school and homework began. Nat's family was having a cousins' reunion, and relatives were coming from all over, so Buck didn't see much of his friend.

Impatient for the headlamp to come, Buck even went to the little post office attached to Bealls' and asked if a package was there for Joel, that he had permission to pick it up if it had.

Mrs. Beall gave him a half smile that meant, *not on your life.* "Now, Buck," she said, "you know that even if I had a package here for your brother, I couldn't give it to you. Not without his signature. You'll just have to wait till we put it in the box at your driveway. If they said it was on order, it'll come, don't you worry."

As he walked back toward his bike, hands in the pockets of his jacket, he heard a woman call, "Excuse me . . ."

Buck turned quickly, thinking it was Mrs. Beall, telling him the package was there after all, but it was a brown-haired woman in pants and a jeans jacket who had been sitting on a bench outside Bealls' when he entered. She was no one he'd seen before, because he would have remembered; she was as freckled as a speckled egg. Her wavy hair was cut short and fell loose over her ears, and a cloth bag hung on her shoulder. She was smiling at him tentatively, and Buck walked over.

"Ma'am?"

"Hello. You're Buck Anderson, I think, and I wondered if you had a few minutes to talk," she said. "I'm Karen Schuster, Jacob Wall's daughter."

Buck studied her face, unable to see any of Jacob in her features, except for the eyes, perhaps, the same shade of blue. Jacob didn't smile enough for him to tell whether her smile matched his or not.

"I g . . . guess so," Buck said, and she motioned to the bench beside her. Buck sat down, leaning forward awkwardly, ready to leave at his first opportunity. Yet he had to admit he was curious.

"The Bealls tell me that you and your uncle are dropping in regularly to help my dad out," Karen said. "I wanted to say thank you in person."

"It's okay," said Buck.

"I haven't . . . haven't been able to see him yet, and I just wondered . . . how is he doing? His health?"

Buck's shoulders gave a little shrug. "He ggggets around—we just do the things he ccccan't do—pick up his mail and everything."

She nodded, her blue eyes searching Buck's face, taking in every little nuance of expression, as though that would answer whatever she couldn't get up the nerve to ask.

Then she leaned back suddenly and looked out over the parking lot. "I write to him, but he returns my letters unopened. I suppose you knew that?"

Buck didn't answer. He was uncomfortable talking with her, not that she wasn't nice enough, but he didn't want to tell her anything Jacob wouldn't have wanted her to know.

Karen sighed. "I just can't get him to forgive me, and you've no idea how that hurts."

Wow! Now he *knew* he shouldn't be listening, and he shuffled his feet as though he might stand up, but he didn't. Resting his arms on his knees, palms together, he studied his fingertips.

"My husband is—*was*—a financial advisor, and three years ago, Dad put all his money, and all his trust, in us. Gary, my husband, had a plan all worked out so that when Dad retired, he could buy himself a small farm and raise horses, a few, anyway, something he'd always talked about doing. He loved the country. He even had the land picked out and was going to hire a couple of men to help him."

So what was the problem? Buck wondered. This was country, but probably not what Jacob had in mind. . . .

"We really, truly, wanted the best for Dad. He deserved it—he was so lonely after Mom died, and his rheumatoid arthritis made him take early retirement. But . . . at the last minute . . . Gary impulsively invested most of Dad's money, and most of ours, in a new business venture he didn't think could possibly lose. Something that would bring Dad, and us, even more retirement money than he had thought. And . . ."

Buck guessed.

"We lost everything. Well, not quite everything, because there was enough left . . . just enough . . . for Dad to buy the house and the little piece of land he's on now. No barn, no horses, no fencing, no pasture . . . We had to sell the place where we were living and move to a condo ourselves. We're in North Carolina, Dad's here."

Buck glanced over to see a tear slide out of the corner of her eye and make its slow way down her cheek. Her hand came up quickly and brushed it away.

"We want to do whatever we can to make it up to Dad and prove that we're sorry. We'd like to start putting a little of our money in his bank account every month, but we don't even know what bank he uses, or if he'd allow it. Most of all, we just want him back in our lives, to take care of him if he ever needs it, but he won't take my phone calls, won't read my letters, and won't even answer the door. He's furious about what happened, and I don't blame him."

"That sssssssounds . . . really bad," Buck said.

For a while they sat without saying anything, and then Karen turned again to Buck.

"Do you have any suggestions? I mean, is there something he really wants or needs that we could buy for him—that you could give him for us?"

Buck shook his head. "He'd know."

"Yes, I suppose he would." Karen adjusted the bag on her shoulder. "Well, I shouldn't be bothering you with all this, and I just appreciate your listening. I simply can't bear the thought of Dad getting older and more crippled—not having people around who love him. It was awful what we did. What . . . Gary did. He lost his job over it too and is working somewhere else."

She stood up, and so did Buck.

"Well, again, thanks for listening. Hope you enjoy the rest of your vacation. Guess school starts pretty soon?"

"Yeah," Buck said. "Nice to meet you."

"You too."

• • •

He couldn't help but think about it when he went to Jacob's the next morning. Only a few days left before school started, and Jacob was working him hard—not in chores but his speech.

It had changed, he knew that. *He* had changed, and when he recited stuff aloud in front of the big mirror still propped against the wall at Jacob's, he was pleased that he looked like a guy named Buck Anderson, not a guy in a Halloween fright mask, his mouth pulled to one side, his jaw clenched, eyes blinking like a tavern sign.

Crutches, Jacob called them, used to help get the words out. Except that they didn't. No more *decoys* either, the pulling at one ear, the scratching of the head, the shifting of the feet, all the little things he might have hoped, unconsciously, would distract the listener from his stuttering.

Jacob even relented and played a DVD that he'd made for his patients at the military hospital, parts of speeches by famous people—a president, a general, a senator, a movie star—each one demonstrating "normal disfluency," as Jacob called it, showing that everyone is disfluent once in a while. "They just don't have a fit when it happens, that's all."

But today, because Buck's mind was on Karen, he wondered if Jacob could possibly be happy, cutting her out of his life. He wasn't paying enough attention to his stuttering, and when he made phone calls and Jacob raised a finger, he sometimes reverted back to his choking repetition of a sound before he said a word, instead of letting the stutter come out slow and natural.

"Running backward again," Jacob told him. "You fight it like that, you're stuck in the same old rut you used to be."

Buck turned toward the mirror and saw the weird set of his jaw, and relaxed it, but he felt on edge, and saw that Jacob was too. He was wasting his time today, and Jacob's as well.

When the session was over at last, Jacob slowly got to his feet and said, "You want to come maybe once a week after school starts and we'll work on it? You've got to do your part, though, Buck. Practice at home. Practice on friends."

"Yeah, well . . . ," Buck said, and picked up his jacket. It was the same jacket he used to wear searching for caves, he and David, only reminding him that the cold spell was sticking around, cheating him of some last warm days of vacation, and it didn't help his mood any.

He walked over to the door without saying good-bye, and pulled it open, and there stood Karen, staring past him at her dad.

"Dad . . . ?" she said, pleading.

"Get out!" Jacob yelled, hobbling his way across the room.

"I just want to *talk* with you, *please!*" she begged, still blocking the doorway.

"Don't let her in, Buck!" Jacob bellowed, waving one arm. "Close the door! Now!"

But Buck couldn't. Wouldn't. And suddenly he wheeled about and faced Jacob. "Who's running backward nnnnow?" he shouted. "All she wants you to do is listen to . . ."

But Jacob's free hand gave him a push and Buck almost collided with Karen as he tumbled to one side, the door banging shut behind him.

Karen stood with one hand over her mouth, eyes brimming, and Buck didn't know what to do. He'd almost knocked her down.

"I'm sssssorry," he said.

She nodded as she turned and went back down the steps, and Buck watched as she slowly got in her car and drove away.

32

FACEDOWN

The old fool! Buck was thinking as he pedaled home. *Serves him right to spend the rest of his life alone with his anger.* Buck had a notion not to show up for the next session. Now that the carnival had moved on, he was determined to go back in the Hole again whether he had the headlamp or not. Also, there were two movies showing at the Palace on Saturday, and he and Nat, and probably Katie and Colby, would be going. He'd tell Jacob his dad needed him to crate up the last of the vegetables for market, which was also true.

He spent the rest of Friday morning packing lima beans, a pound to a plastic bag, and placing them in a box. Then the last of the pole beans, and finally carrots.

"How'd we do this year, DDDDad?" he asked as he lifted a heavy box to make room for another.

"Better than last year," Don Anderson said. "Be nice to have a job that pays year-round, but then it's nice to have some time off too. Not that I get much time off at the mill."

Buck found his dad giving him a sideways glance. "How was *your* summer? You know, Buck . . . seems to me your . . . stuttering's . . . well, better. Have you seen a difference yourself?"

"Yeah, it doesn't bother me like it used tttto," said Buck. "I just . . . llllllllllet it come," and he purposely stuttered on the *L* and grinned at how easily he could do it.

His dad returned a quizzical smile. "Whatever works," he said.

And that afternoon, after a big ham sandwich and one of Katie's homemade milk shakes, Buck walked down to the mailbox, the early autumn wind whipping his hair, making goose bumps on his arms, and found that the headlamp had come. And because he had Joel's permission to open the package, he raced back to the house and up to his room to rip the package open.

He stood in front of his mirror and slipped the harness over his head—one strap going around the front like a headband, the other strap beginning at the lamp in front, then going backward over the top of his head and connecting with the strap around in back. It was loose now, but would be nice and snug over his bicycle helmet.

Then, his shoulders erect, eyes on the mirror, he flipped the switch.

Nothing happened. No light.

How could this be? After weeks of waiting . . . ! Yanking off the harness, Buck checked the little folded slip of instructions and found that batteries were not included.

He realized that it was the more expensive headlamp he'd wanted first that came with batteries, but not this cheaper model.

No problem. He still had money from his work that summer. He grabbed his jacket, took money from his top drawer, and stuffed it in one zipper pocket. Then, unable to let the headlamp out of his sight, he folded it up the way it had come and stuffed it in the other pocket, zipping it closed.

"Want some?"

Buck jumped at the sound of Katie's voice in the doorway, and turned to see her holding out a giant bag of M&Ms, in tiny chocolate-colored packages.

"Sure," he said, and took a handful. "Halloween already?"

She giggled. "My favorite holiday. Where you going?"

"To BBBBBealls'," he said nonchalantly. "Want anything?"

"No. We just got a ton of groceries yesterday," she said, and went on down the hall to her room. Then, "Close the door when you go out, will you? Dad doesn't have the furnace running yet, and it's freezing in here."

"Sure," Buck said.

He whisked up the wrapping paper and went downstairs, careful to close the back door after him, stuffing the wrapper in the trash can by the side of the house so there would be no questions from Mom or Dad or Mel: *What the dickens do you need a headlamp for? You shouldn't be out on your bike after dark, and you know it.* And then, fastening his helmet under his chin, he was riding his bike to Bealls', the afternoon shadows lengthening on the dirt lane before him.

He needed two double A batteries, and for one brief moment he imagined Mr. Beall saying, "Well, dang it, Buck! I was sure we'd ordered some more, but I don't see them around here." *Don't even go there,* he told himself. *You worry like David.*

There were few people in the store, and the Bealls were using the free time to restock their shelves.

"Hi there, Buck. Be with you in a moment," Mr. Beall called from a rolling ladder suspended from a rail that ran all along one wall under the ceiling. He had carefully re-arranged some large packages of paper towels to make room for others. "Now what can I do for you?" he asked, climbing down, one scuffed brown shoe following the other.

"I'd like a ppppackage of double A batteries," Buck said.

"Sure thing." Mr. Beall turned and faced the battery case, running his finger along each tiny row. His fingernail had dark vertical lines on it. "A two-pack, four-pack, or six?"

"Uh . . . make it four," said Buck.

"There you go." Mr. Beall placed them on the counter, and Buck's heart did the little pleasure jump. As he rang up the sale, the man said, "You seem to be doing all right these days, Buck. Glad to see it."

Buck gave him a puzzled smile, then realized he meant the stuttering. Weird that people didn't come right out and say the word, like it might be catching or something.

"Yeah," he said, and then, mischievously, "I'm dddddddo-ing okkkkkkkay."

• • •

He pedaled along the road, wild to get home and try it out—in some really dark place, and he wasn't about to wait until evening. A closet, maybe. Or the basement. Yeah, that was it. In the old windowless coal bin that hadn't been used for maybe eighty years.

Was it really as powerful as the advertisement said? Would it shine light eighty yards out in front of him? Think what the inside of the Hole would look like if he came to an opening in the rock and could really see all around him. It hadn't rained now for over a week. So, tomorrow? Could he possibly sneak off tomorrow? Mel was coming home, but that shouldn't matter. And maybe Dad would be at the sawmill helping Gramps and Joel. It might work. . . . And Jacob? To heck with Jacob.

He was riding down the long stretch of pavement bordered by tall pines on either side, making it seem as though evening had come already, when he heard an engine noise from behind. He edged over to the right, carefully steering his way along the narrow strip between the white line and the edge of the paving, waiting for the vehicle to pass.

But it didn't.

Buck could tell by the sound that it was slowing as it came alongside him, and suddenly it was so close that he struggled to steady his bike.

He glanced over to see who was driving and saw Pete Ketterman at the wheel of his dad's Nissan pickup, an old 1990 model. The next thing he knew, his bike was bumping and bouncing along the shoulder of the road, and then he was tumbling down into the gulley, his bike on top of him.

"Oh, gee, looks like you had a little accident!" Pete called, getting out and coming around. "And here we are, ready to help." Then, looking quickly up and down the deserted road, he said to the others, who had climbed out too, "Get him in the truck, guys, and throw the bike in back. We'll give him a ride."

"No, I cccccan get home myself," said Buck, his leg entangled in the frame of his bike, one pedal still spinning.

"Hey, what are friends for?" Pete said, and to the others, "C'mon, hurry."

"Where are we supposed to put him?" asked Rod. "In the cab?"

"Where else? Sit on him, if you have to. Hurry."

And suddenly four sets of hands were grasping Buck's arms and legs. "Get *away* from me!" Buck yelled, kicking. But with eight hands on him, yanking him up out of the weeds and carrying him to the truck, it was no use.

He was wrestled to the small floor space between the back of the front seats and the two jump seats in the rear of the cab. Buck heard the clunk of his bicycle as it was tossed in the bed of the pickup, and then he felt knees and feet stepping on and over him as Rod and Isaac worked their way into the jump seats.

He heard Pete climb back into the truck, heard Ethan's laughter coming from the passenger seat, and he lay facedown, scrunched into an awkward position, legs bent backward at the knees, feet over his rump.

The engine started up, but the pickup didn't move, waiting for another car to pass, and then it shot forward with a squeal of tires and headed up the road.

"So, where we going?" asked Isaac above the truck's rumble.

"I'm thinking," said Pete, and drove on. And then, in a

falsely cheery note, he called to Buck, "Hey, Buck-o, we're your *friends*, remember? The nice guys whose duck blind you demolished? Just going to help you out, buddy. One good turn deserves another, right? Going to give you a little sp . . . sp . . . sp . . . sp . . . speech lesson, that's all."

Frightened as he was, and smushed beneath two pairs of dirty sneakers, Buck managed to say, "Wasn't your plywood."

"Yeah? Wasn't your land either. You know how long it took us to make that duck blind?"

Buck could have made a comment about how it sure didn't look like a duck blind to him and Mel, and did they have hunting licenses, but he didn't.

"Eleven weeks! Yup! Eleven weeks of hard labor, all torn down in one afternoon, by El Creepo and his big bad thug of an uncle."

How did Pete manage to be driving his dad's pickup? Buck wondered. *And with all his friends onboard?* You couldn't get a driver's license in Virginia until you were sixteen, but you could get a learner's permit at fifteen and a half. Most kids entering high school were thirteen or fourteen, but if you'd been held back a year somewhere along the way, usually kindergarten if your birthday didn't quite make the cutoff for first grade, you could end up the oldest, strongest, tallest, and possibly brightest kid in class from then on. Buck didn't know about smartest, but Pukeman was probably one of the bigger, stronger boys going into high school. Still, he wasn't just running a quick errand for his dad. He had all his friends on board.

He wondered about his bike, if anything was broken.

Where *were* they going? They sure weren't taking him home because they'd have reached his road by now, and he had felt the truck making no right turns.

There was no point in wrestling with them. No way he could reach the windows to signal for help, and he could yell all he liked, but no one would hear.

They were probably going to pour beer down him again, and leave him way out in the country to make his way home, royally drunk. What if he refused to swallow, and just let the beer pour down his chin? Could they *force* someone to swallow? He didn't think they'd beat him up. Not even Pukeman would stoop so low as to put one guy up against four. But one at a time?

Another stab of fear coursed through him, and his breath came in short hurried gasps, keeping time, it seemed, with every other beat of his heart. He inhaled the dust and dirt on the floor, the smell of Isaac's sneakers.

"Where we going, Pete?" Rod called after five minutes or so of winding around and around. If they had skipped the turnoff to the Andersons' place, then they must have missed the turnoff to the Kettermans' as well, and were heading out into more rocky terrain. Every bump in the road made Buck's forehead bounce. He turned his head occasionally to work out the crick in his neck, but it didn't help. There were Hostess cupcake wrappers on the floor, and an empty pop can that rolled and lodged against his face from time to time.

"Yeah, where we heading? The boondocks?" said Ethan.

"Got an idea," Pete told them. "A *really* good idea. Little Buck-o's going to get a super-duper lesson. Heck, we might even cure this guy in a single afternoon. Now wouldn't *that* be something? He *might* even learn something about not messing with other people's stuff." Over his shoulder, he asked, "Did anyone notice if there was rope back there along with the other stuff we picked up for my dad?"

Isaac twisted himself around, one foot digging into Buck's back as he turned to look out the rear window. "Yeah," he said. "There's rope. Whole coil of it."

"What are you going to do with it?" Rod asked, and Buck could tell that even he sounded wary.

"You'll see," said Pete, and there was a steel cold tone to his voice that didn't sound like kidding any longer.

A few minutes later the truck turned sharply and the road was definitely rougher, if it was road at all. It seemed to go on forever.

"You know where you're going, Pete?" asked Ethan.

"Almost there," Pete answered. And suddenly the pickup came to an abrupt stop with a jerk, and everything shot forward, including Buck's head against the base of the driver's seat.

"Okay. Everybody out," Pete said. "See if the creep has peed his pants yet."

"What *is* this?" asked Isaac. And then, "The Pit!"

33

DARK

"Listen, man . . . !"

Buck couldn't tell whose voice it was this time, but Puke-man wasn't listening. "C'mon, drag him out, we've got to take off pretty soon. Ike, get the rope."

The thump of Buck's heart was almost as loud in his head as it felt in his chest, and he broke into a sweat, even though he'd been too warm down there on the floorboards in his fleece-lined jacket.

Pete was giving orders like a master sergeant, and the other guys obeyed like privates. If he was trying to scare Buck out of his wits, he was doing a pretty good job of it, Buck decided, but he wasn't about to let Pete know.

Still, after they yanked him out of the cab, he tried to

make a run for it, but Ethan dived for his legs and brought him down. All Buck got out of that were a bruised chin and a twisted arm.

Pete had one hand on the back of his neck now, and was pushing him toward a bare spot in the underbrush, about as wide as a card table. It was bordered on one side by the base of a rocky cliff that blocked out what was left of the afternoon sun, weeds on the others. The bare place itself was covered with a six-inch-high wooden frame, with boards nailed across the top, and a yellow DANGER, KEEP OUT sign nailed to a wooden post at one side.

"Nobody's allowed in the Pit, man!" said Isaac. "You know what happened to those frat boys. . . ."

"So they got kicked out of their fraternity," said Pete. "We're not a fraternity. Hold him while I get the hammer."

Pete made his way back to the pickup, opened the truck's toolbox, and returned with a builder's hammer. There was already a small space between two of the boards, and Buck watched as Pete inserted the hammer's head in the narrow opening and yanked up the end of a board. It took several minutes, but the first wide board came off, then the second, leaving a rectangular opening about a foot wide.

"Now," said Pete, "the rope . . ."

"Lllllet me alone," Buck said, and hated the tremor in his voice. "You've already ggggggot me all the way up here." As though he even knew where he was. He'd heard about the Pit but had never been there. They weren't going to hang him, were they? Was Pete really that crazy mad?

But while the other boys held his arms and legs, Pete looped the rope under Buck's arms and around his chest and tied a knot.

258

"Stop it!" Buck yelled, twisting and kicking, but they wrestled him down and held him.

"Now, you guys hold the rope, and, Ethan, help me lower him through the hole."

Well, he was going to make it as hard as he could for them, Buck decided, and lived up to his name, bucking and kicking. He was gratified to hear Pete's teeth click together once when his head collided with Pete's chin.

Despite his struggling, he was pushed to the edge of the opening and Pete buckled his knees from behind so that he sat down. And then, with the other three boys holding the rope, Pete pushed him over the side. Scraping the wood planks as he fell, Buck found himself dangling, his body turning this way and that, over the dark of the Pit.

Instinctively he reached up and gripped the remaining boards on each side.

"Oh, no!" said Pete. "Lower him another foot, guys."

Buck felt the rope slacken and then, when Pete stepped on his fingers, Buck let go. Five feet down, all he could see now was the rectangle of light above him and Pete's face leering at him.

He was immediately engulfed in a damp earth smell, and could make out nothing at all below him. He had only heard rumors about the fraternity guys holding a party down there. Whether it was rocky at the bottom or flat, whether it had fissures or drop-offs, he didn't know.

"What do you wwwwant from me, anyway?" he called up. If Pete asked for an apology, could he do it? Could he not do it? Could he say he was sorry for all the work they'd put in on the duck blind without saying he was sorry he and Mel had torn it down? Because he wasn't.

259

But Pete wanted something else, and his face seemed to fill the whole rectangle at the top.

"Repeat after me, creep. 'I . . . am . . . a . . . stupid . . . weirdo.' Without stuttering. Every time you stutter, we lower you a foot."

Buck heard Ethan laugh.

Never.

"Come on, Buck-o. Time's a'wastin'. We're trying to help you! You can do it. 'I . . . am . . . a . . . stupid . . . weirdo.'"

Silence.

"Lower him," Pete instructed the others, and with a sudden jerk, Buck found himself a foot lower, the rectangle of light above him growing smaller.

"Whas a'matter, Buck-o? You shaking so hard you can't talk?" Pete reached down and gave the rope a little jerk.

Buck pressed his lips together tightly. If Katie were watching, she'd probably say, *Buck, don't be stubborn! Say it! Say anything!* No way. His anger was even stronger than his fear.

Pete was bluffing; he felt sure of it. Frightened as he was, Buck knew they couldn't hold on forever, and Pete was anxious to get back. They'd *have* to pull him up.

"Okay, how about 'I'm a stinkin' creep.' Come on, Buck-o. Don't make me angry. Say it. Try not to stutter now. 'I'm a stinkin' creep.'"

And Buck couldn't help himself. "Yeah, you are," he said.

"Lower him another foot! No, two feet," Pete said.

And the rope jerked some more.

Two feet, three feet, then four . . .

"Help me hold the freakin' rope!" Ethan bellowed.

"It's going! There isn't any more!" shouted Rod.

"Hold it! *Hold* it . . . !"

Buck was falling, jerkily falling, and a moment later, he hit a muddy surface, one leg twisting under him, his arm scraping a rock.

"You dropped him, you jerks!" Pete yelped.

"There wasn't enough rope!" Isaac yelled back. "You kept saying 'lower him.' What'd ya expect?"

There was a lot of scuffling from above; then four faces crowded over the rectangle.

"Buck?" called Rod.

"Shut up. Just get a flashlight. Check the toolbox," Pete said. "What the heck . . . ?"

Buck tentatively pulled his leg out from under him and rubbed along his shin. Then, without shifting his body more, he felt the surface all around him to see how much room he had to move. Rock and mud. After that he lay on his stomach, his arms outstretched, and gingerly explored some more. Crawl space, as far as he could reach in all directions, except for rock wall at one side. No drop-off.

The sound of feet on the boards above. Then the beam of a flashlight caught him in the face, and he estimated that he was about fifteen feet down.

"Hey, Buck," called Ethan.

Buck refused to answer. Rubbed his ankle.

"You okay?" asked Rod.

No answer.

"What are we going to do, Pete? Get another rope and make some kind of ladder?" Rod asked.

"You kidding? I've got to get Dad's truck back before he

gets home," said Pete. "Buck's okay. Give the little creep time to think about what he's done. We'll come back tomorrow with . . . I dunno. Something."

"Leave him here all night?" Rod asked.

"You got a better plan? What else are we going to do? You guys dropped the rope, not me." Pete's voice sounded angry. He knelt down and addressed Buck. "Here's the story, and you better listen: you decided to ride out to the Pit and look it over. But you were fooling around and fell in, see? You tell anybody we had anything to do with it, and you are going to be one sorry mess. Got it?"

Again, Buck refused to answer.

"Okay. Play it your way, and maybe we won't come back at all. Let's go, guys. I mean, we've got to hustle."

The square of light grew bright again as the boys moved away. But then Rod leaned down and said, "Buck. Catch." And the flashlight came tumbling down, landing at Buck's feet.

"Come *on*!" Pete was yelling.

The slam of the truck's door, then the other. The sound of the engine starting up, backing up, then the rattle as the truck made its way over bumpy ground, back toward the dirt road some distance away. And finally, there was no sound at all but a distant chirp of insects in the field above.

Buck felt a momentary wave of panic. Maybe he should have obeyed Pete. What were words, after all? Wasn't he used to people calling him names sometimes when he stuttered?

What if they didn't come back tomorrow? Couldn't, for some reason? What if Pete couldn't get the truck again, and the longer it went on, the police looking, the more frightened they were to say anything? They'd left his bike—he'd heard it clatter right beside the platform above, so in the unlikely event that someone would come looking for him here—the boards lying to one side—they'd figure this was where he was.

What would happen when he didn't come home tonight? His folks would be frantic. He hugged himself with his arms. He had to think. The last person who had seen him was Katie, who had offered him M&Ms. . . .

And then he remembered the headlamp.

Buck turned the flashlight on, but the battery was weak and the light went on and off. Quickly, he propped it beside him at an angle to shine on his lap, and then carefully, very carefully, he unzipped his jacket pocket for the batteries. . . . Little packets of M&Ms slid out with them onto the rock, and Buck put the candy back inside and zipped the pocket up again. Then he took out the headlamp from his other pocket. Would it even work now, after his tumble down into the gulley and being squished on the floor of the truck? There were no cracks that he could see, though it had been bent slightly to one side. He secured it between his thighs.

Using what little light he had from the flashlight, he opened the package of batteries and took out two, then pried open the back of the headlamp and slid them in place.

Lifting the harness strap, he slid it over his helmet like a headband. And when it was adjusted and the headlamp was secure, Buck reached up and turned the switch.

Instantly the walls of the Pit became the muted browns

and beiges and white layers of a fairly large cavity—the size of a large living room with a fifteen-foot ceiling. The flat surface where he was sitting was itself not much wider than an elevator, but the rest of the space was filled with ridges and ledges, with an enormous rock slide filling one corner. There were initials carved into a large rock just ahead of him, a couple of empty beer cans, a cigarette wrapper on the ground, and the smoky smudge where a bonfire had been.

Any other time, Buck would have been delirious with excitement to explore, but right now, all he could think about was home, and if they were watching for him at the table. They'd probably call Nat's house, wondering if Nat had seen him. Mel might even call Jacob, and . . . Oh, man. Jacob's "Get out" still rang in his ears.

And of course, there was no note on his pillow giving any hint of where he might be, not that it would help this time, if there were.

34

TOO LATE

His first thought was to check for his cell phone in his back pocket. Mom had chewed him out the last time he was late for dinner, so he'd been making a point of keeping it in a back pocket no matter where he went. But he already knew what it would say: *no service*. If there had been, he could have dialed 911 and told them where he was. No, actually, the first call he would have made would have been to David: *u won't believe where I am!!!!!*

He couldn't believe it either. Slowly he turned himself around, and this time he took in everything—the tumble of rocks in one corner, the dark crevasse above it; the various colors of limestone layering the walls. A few large rocks littered the floor, like furniture; one had initials carved into it, with the fraternity insignia (the evidence that had gotten them busted). Buck also made out a dark stream of water—so dark it was easy to overlook—that flowed from behind a huge boulder and silently disappeared again into a wide slot in the wall six yards away.

He reached down and rubbed his ankle, relieved to find that by changing positions, it felt better. He didn't think he had sprained it when he fell. It wasn't the pain that bothered him but the humiliation he'd felt, dangling there like a worm on the end of a line. And Pete's ugly face above him—all four of them—taunting.

Say it! "I am a stupid weirdo."

Well, no freaking way was he going to say that. Still . . .

He stuck his cell phone back in his pants pocket, then thought better of it and put it in one of the zippered pockets of his jacket. At least he could see what time it was on his cell, but it was no help right now.

He knew he'd feel less panicky, and warmer, if he moved around—pretended he'd been exploring this on his own and did what he'd do then. Except that he had no knee pads with him, no arm pads, no gloves, no canteen, no tape, and no food, other than three small packets of M&Ms. And, of course, Pete's rope, though he saw no way he could use it now. At least he was still wearing his bicycle helmet, and best of all, he had the headlamp.

The Pit was drafty, which meant there were holes and leaks, letting air through somewhere. A chilly spot to spend the night, which was probably why the frat boys had built a fire.

Buck got to his feet and tested the mound of rocks to see

if it was stable. Nothing moved or jiggled, so he carefully began to crawl, foothold by foothold, toward the dark, cavernous shadow at the top, and found that it was only three feet deep. A frat boy had obviously climbed up there too, because he'd left a cap at the back, like a flag.

No bats here, clinging to the high ceiling. Mold and moss, making the rocks slippery underfoot. Finally he climbed down, leaving the fraternity cap behind, out of respect for the guy who had been here first.

He took out his cell again and checked the time. Seven past six. The family would be gathering for dinner, and he imagined that at this point, his mom would be more annoyed with him than angry.

Gramps would probably say, "Let's go on," before he bowed his head, and—referring to the food before him— would say, as always, ". . . bless it to nourish our good. Amen."

Buck tried not to think about food, however. The big ham sandwich he'd had for lunch and the strawberry milk shakes Katie made had filled his stomach, but now he was definitely hungry. If Pukeman didn't get back here with another rope until tomorrow night, those little packets of M&Ms were going to have to be rationed out slowly.

He turned off the headlamp to save the batteries and felt around for one of the little M&M packets, slipping it out of his pocket. Then, without opening it, he tried to count the number of candies by pressing down on them through the wrapper. Were there eight? Ten? They kept sliding away from his thumb and forefinger and he was probably counting some of them twice. Ten at the most. If Pete came back the same time tomorrow afternoon in his dad's truck, that would be about twenty-two hours from now. So if he had thirty M&Ms, the most he could eat was one an hour. Buck left the packet in his pocket and zipped it up again.

He turned on the headlamp and crawled over to the quietly moving stream, wishing he had a stick to test the depth. He directed the beam straight down into the water and saw the sharp decline of the rock beneath, that quickly turned the water from clear to black, and he was glad he had not fallen or rolled into that when the rope dropped.

Buck wondered what cavers would do with the Pit if they got permission from the county to explore it. Have a cave diver go under the rock to see where the stream led?

He followed the wall along its rough circumference, crawling around boulders, climbing over ridges, shining his headlamp into every possible opening. So thoroughly did he inspect and explore that when he checked his cell phone again for the time, he was amazed to find it was after eight. But he wasn't tired. He had to memorize everything he found so he could describe it to David.

Buck had squeezed into an especially tight corner to investigate a small dark area in the rocky wall near the floor. He got down on his knees and felt around, and then, detecting a hole, took off the headlamp and lay on his side, body bent at a right angle. Carefully, he trained the light directly into the hole. The drafty passage was open as far as he could see and—on ahead—was much larger than the opening. It could lead almost anywhere, perhaps a drop-off or a dead end. Or—and his heart raced with excitement—other galleries, even bigger than this one. Could he possibly, *possibly,* fit himself through this hole?

He took off his helmet and pushed it into the hole to see how many inches of clearance he had. A few. But enough for his shoulders? If he really scrunched? *Think!* he told himself. What would David say?

David, he was sure, would say no. He was positive that David himself wouldn't try it. But people did know that Buck was here. Eventually someone would come, and Buck didn't want it to be before he'd had a chance to explore a little. He decided to take a chance.

He went back to the center of the Pit and, picking up Pete's rope, tied one end around his ankle and let it drag. Then he opened a packet of M&Ms and allowed himself one piece, just to quiet his nerves. Finally, he crawled back behind the boulder and lay down on his side again, contorted his body into a right angle, and, pushing his headlamp and helmet in ahead of him, slowly, carefully inched his way into the opening, arms first. Then his head, turned sideways, his ear scraping along the cold rock.

Buck concentrated on curving his shoulders inward, one at a time, as close to his chest as he could get them, requiring the smallest possible space. Moving like a centipede through the narrow opening, he felt it sharp and unforgiving all around. But then . . . then . . . his shoulders were free and he was able to drag his hips, his knees, and finally his feet in after him.

Just as his headlamp had shown, the passage was getting wider, though he had to crawl some distance before he could raise his head more than a few inches. But finally he was able to sit up, his back against the wall, and he could almost stretch his legs out in front of him.

Buck put on the helmet and headlamp again, and treated

himself to one more M&M, wishing that he had water. If he found any dripping down the rocks, he would drink it, because water filtered through the ground, the rocks, the sand, and into a cave was usually, he'd read, safe to drink.

He trained his headlamp on the area around him, debating which way to go. There was no clear passage—rocks and boulders protruded at odd angles no matter which direction he went—but there was one possibility that seemed more open than the others, a higher ceiling than the rest, though the terrain itself looked rougher and more jagged than the ten or twelve yards he'd traveled so far. *Go for it,* he told himself, and he had just maneuvered around a corner when he thought he heard someone calling his name. He slowly sat back down.

"Buck!" Now two voices were calling.

He turned his head and listened.

"Buck, we've got more rope. Come on." Pukeman.

"Yeah, come out, come out, wherever you are." That was Isaac.

The sound was obviously some distance away, yet he could hear the words clearly.

"Hey, Buck!" Pete yelled. "We put some knots in the rope, so you can climb it. Let's go!"

They must both be leaning over the Pit, Buck decided, because he could hear much of their conversation.

". . . think he got out?"

"How? . . . Bike's still here. . . ."

"Shine that lantern all around down there. . . . any way he could have . . . ?"

"Buck?" Pete was calling again. "Nobody knows I've got

the truck and I won't be able to get it tomorrow. C'mon, man. We were just messing with you."

Yeah? Buck thought. *Tell me about it.*

Their conversation again.

Pete: "There's our flashlight."

Isaac: "Where?"

Pete: "There! Look! You'd think . . ."

Isaac: "What's that dark over there? Looks like water. Over to the right . . . Man, it *is* water. . . . You don't figure . . . tried to . . . swim out?" More silence. "What if he didn't *make* it, Pete?"

"Shut up! Just shut up!" Pete's voice. "Why don't you climb down there and check it out?"

"Why don't *you*? This whole thing was your idea. . . ."

"I weigh more than you. . . ."

"So what? Neither of us can hold the other. . . ."

"Buck!" Pete was bellowing now. "Enough already. Just climb the frickin' rope if you're down there. Your folks are going a little nuts. . . . Calling everyone. . . ."

Buck leaned back against the rock wall and buried his face in his arms. He hadn't wanted his folks to worry, but of course they were. What did he expect? He remembered Katie standing there with that bag of M&Ms, holding it out for him, probably blaming herself over and over now for not asking him more questions when he said he was going to Bealls'.

He knew that Mr. Beall would be questioned, and he would tell them he'd sold Buck four batteries. Then Joel would tell them about the headlamp, and—thinking that Buck was fooling around in the woods at night—Mel, when

271

he got home, would be searching every path along the river. How could he let them go on worrying like this when all he would have to do was go climb up the stupid rope and let Pukeman drive him home?

He looked back the way he had come . . . then the other direction, with more and more openings to explore. . . . When would he ever get down here again? When would he ever get another chance? Still, how could he let the family worry like this? Katie would probably have told them about that note to David and the police would be searching for him in the old Ambassador hotel. Made perfect sense. He'd wanted the headlamp to explore that old hotel at night.

"Okay," he called finally, and turned himself around. He'd go home.

He slithered a few yards back into the narrow passage and then, getting no answer, called to Pete again.

"Okay," he yelled, louder, but the last syllable was drowned out by the distant sound of an engine starting up, the noise growing fainter and fainter, and then Buck was alone for real.

35

PASSAGES

Now he'd done it. *Stubborn, stubborn, stubborn.* All the breath seemed to go out of him, and Buck lay motionless on the cave floor, trying to think.

Maybe they'd gone to get help? Not bloody likely—not yet, anyway. Maybe they figured that someone else had come along, heard Buck yelling, and had gone for a ladder and got him out. A tall roof ladder might have done it. No, probably not. If that had happened and he'd been rescued, wouldn't his bike be gone too? No, Pukeman *had* to know that he was still down here.

What chance did he have now to get out? Who would likely come all the way out here? There wasn't even a road leading back to the Pit, just a trail in the weeds where people had come to gawk before the county boarded it up. Buck didn't even know how to get here himself, except what he'd heard Pete saying to the other guys, something about Brandon Junction and Mountain Road. . . .

He crawled backward until he could sit up, then reached for his cell phone again to see what time it was. Did he only imagine it or was the time display getting dim? It was five after eleven, but . . . He snapped it open and punched in "phone information." The battery was low. Very low. Only one bar left and it was flickering off and on. At some point, even the time and the light from his cell phone would be gone. It was his only backup if something happened to the headlamp. He closed it quickly. Now he *really* had to be careful.

Okay, stay calm, he told himself. What was so different from a couple of minutes ago, when he was debating whether to answer Pete? Nothing, except it would be a while longer before someone called the rescue squad. Meanwhile. . . .

He ate another M&M to give him energy, got on his knees again, and began a crawl. It was murder on his kneecaps, but at least he was making better time than when he was flat on his stomach, trying to get through. And he was cold. He had to keep moving.

Each time he came to a wider passage, he stopped and sat back to rest. Sometimes it was only a place he could stretch out one leg, not both. And sometimes he could stand up if he bent double at the waist. Or the only way he could sit was in the knee-chest position, looking up through a narrow chimney of rock, ending in darkness, whether rock or night sky, he couldn't tell.

There were two distinct places he made a choice which way to go. At each of those points, Buck built a small tower of rocks and then, in the clay nearby, scratched an arrow to show the way he was going.

He was tired, though. And cold. And hungry. Excitement could keep you going for a long time, but it couldn't fill your stomach. How long would his batteries last? he wondered. Seventy-two hours, the instructions had read, on low beam. But he needed to keep it on high occasionally to check for danger ahead. He had one more set of batteries; that was it. He tried not to punish himself for having bought the four-pack instead of the six.

In some places the passage, if he could even call it that, had walls that were wrinkled like corrugated tin. *Like crawling through someone's intestines,* David would say, and Buck smiled at the thought. David could turn almost anything into something gross. Buck remembered the time they'd been looking at a photo of a once-submerged cave, with knobby calcite growths on the walls and floor, and David had called it cat barf.

He was grateful when he made another turn and found that not only was the ceiling high enough for him to stand, but there was a thin stream of water trickling down the side of the rock. He cupped his hands to catch it but got so little that he finally took off his helmet, pressed his cheek against the rock, and lapped at the water with his tongue, leaving the sharp taste of cold chalky rock in his mouth until he had just enough to swallow. It was delicious. He closed his eyes and swallowed again, and again, and again, one hand on the front of his jacket to keep it dry.

He took a new direction and started forward, then gave a sudden yelp. Two black eyes were coming directly at him, almost colliding with his face. Then, with a swoop, they flew upward, grazing his forehead. *Bats.*

Others clung like beans on a vine to the low ceiling ahead, only occasionally twitching, turning. Buck knew that if he didn't disturb them, he could get by without incident.

Every so often the passageway opened into a larger space, almost room size, and that, in turn, was connected with another passageway farther on, like galleries in a museum. He crawled into one where the flowstone was more like ruffles—brains, David would describe them—ridge after ridge to crawl over, and Buck couldn't be sure he wasn't just going around in circles, stumbling and lurching toward any smooth surface where he might be able to stand up. He didn't dare make any turn he couldn't remember. How did he know it was already too late to find his way back? A quick stab of fear made him suck in his breath. An insect dropped on him, down the neck of his shirt. Buck had no free hand to dislodge it. Several minutes passed before he found a level spot where he could stop and shake it out.

He tried to see everything, memorize it so he could describe it to David. Buck had never thought of himself as lucky—not until he'd discovered the Hole—but now, coming to a huge rock that looked as though it had been split in half, he was amazed to see what he guessed was the faint imprint of a leaf—part of a fern, he thought, about as big as his hand.

He maneuvered himself a little closer until both feet were solid, then stood transfixed, wanting to run a finger over it.

He blew on it instead. A thin cloud of clay dust rose in the air. And then, to his wonder, he saw that it wasn't a fern at all, but the fossilized skeleton of a trilobite—three fourths of one, anyway—one of the earliest creatures to inhabit the earth. Its three segmented lobes were unmistakable. He had seen photographs of them in almost every caving book he had studied. He knew he was standing for sure where a sea had once been.

"David," he said aloud. "I'm naming you David."

He took out his cell phone to take a photo. There was a click, but no flash. Now, when he tried to check the time, there was no time at all.

• • •

He had no way of knowing whether it was the middle of the night or the middle of morning. Whether it was still Saturday or Sunday now. All Buck knew was that he was more tired than he could ever remember being, his thigh and calf muscles aching with the strain of keeping his balance, crawling sideways or up and down.

He found a spot smooth enough to sit on, and folded his arms across his chest, but he was too cold, especially his legs. He took the rope and wound it around and around his calves, pressing his jeans more tightly to his legs. Taking off his old jacket, he examined it for zippers, and discovered a long one under the collar. When he unzipped it, there was a hood, tightly rolled up, that he unfurled. He looked for more pockets, more zippers, and found two more on the inside, left and right.

There was nothing in the right pocket. But in the left,

he pulled out the half piece of cheap survival blanket that David had given him once, which had torn on the center crease and, he saw, was threatening to tear on the other folds as well. He put his jacket back on, drew the hood over his head, pulled his knees up, and, as gently as possible, covered himself with the piece of Mylar blanket. His head dropped. Ten minutes, he promised, and then he'd keep going.

When he woke, however, he could tell through the fog of sleep that it had been longer than that. Perhaps much longer. He'd dreamed too, a weird dream about trying to find something. Yet when he found it, whatever it was, it belonged to someone else.

Carefully he straightened up, rubbing the crick in his neck, and refolded the survival blanket. He unwrapped the rope from around his legs, and when he finally got to his feet, he relieved himself against the boulder where he had been sitting and moved on, to see as much as he could before rescuers came.

Another thought, and this time it was like a punch in the gut. Maybe no one was coming. Maybe none of the guys had told. If Pete and Isaac started to think that Buck had fallen in that stream and been sucked under, or tried to swim his way out and didn't make it, maybe they wouldn't tell anyone. Wouldn't want it known that they were responsible. And by the time one of them cracked, it could be days from now. A week. Much too late . . .

"Stay calm," he said, aloud this time. Or, as Gramps would say, *Settle yourself.* Wasn't that the first rule of caving? Almost anything you could do when you were super scared would be a huge mistake.

Better to keep himself busy, keep moving, backward or forward, what did it matter as long as it could disguise the thumping in his chest and keep him warm. He knew this much—there were no footprints here but his own. There was no graffiti on the walls, no beer cans or gum wrappers or cigarette butts on the floor. Nothing that gave any evidence that anyone had been here—ever.

Occasionally Buck came to a small stream or a pool, enough for a long drink. When the path divided again, he left another little tower of rocks and, this time, the wrapper of one of the three precious M&M packets to show the way he had come.

He was hungry, no disguising that. His stomach grumbled and ached, and he finally gave in and opened the second pack of candies. He remembered the way Katie had held them out to him, wishing his hand had clamped down on more of them. The next time he made a turn, he was both thrilled and dismayed to see that his path was almost completely blocked except for a tall lopsided V-shaped slit in the rock, about four feet off the cavern floor. Poking his head into the opening near the bottom, he could see a high-ceilinged gallery ahead, and the headlamp shone on crystal soda-straw formations hanging from the ceiling like clustered subterranean chandeliers.

He gasped, gaping in wonderment. The Hole was nothing compared to this. He *had* to go through. Had to see it. This was the most wonderful thing he'd seen yet, and *he* had discovered it! It was incredible! Wait till he told David! But how to get over there? It was too high to step over. Too narrow and jagged at the bottom to slither through on his stomach. Gravity alone would pull his body downward, not only shredding his clothes, but possibly entrapping him. With his feet off the floor, he would not even have his knees available to propel him over to the other side.

In a cave, you had to plan every single footstep before you took it; you had to know exactly where each foot would go. If he crawled up the wall on this side and tried stepping into the V with his foot, leaving his other foot free to swing himself over, his sneaker might turn sideways, down into the point of the V. If that happened, he could be stuck there with no easy way, if any, to pull himself out.

Directing the light from his headlamp straight ahead, he could see that this cavern seemed to go on and on. There was no way of telling how far he had come already. It was the chance of a lifetime. His skin tingled with excitement. He decided he had to try.

36

THE LAST
OF EVERYTHING

Correction: He *wanted* to try. Nobody had a gun to his head. Still . . .

He could tell by the pounding in his ears that he was scared, with good reason. He didn't even try to convince himself he shouldn't have left the Pit. Should have stayed right there till someone found him. And then . . . to lose his chance to go back with Pete and Ethan . . .

If only he had put on hiking boots that morning instead of his sneakers. If only he had knee pads and arm pads, he might be able to slither his body across the sharpest point of the V. But he didn't, and if-onlys didn't help. He was here, and this was his chance.

He took the rope and stuffed it between some of the sharp

spikes at the bottom of the V, packing it down to make a small platform. Then he scrambled his way up the rocky wall till he reached the bottom of the V and could see the floor on the other side.

Still, he clung to the wall and reconsidered. Even if his right shoe balanced perfectly level on the platform he had made, the other leg had to come forward and pass it in that narrow space. His entire weight would be on the foot in the V. And it was that foot that had to push off and propel him over. What if his legs became entangled and he tripped? What if the right foot tipped sideways anyway and got wedged between the rocky spikes?

There was no other way to get through, and it was either try this or go all the way back to the Pit and wait for rescue, without exploring the most important part of his discovery.

He made the decision to go ahead. If he could brace his hands or forearms against the rock wall of the V to take some pressure off his foot, it might work. It would require all the arm strength he had.

Buck gingerly extended his right foot. He placed the sole of his sneaker lightly down on the rope platform between the spikes. *Wait*, he told himself, bracing his arms on the rock wall before putting more weight on his foot.

Carefully . . . carefully . . . pushing harder and harder against the rocky walls with his arms . . . he brought the left leg forward. . . .

But there wasn't enough space for his legs to pass without raising his left foot higher . . . higher still. . . . His right foot began to sink.

And suddenly the rope platform shifted. His right foot

tipped. He felt the jolt as his sneaker settled sideways, the left foot suspended in midair with no place to go.

For a moment he couldn't breathe. His sneaker was growing tighter around his arch. Every second he perched there, the weight of his body on a single foot, gravity was at work.

Far more experienced cavers than he had been trapped in a similar manner. Using his arms, he pushed against the walls of the V with all his strength. Buck attempted to lift his foot even a centimeter, and tried to rock it gently toe to heel—back and forth, back and forth . . .

His shoulders throbbed, his biceps ached. His arms began to tremble with the effort he was expending to take the weight off his foot.

"C'mon, c'mon!" he said aloud. He felt his foot begin to move as the shoelaces loosened. Suddenly his foot was out of the sneaker. Using the trapped shoe for a launch pad, he gave it one swift downward push and propelled himself over to the other side.

For a minute or so, he just lay on the limestone floor, too freaked out and shaken to sit up. But gradually, as he felt his heartbeat begin to slow, he raised himself up on one hand and looked around.

Ahead of him, he could see the largest gallery yet—not as big as the Pit, perhaps, but the most fantastic. It was even awesome where he sat, with knobby formations protruding from the ground like pale carrots. He rose up and crawled back to the V to free his sneaker and the rope. Then, carefully, he made his way through the stalagmites toward the delicate crystal straws hanging from the ceiling in the room beyond.

How far did this go? Once again, the headlamp captured a long crooked passageway of sorts, like a mirror seen in a second mirror, where one reflected tunnel displayed another reflected tunnel, and they would go on into infinity. He was careful not to touch the seemingly translucent straws, and was mindful of where he put his feet.

"Awesome!" he said aloud. "Oh, man, David. You should be here."

He wished he had a caving book with him to identify some of the structures. He should be taking notes, drawing maps or diagrams for the cavers who would come here next. Buck felt almost as eager to get out and tell people about it as he had been to explore in secret.

There were rocky formations that resembled familiar objects if seen from the right angle—a car . . . a boot . . . a head. In another gallery, he came across a few fallen rocks that resembled, from almost any angle, a huge chair. There was the back, the seat, two arms on either side, one a little lower than the other. He was almost tempted to climb up and sit in it.

On a rocky bridge, he stopped to reconnoiter, and looked about for the place he had entered this part of the cavern. For the first time he realized a basic of caving he should have learned long ago: an entrance doesn't necessarily look the same going back as it did when you entered.

He had figured that the tall V in the rocky wall would be unmistakable from any angle. Now, even from here—five feet or more above the cavern floor—there appeared to be many different directions he could go.

Had he truly not marked the direction he was taking

once he had freed his sneaker and moved on? Buck climbed down off the bridge the way he had come, foregoing an even larger gallery beyond. He looked for the pointed rock with the three dangling stalactites he had seen shortly after he made it through the V.

There—he saw them, not ten feet away. No . . . the rock wasn't the same. As he moved forward, he saw another three to his left. . . . No, not them . . .

He suddenly felt overwhelmingly tired. Without food, he was easily exhausted. It was a mistake to try to find his way back when he was this weary, so once again, he found a smooth place where he could sit. This time he made a cushion of the rope for insulation, sat down on that, drew up his legs, and wrapped what was left of the fraying piece of survival blanket around him, tucking it in under his thighs. Almost immediately, his chin dropped down on his chest, and he slept.

• • •

He awoke in total darkness and was completely disoriented. The only sound he heard was his own breathing, that and an intermittent growling of his stomach. He had never seen the world so black. Blacker than black. For a minute he wondered if he might have gone blind, and rubbed at his eyes, for there was no vision at all, even though he could feel his eyes wide open: no specks, no dots, no traces of light. He brought his hand up to within inches of his face but saw nothing, and finally realized that the headlamp had gone out.

Buck had nothing to rely on now but touch. There were

two batteries left. If he lost even one, the headlamp wouldn't work. His cell phone was dead—no light there.

It took a few moments before he had the courage to move again. Then, carefully, carefully, in slow motion, he lowered the hood of his jacket, lifted the headlamp band from around his helmet, and placed it in his lap. Feeling for the latch of the battery case, he opened it and removed the dead batteries. Unzipping his pocket with the cell phone in it, he dropped the batteries in and zipped it up again. Then, his pulse quickening, he unzipped his right pocket and took out the two new batteries—the last two—and transferred them to his left hand.

Carefully, he took back one battery, explored it with his fingers, and delicately, like a surgeon with a scalpel, he pressed it into the case until he heard the snap. Then the second battery, and with trembling fingers, he . . .

He dropped it.

No!

Don't move, he told himself. With one hand, he felt to the right of the headlamp. Then the ground to his left, and could tell that it sloped, to where, he didn't know. Felt around to his right again. Dust, clay . . . No battery. He gingerly lifted the headlamp in his lap, and felt between his thighs. Nothing. *Oh, please! Please!*

The left hand roaming again. Then the right. And finally, tucked under one thigh, he found the last battery. Holding it tightly between two fingers, he felt for the positive end and thrust it into the case. Then he closed the lid firmly, checked that it was locked, and flipped the switch.

Instantly the world of tan and gray and white and brown

returned. Buck tipped his head back against the rock wall, taking big gulps of air, waiting until the pounding of his heart had subsided. Then he slipped the headband over his helmet, pulled up the hood of his jacket, and finally got to his feet.

He had no idea now what time it was, what day it was. His teeth chattered with cold. All he wanted was a marker showing the way back to the Pit—a little tower of rocks, an M&M wrapper, a sneaker print or arrow in the clay . . . How he would get back over the V he didn't know. Make a platform of the rope, his shoes, his jacket, perhaps . . .

As he moved from one rocky gallery to the next, climbing, crawling, slithering, rolling, squirming, he found the air growing misty with fog, and wondered if he was going deeper and deeper, expending all this time and energy getting farther away from the one place he could be rescued. When the new batteries gave out, he absolutely would not be able to find his way back in the dark.

He had made one bad decision not to get out when he could, when Pukeman had offered; he couldn't compound it now by making another. He had to get back to the Pit. He decided to allow himself one hundred steps or paces away from the bridge, and if he found nothing familiar or promising, he would start the slow journey back to the bridge and try another route. From now on the bridge would be his focal point, and he'd never get so far away he couldn't find a path back.

Buck counted as he went, taking slow, measured steps, shoulders bent to avoid overhanging rocks, neck aching. He was overwhelmingly hungry, and his mind kept focusing on

Holly Homestyle's chicken pot pie. He thought of the buttery crust, the rough chunks of potato and onion, and could feel the saliva gathering in his mouth. That and a chocolate soda, the kind you could only get at the marble soda fountain in Talbert's Drugs. *Oh, man.* He fantasized about holding those long spoons with the small scoop at the end so you could pry out the last of the chocolate syrup at the bottom of the tall soda glasses, the little dab of real whipped cream that he'd save till the very last. . . . And finally, unable to stand it any longer, he reached in his pocket and ate the last of the M&Ms.

His strength was giving out, however, and he reached the count of eighty-six and knew he had to rest. He slid down to the cavern floor, his cheek against the wall, licking the tiny veins of water that trickled into his face. Then he surveyed his outstretched legs with half-closed eyes.

He was more than filthy. His jeans were worn through at the knees, and his kneecaps were bruised and a little bloodied. One pant leg was so covered with wet clay that he couldn't even tell what color it was supposed to be. The laces of his sneakers were caked as well, and the canvas along the top had torn. The hands in his lap were as rough as sandpaper, and blistered too.

Perhaps he should just stay right here, he thought. He could not imagine that one of the boys had not told by now. But even the roof of his mouth felt dusty, and he was almost too tired to sleep. How many times had he heard his mom say that after a hard day at Holly's—"I swear I'm almost too tired to sleep."

He felt his head nod and he jerked it up again. He really

288

shouldn't let himself fall asleep without the Mylar blanket. It had torn again, and soon there would be little left. If he didn't keep moving he could develop hypothermia. But his eyes closed in spite of himself. And once again, without the sound of his own grunts and footsteps, all he could hear was his own breathing and the faraway ticking of a clock. . . .

A clock?

Buck opened his eyes suddenly and listened.

It wasn't a clock. Too irregular for that. *Plip, plip, plip . . . plippa plop. Plip, plip, plip . . . plippa plop . . .*

He rose up on his knees, eyes enormous. *Plip, plip . . . plippa plop.* And with each drop, there was a slight echo.

He was on his feet again, following the sound. *One in a million . . .* The rhythm stopped, then quickly resumed again after a moment or two, but as he propelled himself forward, lurching toward any handhold he could find, he could tell that the sound was getting louder.

Plip, plip, plip . . . plippa plop . . .

There could be a hundred places here in the cavern where water was dripping. He'd already reached his limit of one hundred paces from the bridge, and if he kept telling himself he'd go back and didn't . . .

Approaching the sound, he scrambled over two huge rocks in his path. At the crest, the beam of the headlamp shone on a trickle of water sliding down a high rock wall—a long drop at the end—six or seven feet . . .

And as Buck lowered his eyes to the pool below, the light full on the water, he saw beautiful sparkles of color around one edge—the only bright colors he had seen in days. Green here, yellow there—a twinkling of red and orange, gleaming at him in the light of the headlamp, some of them reflected back in the water. Was he hallucinating? If you went too long without seeing color, is this what happened?

Unable to take his eyes off the strange-colored dots, he carefully descended the other side of a boulder and approached the pool. The colors were coming from tiny round disks scattered there on the rock. So thirsty he fell to his knees, his cupped hands bringing water to his mouth as fast as he could drink, again . . . and again . . . and again. And when he was satiated, he raised himself up and looked about. The colors were still there.

Suddenly, disbelieving, Buck leaned over and studied them closely. *Skittles!* His mouth fell open, and he looked up, training the headlamp on a small passageway that went up, up. He threw back his head and yelled with delight. It could only lead to the Hole. And home.

37

ROPE TRICK

First things first.

Buck walked all around the pool, his sneakers making deep imprints in the wet clay, and gathered up the Skittles, one by one. The first disk on his tongue tasted of grape and made his stomach rumble in anticipation.

He had to get them all—the lemon, the green apple, the strawberry; the orange was so close to the water that he got the sleeve of his jacket wet in retrieving it, but he didn't care. He knew the way home, and, meager as the Skittles were, they were his fuel for getting there.

But it wasn't so simple.

The high ceiling above the pool dropped dramatically at one end, with just enough space for Buck to walk beneath it. It was here that the chimney began, but how far up did it go? He strained his memory, trying to remember if he had heard a splash or a ping when the Skittles fell out those many weeks ago. Had he heard anything at all? Or had he just felt them slipping from his overalls pocket?

Think! he instructed himself, but his brain was useless. He wanted another Skittle—lemon this time, then another.

He crammed the rest of them, sticky now, in his pocket and zipped it up, trying to devote his full concentration to getting out. It was like a trapdoor in a ceiling, with no way to crawl up the walls.

How could it be that he had come this far—all the way from the Pit—and had unknowingly discovered a cavern under the sliver of Blue Ridge Mountain that had diverted their country road eleven miles around it—only to find that he couldn't get out?

If ever he needed Katie to tell their parents about the note, it was now. *Please,* he thought, *please call David. Forget the Ambassador Hotel. Tell the rescuers to comb through Wilmer's meadow till they find the outcropping of rock, and feel the cool air coming up out of the hole. If they crawl in, if they call my name, I might be able to hear them.*

But how would she know all this? Why would she even call David, or believe anything other than what he had told her? And, worst luck of all, David was at Survival Camp, ironically, and his mom was on a trip.

One more Skittle—orange—and he would stop. He remembered now that when he'd looked down after the Skittles fell, there was a sort of shelf, perhaps ten feet below. Some Skittles must have missed the shelf and gone on to fall around the pool. Looking up again, he could see the shelf, and that there was room to get around it if he was climbing the chimney, but how could he get inside it at all?

He had a rope, and he knew how to make a knot or a loop in it and heave it up a hillside during a rock climb in hopes it would snag on something strong enough to hold his weight. But how do you throw rope up a hole only two and a half feet wide?

He squatted down, arms on his knees, forehead resting on the backs of his hands. He was too tired, too hungry, too cold, and now that his feet were wet, colder still. The gnawing in his stomach was painful, but even worse was the knowledge that he'd had a chance to get out when Pete called to him and he hadn't answered soon enough. He might have ruined his only chance of rescue.

He had to face it: He'd wanted Pukeman to worry. Wanted Pete to suffer. Buck was too freakin' stubborn to save his own neck. His mind just wasn't functioning right, he knew. Lack of food, lack of sleep. He turned back to the pool and drank handfuls of water to keep hydrated. *Think,* he commanded again.

There had to be another way. Maybe he had overlooked the simplest solution—find something to stand on. At this point, if David were here, his friend would say, "Yeah. Anybody happen to have a stepstool?" And make them laugh. Or not.

Buck gave a low moan. Everything around him had been molded in place millions of years ago. There were jagged rock formations at the other end of the pool, but he could no more tip one over than he could have tipped over the

Washington monument on his class trip. He stroked his closed eyelids, which felt heavy with the sleep he wouldn't allow. Hadn't he, when he'd last left the bridge, come upon a rock slide? Reddish-brown rocks at the foot of a boulder? If he could find one about two feet high, and roll it . . .

Maybe he had seen those rocks when he'd first entered this gallery. Or maybe they were a lot farther back than he could remember. He realized now how disoriented he had become, because when he headed in what he thought was the direction of the bridge, he came to the rock slide first.

Never mind. All he had to remember were the pool and the chimney.

There were, of course, no round rocks. There were huge square blocks, and diamond-shaped rocks, and rectangular chunks of limestone. The best Buck could find amid the tumble was an octagonal rock, perhaps two feet in diameter, that was sunk several inches into the clay floor.

He sat down on the square block and counted the Skittles in his hand. Four left. One now, one when he got the rock out of the clay, one when he got the rock beneath the chimney, and the last one when he'd climbed the chimney.

He chose a purple Skittle and waited until it was only a memory on his tongue. Then he lowered himself to the floor with his back against the square rock, feet against the octagonal rock, and, lifting his butt off the floor, pushed with his feet as hard as he could. He felt the rock move. Only a centimeter, but it moved. If he had to do this all the way to the pool, he would do it.

Five hard pushes and it was out of its hole. Buck turned around and stood up, leaning over to brace both hands against the rock, and pushed as hard as he could. It moved a couple of inches. Pushed again. An inch more. Again. Again. Finally, Buck stopped counting and just pushed.

• • •

How long had it taken to push the rock to the pool? Hours? Half a day? Buck had never appreciated before just how much all that hoeing of bean rows and lifting of crates and biking uphill had done for him. For his biceps and hamstrings.

The octagonal rock was in place below the chimney at one edge of the pool, and Buck ate a strawberry Skittle and rested.

When he was ready for the next step, full of all the water he could drink, he found that even though the rock seemed to settle into the damp clay, it moved whenever Buck tried to stand on it. He gathered a few smaller rocks to place against it—but again, each time he tried to mount it, it moved, and he fell off.

Buck had one more trick to try. Taking the rope, he wound it around and around the base of the rock, as close as he could get it, pushing it in with his fingers to fill up every small space in the clay. And this time, when he stepped on the rock—first one foot, then . . . slowly . . . the other . . . the rock barely moved.

He took a few breaths, then set his sights on the ridges above him. His head, his shoulders, his arms were inside the chimney, but everything depended on getting a foothold. Reaching as high as he could, he grabbed the stony projections on either side and tried to pull his feet up into the chimney, but he was too low. Not even Pukeman could climb up a chimney with his hands alone.

He rested a moment, and then he jumped. The next thing he knew, he was tumbling onto the rock below, scraping his ankle as he fell. One leg of his jeans got wet in the pool.

Buck rolled over on the clay bank, head buried in his arm, almost too tired to think. There was no other way out. He had to do this. *Rest,* he told himself. *Just rest a minute.*

The minute turned into several minutes, but when he opened his eyes again, conscious of the cold, he was also refreshed, and he knew he would try as long as it took.

First he made sure that the rock was secure in its rope and clay base. Then he gingerly climbed on again, balancing his feet just so, and with the beam of his headlamp, he scouted out the knobs and ridges to aim for. He bent his knees slightly, his body in a crouch, and he jumped.

His right hand grabbed a stony knob and held on; his left hand missed, but his arm came down on a ridge that supported his weight—at a crooked angle, to be sure, but he was higher now than before.

Carefully, carefully, he drew up one knee, searching out a landing place for his right foot. He couldn't see anything below him, but he felt the toe of his sneaker strike the wall at some point. Buck braced his back and shoulders against the wall, his foot pushing hard on the wall across from him. The other foot came up to join it, and Buck was scrunched inside the chimney as tight as a boxer's fist inside a glove.

For a minute or two, Buck let his arms rest, his back and legs doing all the work. Then, slowly, he began the difficult job of maneuvering his body up the shaft. A foot moved, then a shoulder, an arm, a hand. . . . At times his thigh and calf muscles seemed to be going numb, and once or twice his body slipped, and he had to tense every muscle he owned to keep from going down. A foot, a shoulder, an arm, a hand . . . up and up, no more than an inch at a time, Buck "chimneyed" up the rock.

"Don't let go," he told himself, gasping. "Keep pushing! Push!"

And he did. If he got to the ledge, he could rest. He could not give up. He'd come too far for this. He pretended that David was there at the top, looking down at him, yelling instructions, encouragement.

Almost there! David would say. *You're going to do it, Buck! Get your butt up here. We're gonna make history!*

When he was high enough to reach the ledge, Buck pulled himself onto it, breathing through his mouth in loud gasps. He was rewarded with three Skittles that had landed there, and he ate them all. But after he had sat, legs dangling, for two or three minutes, he was ready for the homestretch. Pulling himself up until he could stand on the ledge, he lifted one foot and placed it against the wall. Then he braced his back and lifted the other foot. Up the shaft he went in a slow, laborious climb.

Finally his hands reached the top, and then, just like crawling out of the Hole, he hoisted himself onto the rocky floor—first his trembling elbows, then his knees, and he was out.

He ate a green apple Skittle.

• • •

His legs were so shaky he didn't know whether he should rest for a while or go on. The headlamp made the decision, for the beam was so faint now that there was only a dim circle of light on the walls of the passageway, almost none at all up ahead.

Buck made it as far as the first turn, and then, like the closing of a curtain, the batteries gave out. He had used so much power on high beam that there was nothing left.

Darkness all around him. Was this the final test, he wondered? The final punishment? He had only been here once, but he trusted himself now to find his way out. If he moved his left hand along the rocky wall, looking for the turnoff to the Hole, and his right hand along the ceiling, to warn him when it was time to crawl or, lower yet, to slither along on his stomach, he could do it, he thought.

Yes, there were the arrows! He could feel their taped edges, even though he couldn't see them. And eventually the blackness that kept his eyes huge turned to a midnight gray, and then a smoky gray, and finally he detected the most welcome sight he had ever seen: the little patch of light beneath the Hole.

38

IMPRINTS ON STONE

Forty minutes later, Buck smelled the scent of meadow grass, as wonderful as anything he could remember smelling in his life. Well, maybe not better than chicken pot pie. He could hear the buzzing of a bee and the distant noise of a car on the road as he emerged from the Hole, like some newly hatched grub, half blinded by sunlight.

He couldn't believe the colors! It was as though the world had turned brighter than it had ever been before—the orange of an autumn tree was more orange than he could remember. A yellow bush, brilliant in the afternoon sun. The greens—a fantastic variety!

And the heat! Why was he wearing a jacket?

Buck shaded his eyes with one hand as he turned and

stared up at the hump of mountain under which he had crawled, that somehow connected the Hole to the Pit on the other side.

How far was that? How long had it taken?

He was too tired to figure it out. Buck folded up the headlamp and slipped it in one pocket, then removed his helmet and jacket and climbed over the rocky entrance of the Hole. Weaving slightly from fatigue and hunger, he stumbled into Wilmer's meadow and grabbed a handful of daisies, remnants of summer, and stuffed them in his mouth, barely chewing in his eagerness to swallow them down and stop the ache in his stomach.

He could tell that his mind wasn't computing quite the way it should. As though he was slipping in and out of sleep. He knew he was hungry, knew he was sore all over, that he had to get home, but somehow felt he couldn't go home without his bike.

Buck made his way along the line of woods until he came to the road. It took all his energy to go down in the gulley and then up onto the shoulder, where he stood with his thumb outstretched, waiting for a ride. Cars didn't come by all that often.

The first one that passed him whizzed on by, but the second—a beat-up SUV—slowed to a stop, and the driver leaned toward the passenger window, looking him over.

"What the heck happened to you?" he asked jovially. "Looks like you had a little accident. Come on, get in. But you better get a potato sack from back in there and spread it on the seat. You're muddy right up to your armpits."

Buck did as he was told and exhaled with relief as he sank

into the seat. When did car seats get so soft? Hitchhiking was another thing he was forbidden to do, however. How many rules had he broken since he'd started caving without David?

The car moved forward, but the man glanced over. "Is that what happened? You in an accident?"

"Yeah," said Buck, and leaned back, eyes half closed, his limbs absolutely exhausted.

"Where you headed?"

"Uh . . . BBBBBBrandon Junction."

"Whew! That far, huh? Somebody waiting for you there?"

"Yeah." Lying came easy now. Easier than answering questions. Buck honestly did not think he had the strength for that.

"Well, that's a couple more miles than I was planning on going, but I think I could run you that far. Tom Hoover, by the way."

"Nice to meet you," said Buck, and closed his eyes completely.

They rode another few minutes in silence and the driver said, "Been strange weather, hasn't it?" And when Buck didn't answer, he said, "Seemed like fall was here for sure, and now it's summer again."

No reply. *Don't fall asleep,* Buck told himself. He had to get his bike.

"You know," Tom Hoover said, "you look like somebody who could stand a little lunch, and I got half a beef sandwich back there." He reached around behind his seat as he drove and pulled out a small white sack with a mustard stain on the side. "You want it?"

Buck's eyes opened and he reached for the sack, nodding. And then he was pushing the bread and beef toward his mouth as though he couldn't get it in fast enough, and the man said, "Hey, hey! You don't wanna make yourself sick now. Go a little easy."

Too tired to be embarrassed, Buck swallowed, almost without chewing. Another bite and another, before he finally began to slow, and shoved the remaining crust in his mouth.

"How long since you've eaten, buddy?" the man asked.

"It's . . . bbbbeen a while," said Buck.

"I can see that." The man had red hair on his arms and the backs of his hands, and Buck's head nodded as he stared at the glow of those hairs in the afternoon sunlight. At least, he figured it was afternoon.

"Well, wish I had something more to offer, but all I've got is coffee. You want some of that?"

Buck nodded again, and when Tom handed him the thermos, he didn't even bother to pour the coffee in the plastic cup that formed the top; just lifted it to his mouth and drank and drank and drank until it was gone. Then he lifted it a final time to drain out every little drop before he remembered any manners at all.

"Thank you," he said.

They must have ridden for ten minutes, and then the man said, "Okay, young fella, Brandon Junction coming up. Don't see any car here waiting, though. You sure of where you're going?"

Buck wiped one arm across his mouth and tried to wake up. "Yeah. Brandon Junction and MMMountain Road."

"Well, I don't know that I could get you through on Mountain, because there's all kinds of police cars and fire trucks and I don't know what down that road a ways. You heard about the kid . . . the kid who . . ." The man was studying Buck hard now, and then he said softly, "Holy Moses, Mary, and Joseph . . . You know what? I think I'm going to drive you right there."

He turned the wheel, and finally, a few minutes later when they reached Mountain Road, Buck woke up.

He could see the rotating blue and red lights before he could make out the police cars. Then the fire truck came into view, and after that a rescue squad truck. Little groups of people stood talking among themselves, watching the rescue workers moving about the opening of the Pit. The top had been removed.

As the car came closer, a policeman turned and motioned for them to go around. Instead, Tom stopped the car, and as the officer started over, Buck opened the passenger side door and got out.

Standing there in the field with Isaac and Ethan and Rod, Pete had his back to the car, but as Buck approached, Ethan's eyes widened and his lips moved, but no sound came out that Buck could hear.

Pete Ketterman turned, his face suddenly drained of color, and he stared in astonishment as Buck came up to him.

"Where's my bbbbike?" Buck said.

"B . . . Buck!?" Pete was asking it like a question, as though he couldn't believe what he saw. *"Buck!"* he said again, and then Rod and Isaac said it even louder. "It's Buck!"

And everyone turned—the firemen, the officers, the rescue workers, but the next thing Buck knew, his dad was breaking through the crowd, rushing toward him, and Buck was enveloped in Don Anderson's strong arms, in a hug that almost knocked the breath out of him.

• • •

He fell asleep in the car going home. Vaguely remembered his dad shaking Tom Hoover's hand; might have remembered stumbling up the stairs and onto his bed. He slept hard and deep with only wisps of dreams floating through his head, none of them making much sense.

When he woke again in the early morning, it wasn't because he'd had enough sleep, but because he was overwhelmingly thirsty. He found a stack of cookies and a glass of milk, warm now, on his nightstand. He devoured them, went to the bathroom, then slept some more.

When he woke at last, Buck sat up and saw that Mom had thrown a towel over his bed before he crashed, and he was still streaked with mud. The clock read 5:30, and he was confused. He went into the bathroom and drank two full glasses of water, then rested his hands on the sink and startled suddenly when he saw himself in the mirror.

There were bluish circles under his eyes, yet the eyelids were red. His hair was matted on his forehead and caked with dust, his face streaked on all sides by sweat marks in the dirt. And man, did he ever smell.

Someone had already removed his shoes and jacket, but he turned on the shower and stepped in fully clothed, then watched drowsily as brown rivulets of muddy water streamed off him, pooled around the drain, and were swallowed up in a circular motion. He reached for the shampoo and poured a huge glob over his head, almost too weak to wash his hair, but clawed at it a few times and scratched his itchy scalp, then simply stood with his head down, watching the water stream off the ends of his fingers.

He wondered if he had actually fallen asleep standing up, because he was finally conscious of the water turning cooler, and realized he must have used all the water in the hot water tank. Buck turned off the shower, took off his wet clothes, and dried off.

It was only when he had pulled on a clean pair of jeans and an old Orioles sweatshirt that he realized how hungry he was. Ravenous. He could hear conversation coming from the kitchen and figured that Gramps and Joel were home; heard the clink of dishes and realized that the family was probably eating dinner. What day was it?

He thought he remembered his mom grabbing his face in her hands when Dad had brought him home, thanking God and crying. Knew that Katie and Joel and Uncle Mel had been somewhere in the picture, but he couldn't remember where. Now the clock on his dresser said two minutes past six. The meal was probably half over by now, but Buck started downstairs.

Katie heard him coming and met him at the bottom. "He's dressed!" she cried, and almost knocked him over when she hugged him. And then, jokingly, "He walks! He talks! He's alive!"

He managed a grin. And when he walked in the kitchen, all faces turned in his direction, everyone offering him something from there on the table—Joel with the platter of spareribs in his hand, Mom offering a bowl of green beans. . . .

The air was filled with exclamations and questions, until finally Gramps said, "Will you let the boy eat? Hasn't had a meal in three days!"

Three days! That was how long he was underground?

"What day is it?" Buck asked, running one hand through his hair, totally confused.

"Tuesday, Buck, but you've been sleeping since yesterday afternoon, and we figured you needed that more than food," said Dad.

Buck didn't know about that, because those spareribs sure looked good. He filled his plate with a little bit of everything on the table and let them do the talking while he ate. Katie said that a photograph of him yesterday at the Pit was going to be in the county paper, and that more photographers had been here at the house, taking pictures of him when he got out of the car.

"My bro, the celebrity," said Joel, grinning.

Buck remembered only some of it. Figured he'd been hugged about a hundred times, filthy as he was. What he remembered most was that everybody wanted to know where he had gotten out and he wouldn't tell them, only the police. And they weren't about to broadcast it, because they didn't want anyone else getting lost down there.

"Nat's called at least six times, Buck, and a reporter wants to come by tomorrow and do an interview," his mom said. "I told her it was up to you."

"Sure," Buck said, and tore into another sparerib, the

small bones piling up on the edge of his plate, making Gramps smile.

As for finding out how Buck had gotten into the Pit in the first place, Mel said, Rod was the one who'd finally told his parents, and they had called the police. All four boys had been interrogated at headquarters, where the whole sorry tale had come out. At first they'd said that Buck had been horsing around with them, but then they admitted how it really happened.

Three days after Buck had been dropped in the Pit, rescue workers had swarmed to the scene and were waiting for a professional caver, the smallest man they could locate, to come over from West Virginia and see if he could get through that opening behind the boulder. Scrape marks on the cavern floor had told investigators where Buck had been.

Now, after he finished his mashed potatoes, the best mashed potatoes he'd ever tasted in his life, Buck asked, "So what's gggggoing to happen to Pete and the guys?"

"Well," Dad said, studying him, "the police asked if we wanted to press kidnapping charges. That's what the boys did, you know. We wanted to talk with you about it."

Mom took over, pushing her plate to one side so she could rest her arms on the table. "If something bad had happened to you . . . something worse than what already did, I mean . . . Isaac . . . is that his name? . . . was so upset you might be dead that he threw up during the interrogation."

"And Ed Ketterman settled with Pete, as I knew he would, from the bruise on Pete's face," said Mel. "Not the punishment I'd inflict on a son."

"What do *you* think should happen to them, Buck?" asked Dad.

Well, let's see, Buck thought. *Pukeman has already been crushed by a piano, ground up in a pasta machine, flattened by a pine tree. . . .*

"I don't think they should go to jail or anything," he said. "I just don't want them to bother mmmme anymore."

"I think we can be pretty sure of that," said Joel.

"*I* think they should spend one night in jail, just to see what it's like," said Katie, her eyes flashing. "They robbed the lumberyard too, don't forget."

"Pukeman Goes to Jail." That would make a good strip, Buck thought.

"Their parents have already paid me for the lumber they stole," said Gramps. "I'd like to think that's all behind us."

But there was a lot they hadn't discussed yet, and Buck didn't look forward to it.

By the time Mom served her peach pie, Buck had enough in his stomach that he was willing to do his share of the talking. He told bits and pieces about what he had done, what he had seen, how he had figured out that he could get out through the Hole . . . And that was when the kitchen grew quiet and his own interrogation began.

"How long have you been going down there . . . in that 'hole'?" Dad asked.

Buck tried to think. He knew they had to have this out. If not now, tomorrow or the next day or the next, and waiting for it to happen would be the worst. It was time to tell the truth.

"Since the end of May, I guess. But only tttttttttwice."

Mom let out her breath. "All alone?" She stared at him, unblinking.

He nodded.

"Buck, that was *crazy*!" said Mel.

"I know. I wished David was with me."

Dad leaned forward. "That's what you and David used to do? You think that was any safer?"

Buck sighed and settled in. It was going to be a long evening. "We just like cccccaves! But we never found any of our own."

"Oh, Buck!" Mom said, one hand to her cheek.

"I can't help it. I . . . really . . . llllllllllike to explore," Buck said, knowing he could never quite explain the thrill of being underground, of maybe being the first one to ever be there, any more than Dad and Gramps could explain the thrill of felling trees in a forest. "We used to study maps and things and rrrrrrread up on caves and caving. . . ." He shrugged, and wished David were there to help him out. "And . . . once I found the Hole, I knew you'd nnnnnever let me. . . ." He let the words just hang there. It wasn't an excuse, but it was the truth.

"Joel told us about the headlamp, because the last person you'd talked to was Ted Beall, and he told us he'd sold you some batteries," Dad said.

"You didn't tell me about the caving, Buck," Joel said. "I just thought you wanted to fool around in the woods after dark or something."

"Which is why I checked the woods and every darn place else I could think of," said Mel.

"All these secrets!" Mom said accusingly, looking from

Buck to Joel as though the worst part of it all was that she hadn't known anything. "The *two* of you!"

Buck stared down at the tablecloth. It had happened just like he'd imagined it would, and he couldn't stand the thought that he had caused them so much worry.

"Well, I've got a boyfriend," Katie said loyally, and looked defiantly around the table. Buck had stood up for her enough times in the past.

"What in the . . . what is going on around here?" Mom cried. "I just don't know what to say . . . !"

"We've said enough," Gramps declared, his hands on the edge of the table, ready to push off. "They know how they've disappointed us, and there's no point in talking about it any longer."

Mom's face turned the color of the petunia print on the tablecloth, but she said, "No, Art, I think you're wrong. I think this is the time to hear what's on their minds. If you'd like to leave the room, though . . ."

Buck's granddad sat as stiff as an ironing board, but he finally settled back in his chair without answering.

"Buck, we sure as heck aren't about to punish you for being missing, but going underground not once but twice, alone . . . our never knowing where you were . . . Can you think of anything else that stupid?" Dad asked.

No, he couldn't. But he couldn't think of anything else as exciting either.

"We'll tend to you later, Katie, but Buck . . . what punishment would equal the worry and dread and sick feeling in my stomach for the last three days?" Mom asked, and her voice trembled. "If anything had happened to you . . ."

"Wait a minute," said Dad. "He didn't ask to be put there. . . ."

"And if I hhhhadn't gone in the Hole before, I wouldn't have known how to get out," Buck said, defending what little he could.

But he understood exactly what his mom meant. And he knew that even before the boys had dropped him in the Pit, he had put himself in situations that could have ended badly. He licked his lips. "I really ddddon't want you to worry," he said, and drew invisible circles on the table with his fork. "I guess . . . I suppose . . . I ccccould promise to give it up."

"Of *course* you will!" his mom declared.

But Dad sat shaking his head. He started to speak a time or two, then just shook his head some more. "You could give it up, Buck, but it wouldn't stop the wanting, any more than Joel not joining the navy would stop him wanting to see the world." And then, with a playful scowl at Katie, "or Katie wanting a *boyfriend*, whoever this fella is."

"Well, it's silly to have a rule about what year I can go to the movies with a boy, or what age I have to be to wear makeup, or even why I can't take that design class at the high school next summer! Anyone can sign up."

"Whoa, whoa!" cried Dad. "When did you get interested in that?"

"Only since forever, but Mom said to wait till I was actually in high school, but I really want to take that class, and I could pay for part of it myself and I should be able to spend my money however I want, and . . ."

"You ever hear of negotiating?" said Dad.

"Seems to me that's what you're about to do," Mel said, hiding his smile behind a napkin.

"What we need to find out, though, is what else we don't know," said Dad. "That's . . . what hurts the most."

Mel glanced over at Buck, then down at his own big knuckles on the table, and said nothing.

So Buck began: "I've been ggggetting some help with my sssstuttering from Jacob Wall, too. I should have told you."

The stares he got from his family this time were not angry ones, merely puzzled.

"*Jacob?*" said Dad.

"And I knew about it, and didn't say anything," Mel told them. "For that I apologize."

"Me too," said Katie.

"Well, *I* didn't know anything about it," said Joel. "It's a surprise to me."

"Why didn't anyone tell *us?*" Mom asked, looking from Mel to Buck to Katie.

"Because I wanted to work on it without a lot of questions about how was it cccoming along. Because it's really hard, but . . ." Buck shrugged. "It makes sense."

"To tell the truth, Buck," said Joel, "lately I figured I was either just getting used to it, or maybe you weren't stuttering as much."

"Jjjjjjjjjjjjjjjjust dddddddddoing it bbbbbbbbbetter," Buck demonstrated, purposely stuttering as easily and effortlessly as possible.

Gramps got up from the table, but this time he was smiling a little. "You know, at eighty-three, you can only take so many surprises at one time," he said. "And I think you can do all the negotiating that has to be done without me. So I'm heading for bed."

"Have a good night, Dad," Don Anderson said. "I think we're all going to sleep a little better tonight."

Buck wasn't sure about that, though. How do you make a promise you can't keep? That you don't *want* to keep?

"Listen," he said finally. "Here's a promise I can keep. I won't do any caving by myself ever again. If you let me join a ccccaving club, I'll do all my exploring with them."

"*Let* you!" said Dad. "I'll pay the dadburned fee, if there is one. *Sold!*"

• • •

Buck started to text David, but his cell phone, of course, was dead. He plugged it in to recharge it, and meanwhile, Nat rode over on his bike. Buck went out on the porch as soon as he heard Nat call his name.

"Buck! Man!" Nat said, dropping his bike and flopping down on the steps. "How'd you *do* that? If somebody threw me in a pit, I'd just curl up in a ball. I wouldn't go any-where!"

Weird, Buck was thinking, that what was easy for one person was hard for someone else.

"Well, they dddddidn't exactly throw me. But I didn't want to still be there when school started," he said, and Nat laughed.

But Nat was studying him curiously. "Boy, I don't know. I'd choose a river before I'd choose a cave any day."

"A lot can happen to you on a river," said Buck.

"Yeah, but . . . I'm claustrophobic, I guess. You ever want to build a raft and take it on the river . . ."

It was Buck's turn to laugh. "I'm in enough ttttrouble already," he said.

They talked for about fifteen minutes, then Nat stood up. "Well, I've still got cousins at my house," he said. "Gotta get back. I'll see you at school next week. Maybe we'll have some classes together."

"Yeah. And sit together at lunch," Buck told him.

He sent David a text as soon as he could, but got no reply. The following morning he tried again, and realized David was still at survival camp with no access to anything electronic. So he rode over to Jacob's.

He was remembering the words that had passed between them the last time he was there. The way Jacob had pushed him out and slammed the door. He might do it again.

This time, however, Jacob opened the door before Buck even rang the bell, and put one hand on his shoulder as he came inside.

"Buck . . . ," he said, and gave his shoulder a squeeze.

Buck's return had been on the local news the day before, he was told, and there probably wasn't a person in the county who hadn't heard the story by now. It had even made the city newspapers.

"Wondered if you had any jobs for mmmme," Buck said, standing awkwardly there in the living room, not knowing if he and Jacob were through or what.

"I've got a few," Jacob said. "Need to spruce things up a bit. Got some company coming by next week. But we can talk first. Come on in. . . ."

The armchair looked as though it had been waiting for him. Buck was surprised how much he felt at home, sitting there across from Jacob. He was a little nervous about starting school, but he'd done okay in that reporter's interview the day after he got home, so he figured he could handle eighth grade. With Jacob, meeting the dark head-on made it much less scary.

After they were seated, Jacob said, "I'm sure glad you made it out okay, Buck. Had the whole community worried. You can tell me about it, if you want."

Buck never tired of telling about the Hole, though the person he most wanted to talk with was David. But he gave Jacob a shortened version.

Jacob listened without interruption, and when Buck had finished, he sat shaking his head. "I'm thinking . . . if you can go through all that, you've got the guts to get through therapy."

"Well, I'd rrrrrather be down in the Hole," Buck said, grinning a little.

And that made Jacob laugh. "That's what an army guy told me once—he'd rather be in a foxhole than come to therapy. But . . . there's a happy ending to that story. He advanced through the ranks, and the last I heard, he was a career officer and had just addressed the Joint Chiefs of Staff. Now let's get to work. . . ."

The session ended without any mention of the previous quarrel between them.

"So I can kkkkkkeep coming for a while after school starts?" Buck asked.

"It's up to you," said Jacob, "but I like the company."

"I do too," Buck said.

As he headed for the door, Jacob handed him a few things to put in the mailbox. One was an electric bill. The other envelope, in Jacob's shaky handwriting, was addressed to Karen Wall Schuster, and the stamp had a picture of a bird on it. A pigeon, or a dove, maybe. Buck couldn't tell.

39

BUCK TO DAVID,
DAVID TO BUCK

A powerhouse of a boy, 13, only 4 feet 9 inches tall, climbed his way to the surface Monday after being dropped in a pit by classmates. Missing for three days, Buck Anderson, of rural Virginia, crawled, slithered, slid, and wriggled through a previously undiscovered labyrinth of underground caverns, wearing only a jacket over his clothes and a newly purchased headlamp over his bicycle helmet. He emerged onto private property three and a half miles away, confounding rescue operators at the Pit. . . .

• • •

He was lying on his bed on Saturday when his phone buzzed.

But it wasn't a text, it was a call. And when Buck switched to *Phone on,* he didn't even have a chance to say hello.

"Buck! What in the . . . ? Listen, man, I just got home from c . . . camp and Mom found the news in our paper! You o . . . okay?" David was stumbling over his words he was talking so fast.

"Well, I'm here," Buck said.

"Tell me what really happened!" David was practically shouting. "They put you down in the Pit and you came out some other way? *Where?*"

"Guess."

For two or three seconds, there was no sound at all, and suddenly David yelled, "Buck! The *Hole?*"

"Yeah. . . ."

"*Jeez,* man! That's got to be . . . maybe three or four miles! Under the mountain?" And it wasn't until David finally stopped for breath that Buck could start at the beginning and fill in all the details that a two-inch newspaper story couldn't cover, broken only by David's gasps of "The scumbags!" and "Oh, man!" and "Buck, you idiot!" and then "That's incredible."

"What did Pukeman do with your bike after the rope dropped?" David asked.

"I don't know. I think they jjjjust left it there. I guess the police gave it to Dad or Mel. It was at home when I got bbbb-back, I know that."

"Have you seen Pete since then?"

"Yeah. I went to a show at the PPPPPPalace this afternoon with Nat, and passed by Pete outside the drugstore."

"You say anything?"

"I said, 'Hey.'"

"What'd he say?"

"'Hey.'"

"That's it?"

"Yeah. Embarrassing, though. All four of them cccccame over with their dads—Isaac came with his mom—and had to apologize to me. And they all have to pay their folks for the lumber they stole. Their parents paid Grandpa."

"What I would have given to see Pete and his little ducklings apologize," said David.

"Ethan's dad didn't think he said it lllloud enough, so he had to apologize all over again. I just wwwanted to say okay and shut the door, but it's over now. Listen, how was survival camp?"

"Oh, man. You should've been there. No, you shouldn't. No radios, no cell phones, no TV . . . We had to dig roots to eat, I'm not kidding. Well, potatoes, anyway. And eat berries. I think I lost six pounds. We even had to build our own teepees. I'm surprised they didn't make us carve our own wheels!"

Buck laughed, then said, "Know what? The Virginia Cavers Association got permission to explore the ccccccccavern over Columbus Day weekend. They want me to go with them."

"Get OUT!" David yelped. "Buck! Wow! You're kidding me!"

"And I asked if I ccccould bring a friend, and they said yes. . . ." Buck had to hold his cell phone away from his ear, David was screaming so loudly.

When David stopped yelping, Buck asked, "Do you get Columbus Day off school?"

"If I don't, I'm going to!" David said. "Mom'll let me go. Oh, man, Buck, I think I've died and gone to heaven."

"Well, don't do that. And guess what else? Dad said I could join. I can start doing some caving with them . . . as long as I ppppromise never to go caving alone."

There seemed to be no end of good news. "And you're talking on the phone now," David said.

"Well . . . yeah. Guess I am."

"Another wow. But, Buck, listen! If your family had called me to ask if I had any idea where you were, and if I'd told them to check the old Wilmer place and they found the Hole and they went down and yelled and you heard them and they got you out, you could have told them how you and I used to go exploring together, and we'd both be in the newspaper!"

Buck was grinning. "Wouldn't have worked. You wwwwouldn't have answered. You were at survival camp, remember?"

"Oh, right! Blast it! Are they going to name those caverns for you? I mean, you were the first one down there, as far as anyone knows. A gallery, at least? The Buck Anderson Gallery or something?"

"I don't know," Buck told him, and tried to sound serious. "But I nnnnamed something after *you*."

"You did? *What?* It better be good. Tell me I'm going down in history, Buck. What was it?"

"A fossil. A trilobite named David."

• • •

Buck didn't know what the county would name the caverns. They must have suspected, once the Pit was discov-

320

ered, that something more was down there. But when he explored it with the Cavers' Association on Columbus Day, there was one particular formation he wanted to name—*Jacob's Chair.* And when they asked whom it was named for, he would tell them: a friend.

ABOUT THE AUTHOR

Phyllis Reynolds Naylor has always been interested in things underground and under the sea, as well as out-of-the-way places and the different choices people make in their lives. She is the author of more than 140 books, including the Newbery Medal winner *Shiloh,* and the companion, *A Shiloh Christmas; Faith, Hope, and Ivy June; Emily's Fortune; Emily and Jackson Hiding Out;* and the Boy/Girl Battle series, which begins with *The Boys Start the War* and *The Girls Get Even.*

When her husband, Rex, was alive, he was the first person to read her manuscripts. As a former supervisor of speech pathology at Walter Reed National Military Medical Center in Washington, DC, and a chief of speech pathology at the National Naval Medical Center in Bethesda, Maryland, he devised special programs for people who stutter, but his personality was quite the opposite of that of Jacob Wall from this story.

Phyllis Reynolds Naylor lives in Gaithersburg, Maryland. She is the mother of two grown sons and the grandmother of Sophia, Tressa, Garrett, and Beckett.